Set the Night on Fire

Jennifer Bernard

DEDICATION

To the one who lights up my life. May we always remember to look up at the stars.

Acknowledgments

Thank you to members of the Alaska Forest Service and Kris Dunlap for sharing their knowledge of the "hotshots." Grateful thanks to my editor Kelli Collins, cover artist Dana LaMothe, and proofreader Wendy Keel. To my family, you are the light of my life. Most of all, thank you to my beloved readers. It's an honor and a joy.

Chapter 1

Seven months earlier

Sean Marcus had a knack for impossible situations. So far, he'd survived—usually by the skin of his teeth. But right now, in the Big Canyon Wilderness with the entire world seemingly on fire, he wasn't worried about himself. Only one thing mattered: keeping his crew alive.

He squinted over his shoulder at the towering plumes of black smoke. This wildfire moved like nothing Sean had ever seen. Two minutes ago, he thought they had at least a half hour to get to the black. But the way this thing was eating through the forest, the Fighting Scorpion Hotshots didn't stand a chance of outracing it. Especially when they were already exhausted from three days of backbreaking line work. They'd saved an entire subdivision of two hundred families. But if they didn't get out of here fast, this would be his last impossible situation.

He gave a quick glance at the terrain around them. A thickly wooded ravine to the east, a sheer rock face to the west. The cliff face could provide some shelter against the blast of oncoming flames. This was it. Their best chance, right here. Quick head count. All twenty members of his crew here and accounted for.

"We'll deploy here," he called. Panic flashed across the grimy faces of his fellow firefighters. None of them had ever been in a situation like this—trapped behind the line with a forest fire marching toward them. It was every hotshot crew's worst case scenario. They trained for it, of course, but the fear, the dread, the relentless advance of towering black smoke, the particulate matter swirling through the air, the animal need to flee—how could you ever really be prepared?

"Get those shelters out," he shouted over the rumble of the approaching firestorm. Josh Marshall, his best friend on the crew, stood staring at the monstrous blaze as if he were hypnotized. Sean had never seen the team jokester speechless before. He reached for Josh's pack, unzipped the carrying case that held his shelter, and gave him a shove. "Go, Marsh. *Now.*"

At the sound of his nickname, Josh snapped out of his trance. He shook out the thin aluminum shelter, stepped into it, then dropped to the ground.

His voice hoarse, Sean yelled to the other firefighters, "Stay as close together as you can. Get your face down on the ground. Pin your shelters with your elbows and knees and whatever it takes."

Within seconds, all the hotshots had disappeared inside their silvery tents—except for one.

Finn Abrams—the rookie—backed away, his eyes wild with terror. "No way in hell," he yelled at Sean. "I'm not gonna sit here and get burned up!" He turned and bolted for the ravine, which was already smoking from the first licks of flames.

"Finn! Get back here!" Sean started after him. He'd heard of this happening. Firefighters panicking when faced with the prospect of trusting your life to a thin piece of fabric. He'd tackle him to the ground if he had to. Pin him and force that shelter into place.

But Finn kept going as if a demon was on his heels. And maybe there was—Sean felt it nipping at his back with hot bites of sparks.

Something snagged his leg as he passed a shelter. Josh was half in, half out of his tent, arm stretched to grab him. "Get the fuck in your shelter."

"But Finn—"

"He's gone!"

A blast of hot air blistered the back of Sean's neck. He took one last look at Finn, who was still running, stumbling toward the edge of the ravine, and gave a quick prayer that he'd make it somewhere—anywhere—before the fire hit.

He stepped into his shelter and dropped down. He pressed his face against the earth where the air would be the coolest and pulled the material over his head. To fend off the wind generated by the fire, he used his feet and elbows to pin the fabric to the ground.

He was still shifting around when the most intense sound he'd ever heard swept over him. It sounded like the flapping of ten million batwings pummeling the fabric that encased him. Wind shrieked and roared. Sean closed his eyes against the heat, which felt as if it could melt his eyeballs.

"Holy fuck!" Josh shouted from his shelter.

Amazing that they could hear each other over the din of the forest fire. They were trained to pack their shelters close together to reduce exposure to the heat. Being able to communicate with each other was an extra benefit.

"I gotta get out! I don't want to die in here!"

Sean couldn't tell who said that, but he read the panic loud and clear.

"Nobody moves!" Sean shouted. "You leave that tent, you *will* die!"

Not that he didn't understand the urge to move. To lie here like this—unable to do anything, trapped inside a claustrophobic cocoon while a fire raged on the other side of it—was excruciating. He understood why Finn had run, because every muscle in his body tensed with the need to do the same thing. *Go. Run. Do.* Action. That's what he wanted. That's what he always wanted. But right now, the only possible action was—none.

Well, not exactly none. He could still help his crew.

"When we get out of this, I'm treating everyone to barbecue!" he yelled. "Extra crispy."

Josh, good man, picked up on his lead. "When we get out of this, I'm asking Emma Watson for a date."

"The *Harry Potter* chick?"

"Yeah. She's hotter than this fire, man."

"When we get out of this, I'm gonna quit this shit and be a CPA!" Rollo yelled. "Damn, something just landed on me."

Sean felt it too. Chunks of flaming debris rained onto his body.

He shifted his body to knock the embers off. "Get that shit off if you can but keep your edges tight, guys."

A whoosh of sound stopped him cold. "What was that?"

"Tree exploded!" Rollo shouted. "This is fucking insane!"

"Just hang tight!"

Sean listened in awe to the tornado of noise outside. If the fire weren't trying to kill him, it would be spectacular. So much sound, so much heat. Was this the closest thing a person could experience to being inside a ball of gas? Inside the sun?

His mind drifted as the moments ticked on. He thought of the Yarnell burnover, in which all except one crew member had died. If he died now, he'd be one more Marcus family fuckup. The troubled kid who never got it together. The angry rebel who left Jupiter Point in disgrace. He would never get a chance to clear his name. Never get a chance to prove himself.

When we get out of this, I'm going back—

But Hughie forestalled him.

"When we get out of this," he yelled, panic edging his voice. "I'm gonna propose to Cindy."

"Good," Josh called back. "Because if you didn't, I was going to."

"Yeah right, you might as well propose to your tent."

For some reason, that inspired Josh to sing. "Dearly beloved, we are gathered here today…"

"To get through this thing called fire." Rollo finished off the line. The firefighters laughed, and Sean's heart clenched with pride. Hotshots were tough. Who else would quote Prince while the world was burning down around them?

When we get out of this, I'm going back to—

"How long can this last?" someone yelled.

Sean honestly had no idea. In the Little Venus fire, the burnover had lasted fifteen minutes. That didn't sound like a long time, but right now, he had no concept of time whatsoever.

"I think I can reach my phone. Anyone dare me to take a selfie?" Josh again. "I want proof for when we get out of this."

When we get out...

"Know what I'm going to do?" Sean said out loud this time. He startled at the realization that he could hear his own voice now. The roar had faded. The heat had lessened, too. It no longer felt like a convection oven on high. Was it safe to look outside? Would a blast of heat suck the air from his lungs?

After waiting for what felt like another eternity, he stuck his head out of the opening.

It looked like night out there. Was it night? Or was it simply the thickness of smoke blocking the daylight? The only illumination came from the flames that still flickered in the charred, smoking wasteland. Tree stumps still burned and sparked, hot sap running down their trunks. Chunks of debris smoldered everywhere. Smoke lay thick on the ground, in the air, drifting, swirling.

But the fire had moved on. And it wouldn't be back—there wasn't enough fuel left.

Using his elbows, Sean pulled himself out of the little shelter. He scanned the other tents and saw that everyone had stayed inside. *Thank you, Lord. Please let Finn be okay too, wherever he is.*

"Everyone alright?" he called, his voice hoarse. "You can come out now." One by one, his crewmates poked their heads from their shelters. Streaked black with soot, red-eyed, some tear-streaked.

"What a bunch of beauties, you are," he said. "They should make a calendar out of us."

From the shelter next to him, Josh let out a raspy laugh. "Damn, Magneto. Are we even alive? Or is this hell?"

"Good question." The decimated woodland could certainly pass for hell. Sean turned onto his back and let his head rest on his folded arms. The earth beneath him was warm to the touch. Overhead, twisting masses of gray and black smoke roiled, as if the sky didn't even exist anymore.

Sean vowed never to take the sky for granted again. Assuming he ever saw it again, of course. They still had a long trek to get out of here.

As he watched, the clouds of smoke shifted to make a hole. Through it, he saw a patch of pristine early evening sky, so perfect it snatched his breath away. And there, right there in the middle, he saw a star twinkling.

No, not a star, he realized. It was too bright to be a star. It was a planet. He recognized it from all the nights he'd spent camping on the fire lines, and from the stargazing app on his phone.

That was Jupiter. The biggest, boldest planet in the sky.

"When we get out of this," he said, mostly to himself, but also as a kind of public vow, "I'm going back to Jupiter Point."

Chapter 2

Evie McGraw had barely turned the Sky View Gallery's sign to "open" when the day's drama came pouring into her little sanctuary.

"Have you heard about those firemen coming?" Mrs. Murphy bustled through the door first. She ran the bookstore next door, Fifth Book from the Sun, but didn't ever seem to worry much about sales or customers. Today she had that look in her eye—the one that meant she had big news and intended to share it. Like it or not.

For a moment, Evie considered turning her wooden sign, the one painted with a sun on the "open" side and a moon on the "closed" side, back to moon. "Moon" was so much quieter and more peaceful than "sun."

But a girl had to make a living.

"You're going to be amazed, Mrs. Murphy, but I actually have heard that news already. We're getting one of those hotshot crews that fight wildfires. It's a good thing, with all the fires we've had the last few years."

"No, no, that's not the real news."

Obviously preparing for something extra juicy, Mrs. Murphy settled onto one of the high chrome stools at the espresso bar and dropped her tote bag onto the floor next to her. "Honestly, Evie, these are the most godawful chairs. You should tear all of these out and put in some nice old-fashioned booths. My rear end gives me hell after I get back from here."

Evie drew on the politeness that had been drilled into her since birth. "I'll have to look into that."

"You do that, and you'll see that I'm right."

Evie checked the espresso machine, which was still new to her. Just recently, she'd added the espresso bar in the hopes that it would bring in more customers to her little gallery. She'd opened the gallery as a way to channel her love for photography while still having time to take care of her mother. But now that selfies were all the rage, no one wanted landscape photos anymore. They wanted duck faces and cleavage shots.

"I just turned the coffee on, so it'll be a few minutes. Can I get you—"

"Oh, I'm not here for coffee." Mrs. Murphy adjusted her position on the stool and leaned forward to spill her big news.

But before she could say a word, the door opened again and Brianna Gallagher burst in. With her gingery-sunburst hair, wearing her usual work clothes of grubby overalls, she looked like some kind of comet streaking into the gallery. "I just heard the news, Evie, and I rushed right over!"

Mrs. Murphy bristled like a porcupine ready to defend its territory. "I was just getting to it."

"No offense, Mrs. Murphy." A worried frown drew Brianna's eyebrows together. "But I feel strongly that this should come from a friend."

Evie stared at her best friend. What news could possibly be this momentous? Nothing big ever happened in Jupiter Point. Their little town's only claim to fame was its stargazing, and stars didn't generally change much from night to night.

When the door opened yet again and her cousin Suzanne waltzed in, Evie gave serious consideration to simply closing down for the day. She could spend the time preparing for the dreaded city council meeting, an event that had been giving her nightmares for the past week.

"I can't even believe it!" Suzanne exclaimed, swinging one leg over a stool. She was so tall she made it look easy. "The nerve of that man!"

"Someone better tell me what's going on soon." Evie packed espresso grounds into the portafilter. "I'm starting to fear the worst. Are the firefighters going to take over the city? March naked down Main Street?"

"I like that idea." Brianna cocked her head in a dreamy way, as if picturing it at that very moment.

"You wouldn't find me complaining," Mrs. Murphy agreed.

Evie gave a double-take.

"I can appreciate a fine male specimen," Mrs. Murphy sniffed, then pointed at Evie. "You, my dear, could learn a thing or two from me in that regard."

"I can appreciate…" She trailed off, shaking her head at

herself. Why should she have to defend her personal life? Everyone in Jupiter Point *thought* they knew Evie McGraw. But Evie wasn't sure any of them really did. Not even Brianna, her best friend from the age of four.

"*Speaking* of fine male specimens," Brianna said, stepping into the awkward moment, "let's get back to our news."

"Nice segue." Suzanne reached over for a high five.

"Thanks."

"Sean Marcus is coming back to Jupiter Point," Mrs. Murphy blurted.

The tamper dropped from Evie's fingers and thudded onto the floor. "*What?*"

Brianna glared at Mrs. Murphy. "You didn't have to say it like that." She bounded around the counter and picked up the tamper. "This is exactly what I was worried about."

"She was going to find out sooner or later. I find it's usually better to spit things out." Mrs. Murphy gave Evie an apologetic glance. "I didn't mean to upset you, honey."

Brianna put her arm around Evie and squeezed sympathetically. "Are you okay, Evie? I couldn't believe it when I heard. Of all people to put in charge of the new firemen. Why him?"

Evie gathered her wits together. *Sean Marcus.* Oh sweet heavens, Sean Marcus was coming back. She wasn't ready for this. Of course she was. No she wasn't. *Oh God.*

She focused on tamping down the espresso grounds. "Listen, all of you. I know there was lots of talk when Sean left, but I promise you, he didn't do anything wrong. He has every right to come back here. In fact, I'll be glad to see him."

"You always see the best in everyone, Evie." Mrs. Murphy scolded her as if that quality was a bad thing. "But Sean Marcus was the biggest troublemaker in Jupiter Point. He spent more time in the police station than he did at home."

"I know; he was such a bad boy!" Suzanne bounced on her stool. "So broody and moody, especially after his parents died. I had a huge crush on him."

Evie could imagine that easily. Not that she'd ever had a crush on Sean Marcus—not exactly. But he knew secrets about her no one else knew. And now he was coming back? She had a very bad feeling about this. "Is he a firefighter now? I hadn't heard about that."

"Yes, and he's practically famous." Suzanne tucked her long blond hair behind her ears. "He was in that fire last year, the one where they had to get into those little shelters while the fire burned over them? I heard they're making a movie about it."

"A movie about Sean Marcus?" Evie asked faintly. How far back would it go? Would it talk about his history with Jupiter Point? Would filmmakers be roaming the streets? Asking questions? Panic rippled through her.

"Well, he's part of it, but just a small part." Suzanne shook her head in Evie's direction. "I can't believe you didn't hear about all that. It's like you live in a cave."

Some days, like today, she wished that were true. If she lived in a cave, she wouldn't have to get up in front of the city council tonight and endorse the one person in the whole town she despised.

It would take everything she had to pull that off. The return of Sean Marcus was just a coincidental blip.

"Anyway, thank you all for letting me know." Relieved to find her hands steady, she inserted the espresso holder into the machine and pushed the button to start the brewing process. "Although we probably won't see the firefighters much. They'll be out at the old Army base, right?"

"Yes, but Sean is coming to the city council meeting today." Brianna gave Evie one last little comforting squeeze before heading back to her stool.

Evie jerked and knocked over a canister of espresso beans. Her first city council meeting, and Sean Marcus would be there? It was going to be difficult enough without that added twist. This was a full-on, flat-out disaster.

"Yup, he's going to tell us what to expect from our hunky new firemen." Suzanne grinned. "From what I hear, half the guys in town are going to apply. Everyone wants to be a hotshot now."

"Women can apply, too, you know," Brianna said. "Think about it, Suzanne. You'd be surrounded by hotness. And I'm not talking about the fires."

Suzanne flipped her long hair over her shoulder. "Sweaty men are not my type, you know that. Unless they're sweating over whether or not I'm going to go out with them."

"Oooh, burn."

Evie had never been so grateful for her friends' chatter. She let it flow over her as she fixed her gaze on the dark brew dripping from the expresso machine into two little white china cups. The news about Sean coming back reverberated through her in waves.

Sean had been her older brother's friend, not hers. After the plane crash that killed his parents, Sean had come to live with the McGraws so he could finish high school in Jupiter Point. But he was so withdrawn and distant that she never got closer to him than the dinner table.

Until the Incident happened.

In the chaos and confusion, Sean had lost his cool and gotten thrown in jail for the night. The next day, he disappeared, even though he wasn't the one who had hurt her.

That was Brad White, *only* Brad. But no one knew that. She hadn't said anything, not when it counted, and now…

She picked up one of the espresso cups and took a sip for strength. "Are any of you actually ordering anything? This is a business, you know."

The three women looked at her blankly.

Evie sighed. "In that case, I have to prepare my statement for tonight's meeting. I'll see you all later."

"It should be a juicy one." Mrs. Murphy slid off the stool. "Brad White's in town, I hear."

Evie's heart nearly stopped. "What did you say?"

"Brad White. He's back from all his campaign la-di-da. Everyone says he's walking around with an entourage. They all have Bluetooths and smartphones and—"

The buzz in Evie's ears drowned out everything else. If Brad was in town, he'd definitely be at tonight's meeting. He would want to hear her official endorsement in person.

Brad White and Sean Marcus would *both* be there. This was an even bigger disaster than she thought. Oh sweet Lord above. Where was that cave when she needed it?

As Mrs. Murphy slid off the stool, her skirt snagged on a chrome rivet and rode up her backside. "I'm telling you, Evie, these stools are a menace!"

Suzanne reached over and tugged down her skirt.

Mrs. Murphy pretended to swat her hand away. "Hands off, unless you're a hunky fireman."

"I'll see if I can line one up for you." Suzanne winked. As Mrs. Murphy sailed out the front door, Suzanne looked at her watch.

"Darn it, cuz. I have to get to work. But I'll see you at the council meeting."

Evie shook herself out of her trance. "You're coming to the meeting? Don't you have a date or something? You always have a date."

"I'd skip anything for dreamy Sean Marcus. I bet he's even more of a babe now. Oh, and of course to see my cousin's first starring role as president!" She waved her fingers as she vanished out the door.

Brianna turned to her as soon as they were alone. "You sure you're all right, Evie?"

Evie hauled in a deep breath and called on a lifetime of McGraw tutelage. McGraws kept their cool. They didn't lose their tempers. In fact, they avoided conflict at all costs. It was safer that way.

"Of course. Why wouldn't I be? I don't even know why you're

worried. I barely remember Sean. Honestly, you're being ridiculous."

Brianna fixed the strap of her overalls, which had fallen down one freckled arm. "Evie, I know that you're always calm, cool and collected. I know you don't like drama and you hate making scenes and you want everything to float along smoothly like a nice, calm, stagnant river. You like peace and harmony, and I love you for that. But I will *still* love you if you lose your shit for once. It's okay to be upset and it's okay to show it."

Evie stared at her friend for a long moment. She wasn't upset. Okay, maybe she had been, for a short moment. But she was already over it. "Rivers don't stagnate," she muttered.

Brianna rolled her eyes. "Fine." She hopped off the stool. "Just so you know, I'm here for you. No matter what. And I'll see you at the council meeting."

"*You're* coming to the meeting too? They're deadly dull."

"I have a feeling," said Brianna, "that this meeting isn't going to be dull."

Chapter 3

As far as Sean could tell, Jupiter Point had barely changed in the past thirteen years. The police station certainly looked the same, though he noticed a few flowering shrubs that hadn't been there before. Interesting touch. Were they going for a soothing vibe at the old JPPD? He probably could have used that back in the day.

Funny how that wild kid felt so far away and long ago now. Now he was the superintendent of the brand-new Jupiter Point Hotshots crew, in charge of setting up the whole darn thing. He'd first heard about the proposed crew last year, but hadn't thought to apply until the burnover. Getting run over by a fire had changed a few things in his life.

He'd been back in town for two days, but he and Josh, who'd come with him as crew captain, had spent that time at the old Army base. They'd met with the fire ranger and dispatch staff and started organizing the part of the compound where the hotshots would be located. Tonight would be his first chance to face the actual residents of Jupiter Point. After all the dangerous situations he'd faced, you'd think this one would be tame. But he was nervous as hell.

In the passenger seat of the Ford Super Duty crew cab truck, Josh Marshall had been grumbling since they'd left the base. "Honestly, I'd rather go through another burnover than get dragged to a city council meeting."

"Man up, slugger. You're about to become a superstar. If I know Jupiter Point, that meeting is going to be rocking. Not much happens around here. A new hotshot crew is going to be big news."

"And rightfully so." Josh preened, as he'd gotten in the habit of doing since the *Miracle in Big Canyon* movie was announced. "But I'm not the one in charge of this shindig. You're the superintendent around here. I'm just the minion. Why do I need to strut my stuff for the locals?"

"Because," Sean explained patiently, "I used to live here. They know me as a troublemaker with a chip on my shoulder. Now they're supposed to welcome me with open arms as the guy standing between them and the next wildfire? They'd be more likely to believe I'd *start* a fire than put it out. I need backup."

"Nevertheless, you're the one they hired. You're the hero."

"Fuck that." That was a sore point among the old crew. Sean didn't think he'd done anything special. But another hotshot crew fighting the same Big Canyon fire had lost two members. The media had made a big deal out of that. Then Finn—who had made it to a gravel streambed in the nick of time—got his dad the movie producer involved, and now it had all turned into a nightmare.

"Hey, we survived, and it wasn't because I was cracking jokes. It was because you picked the right spot and you made us stay put. I heard they want Theo James to play you. The one in *Divergent*."

Sean took a corner a little too fast, leaving a streak of rubber. "I'm not talking about that fucking movie, I'm not cooperating with it, and you better not bring it up at the meeting."

Josh laughed. "You're no fun anymore. You're too easy to rile up." He glanced out the window. They'd reached the downtown business district, where the architecture had a storybook flair. Stores were either shingled in cedar or painted in ice cream pastels. Old-fashioned lampposts lined the sidewalks. "What just happened here? Did we drive back in time?"

"No, that's Jupiter Point's thing. It's a tourist town. Big on the quaint and cutesy."

"And this would be Main Street?"

"It would be, in any other town. Here, it's Constellation Way."

"Ex-queeze me?"

"Just go with it. And get a star chart."

Josh was still grumbling as they cruised past the Rings of Saturn Jewelers and the Orbit Lounge and Grill. The Sky View Gallery, with its light blue awning trimmed in white, looked new. It probably catered to the honeymooners who wanted to take home photographic evidence of their trip.

Luckily, the downtown area also contained a Mexican restaurant called simply Don Pedro's and a new 7-Eleven convenience store. The stargazing theme could easily be overdone, in Sean's opinion.

He parked in the side lot of Jupiter Point High School, where he hadn't quite completed his senior year. He drew in a deep breath, wondering how many of the people inside would remember him.

And if they'd try to run him out of town as soon as he walked in.

Josh stepped out of the truck and stretched. "Looks like a full house, man. Maybe it's the welcome wagon. Returning hometown hero, that kind of thing."

"Nope."

"How do you know?"

"Because the last night I spent here was in the Jupiter Point PD's lockup."

~ ~ ~

Evie couldn't believe how many Jupiter Point residents had shown up for the city council meeting. They actually had to move the gathering into the high school auditorium, which buzzed like a hornet's nest of chatter. As she smiled and worked her way toward a seat, isolated bits of talk caught her attention. The new hotshots were definitely a popular topic. The other big news, of course, was Brad White's campaign for state representative.

Brad White, who had asked for the Jupiter Point Business Coalition's endorsement.

And which criminally stupid business owner had just run for president of the coalition…and won? Yep, Evie McGraw. Which meant that she would be announcing the coalition's endorsement of Brad in just a matter of minutes.

How could she endorse the man who'd hurt her so horribly? But—how could she not? No one knew what had happened. Except Sean.

With her heart doing some kind of conga routine, she scanned the crowd carefully. No sign of Sean yet. Or Brad. Near the front of the auditorium, she settled into one of the old-fashioned bucket seats, which still smelled exactly the same as when she'd gone to Jupiter High—like pencil lead. She ran through the statement she'd written. *Happy to endorse…solid leadership…*

Would she have to talk to Brad? Even seeing him sapped her confidence and made her babble like an awkward toddler. Over the years, she'd trained herself to be okay in his presence. Not good, but okay. She could do this. This wasn't about what he'd done in the past. It was about the future.

The usual small-town talk drifted around her. People were anxious about the new roundabout under construction. And then there was the fact that the Milky Way Ice Cream Parlor had shut down for renovations. Some people were saying it might not reopen, a horrible thought that was inciting full-fledged panic.

Maybe Evie should start serving ice cream cones at the gallery. Maybe she should start tap-dancing while she scooped them.

She was smiling at that thought when the fire chief, Doug Littleton, walked into view, with two tall male figures striding behind him. Heads swiveled to watch their progress through the auditorium. A few people stood up for a better look, which blocked her view. She craned her neck to see past them, but couldn't get a clear shot.

Brianna dropped into the seat next to her.

"Yup, that tall, dark and broody man you're staring at—that's him."

Evie's face heated. "How could I be staring when I couldn't even see him?"

"Well, take it from me, he's even better looking than before. I don't remember him being so tall. I wonder who the other guy is. Sweet Jesus, between the two of them…" She fanned herself with the meeting agenda.

"Get a grip. It's not like we don't have good-looking men in Jupiter Point."

"But we *know* all of them. They're all like brothers. How often do we get fresh meat here? Of the beefcake variety? Hardly ever, admit it."

Evie snuck another glance in Sean's direction, hoping to get a good look before the meeting started. She got a glimpse of the other man, who had blond-streaked, chin-length hair and a wide grin. A hottie, no doubt about it, but Sean was the one she wanted to see.

"Face it," Brianna was saying. "Jupiter Point is a cute place to live, but when it comes to dating, it kind of sucks. Why do you think every single woman in town is packed into this auditorium?"

"Maybe they have business on the agenda. Like I do."

"Is that why you're giving yourself a neck cramp? Business?"

Evie didn't hear a word Brianna said. She couldn't have answered if she wanted to. The line of sight finally cleared and, suddenly, there was Sean Marcus.

Her chest tightened as if an iron band had wrapped around her. She couldn't breathe. Her mind went blank.

He looked like a warrior, not the teenage boy she remembered. Every bit of him was hard-muscled and strong and fierce. His dark hair was still thick and unruly, the way she remembered it. But his face had hollowed out, all the youthfulness replaced by lean, rugged lines. He still had that "broody" look, as Suzanne called it, but Evie could think of a much better word.

Sexy.

The man was smoking hot, unbelievably sexy. She actually waved her hand next to her face to send more air to her lungs.

"Wow," she said faintly. She meant to say it under her breath, but Brianna caught it.

"I'll say. He looks like…I don't know, Michael Fassbender, except even better looking."

"Who?"

"The guy who plays Magneto in the *X-Men*. Or no, maybe the one who played the fireman in Magic Mike, I mean, the one who played the stripper who played the fireman. Joe something. Except Sean is *actually* a fireman, and if he strips or starts to dance or—"

"Brianna," Evie said faintly.

"Sorry." Brianna subsided as the city council members filed into their seats. "I'm just saying. It's like Mrs. Murphy says, if you can't appreciate the male form…"

Evie tuned her out. She was too busy appreciating the male form on display across the room to pay any more attention. And that was *so* not like her. She wasn't a man ogler. She didn't flirt. She didn't date much. When she did, she hated it. She didn't enjoy attention from men. It scared her.

But right now, she wouldn't mind a little attention. Would Sean Marcus remember her? Would he remember that she hadn't spoken up for him? Did he hate her?

She found herself biting her thumbnail, something she hadn't done since her teens. Frustrated with her childish anxiety, she shoved her hand under her leg and sat on it.

When she glanced up, Sean was looking at her with those smoky green eyes and a groove had appeared in his cheek. He was smiling. At her. As if he recognized her, and didn't hate her.

It took her right back to that night. Sean peering through the window of Brad's Chevy Nova. Meeting her desperate, humiliated gaze.

All the confusion and fear from that night thirteen years ago crashed onto her like a flood that had been held back by a retaining wall. Brad's hand reaching into his pants. His weird, hot breath against her neck. The helplessness of being pinned, the nasty, mean words spilling out of his mouth.

She snapped back to the present moment. Sean was still looking at her. This was now, not then. His expression held friendliness, not shock.

Smile. She forced her face to obey.

"Evie, are you all right?" Brianna touched her hand, which was clenched onto the edge of her seat. "You look a little ill."

"I'm fine, I'm fine. You know how I feel about public speaking, that's all." She glanced back at Sean and saw that he'd moved. For a moment, she panicked, thinking maybe he was coming her way. But no—he and his friend were following Chief Littleton toward the stage where the city council members sat.

Relief flooded her. She wanted to bang her head on the back of the seat in front of her. Why on earth was she reacting this way to the sight of Sean Marcus? After the Incident, she'd built up a wall against the male gender. The wall helped her deal with seeing Brad around town. It allowed her to go on with her life in peace.

But for some reason, that wall was now shaking on its foundations. Sean Marcus had seen the Incident—or part of it, anyway. He was the only one besides her and Brad who knew anything about it. And she and Brad, by unspoken agreement, had buried it in the past.

Would Sean?

Chapter 4

Sean had expected some stony faces, maybe some glares from his old teachers and various members of the police department. He hadn't expected the crowd to be holding up iPhones to snap his picture, or the high proportion of women packing the auditorium. He hadn't expected...*her*.

He stared...and kept on staring while Josh eyed the seats full of women like a kid in a candy store.

"Is this turnout because of the movie?" Josh whispered.

"I warned you. Not much happens around here. We're big news."

Still, he couldn't look away from the girl at the front of the auditorium. Her chestnut hair was pulled into a low, classic ponytail at the base of her neck. She was frowning intently at her thumb. Who was she? She reminded him of someone...he knew her...but she wouldn't look at him so he couldn't say for sure...

Josh followed Sean's gaze and whistled under his breath. "Do you know her?"

As if she'd overheard, she finally looked in his direction. Her eyes met his in a punch of silvery sage-green.

Evie McGraw. Holy shit.

No wonder he hadn't recognized her at first. She'd only been fourteen when he left. A skinny kid he'd paid no attention to—until the night when everything went to hell.

Now she was…wow, she was an absolute knock-you-off-your-feet beauty. She had the kind of face you'd see in a magazine or on a billboard, all luminous eyes and stunning cheekbones. Did she remember him? Or had she blocked out the trauma of that night? He wouldn't blame her if she had.

Even though she had an air of "don't touch me" vibrating around her like an invisible electric fence, he tried a smile. It took a few moments, but eventually she smiled back. Actually, it was more of a twitch of her lips, but he could read recognition on her face. Her eyes remained cool and wary, as if she was hiding behind a pane of thick, frosted glass.

"Seriously, who is that?" Josh asked again. "Someone you know?"

"I used to."

He didn't know this grownup, frosty Evie. The Evie he remembered was a bubbly, dreamy girl. Young enough so she still read *Harry Potter* nonstop and did her homework on the kitchen table. She seemed very different now, but then again, it had been thirteen years. People changed.

Chief Littleton nudged him toward the stage, and he pulled his attention back to the business at hand. The city council meeting had been called to order, and it was time for them to do their thing. He and Josh followed the chief onstage.

"This is a big moment for us," the chief began. "I've been fighting for this for several years. Here in Jupiter Point, with our urban-wilderness interface, we're sitting ducks for a wildfire. Every summer we get a few that come close. Last year the ranger station even burned down—we all remember that. Finally the bigwigs agreed with me, and we got ourselves a brand-new interagency hotshot crew based out of here. Some of you probably remember Sean Marcus; he's the superintendent of this new crew. That means he's in charge. He sure has come a long way, huh?"

Sean kept his face stony to hide the wince. *Thanks a lot, Chief.*

"Since he left Jupiter Point, Sean has racked up an unbelievable record as a smoke-jumper and hotshot. He's a brilliant and respected leader, he's saved many lives and homes, and word has it he requested this assignment. Let's give him a big welcome home, hey?"

The crowd responded with generous applause. Sean finally cracked a smile and saluted the townspeople. He scanned the faces near the front, looking for Evie, but he froze when his gaze encountered the last person he wanted to see.

Brad White. Right in the front row. The guy had brass balls—he was grinning at Sean as if they were old friends. That cocky smirk made Sean want to deck him all over again, the same way he had that night.

In thirteen years, Brad had grown more polished, and his shock of sandy hair had been ruthlessly cut into what Sean thought of as "news anchor hair." He wore a tan business suit and a royal-blue silk tie. To Sean, he looked like a kid trying on his father's suit.

At least the idiot still had a bump on his nose from where Sean had broken it that night.

He stared the jerk down until finally he turned away and said something to the guy next to him.

Josh hissed in his ear, "Go, Magneto. It's your turn to speak. Make it sing, baby."

Collecting himself, Sean took a step forward. "Hi, I'm Sean Marcus, and it's good to be back in Jupiter Point." He paused until the applause died down. "My job is to put together the best crew I can hire, get us geared up, set up at the new Jupiter Point Fire and Rescue compound—what used to be the old Army base--and do it all by the time fire season comes around in May."

He paused again for a wave of claps and whistles. Brad had a big false smile plastered on his face as if it were glued there.

"The completed crew will contain twenty firefighters. We'll be bringing in mostly fire service veterans, but we're also interested in locals who have their red cards—that's a prerequisite for wildland firefighting. We may be hiring some local ground support from time to time as well. Local knowledge is always helpful. If you know anything about how hotshots work, you know we'll be traveling wherever they need us. Most of the time, you won't even know we're here. And hopefully, when you do notice us, you'll be *glad* we're here. Any questions?"

A young man in a baseball cap got to his feet. "You said you're hiring locals?"

"Yup. I'll be setting up interviews in the next couple of weeks.

Call this number." He handed his card to someone in the front row, who passed it on. "Keep in mind, the hotshot training is extremely tough. You have to be in peak physical condition. You have to pass some pretty harsh tests. And I'm known for demanding the best from my crew."

"Oh yeah." Josh's heartfelt agreement drew laughter from the crowd.

"When it's a matter of life or death, you don't want to be a step slower than the fire just because you slacked off on your endurance training."

A perky blonde in a red tank top asked the next question. "Will you hotshots be living here year-round? Do you have families?"

Sean bit back a smile. Like all firefighters, hotshots tended to get a lot of attention from girls. "This is Josh Marshall, crew captain. Josh, do you want to take this question?"

"Sure. What's your name?"

"Serena."

"Well, Serena, some hotshots have families that they leave behind to go fight fires all summer. Others of us are still single."

"Really?" She batted her eyelashes at him. Sean could sense Josh plotting how to get her number after the meeting. "What about him?" She pointed to Sean. "Is he single?"

Josh snorted. "Yes, Sean is single, but to be totally honest, he's a pain in the—"

Sean elbowed him in the ribs to make him shut up. He spotted Evie a few rows back. Her full lips were pressed together as if she was trying to hold back a laugh. Her eyes brimmed with amusement.

Now that was the Evie he remembered. Teasing, fun, bright.

Was it hard for her to be this close to Brad White? Had he ever faced up to his actions? Apologized? Done time?

Time to wrap things up. "We're going to be very busy over the next few weeks, but my door is always open if you have questions about the hotshots, fire safety, or how to apply. Thank you."

He and Josh left the stage. Josh left to find the men's room. Sean waited in the auditorium, willingly subjecting himself to more city council meeting agenda items so he could steal glances at Evie. Leaning against the wall, he ate up every detail. The graceful arch of her neck, the strand of hair that kept escaping her ponytail, the way her lush breasts pressed against her simple ivory blouse.

Evie was one sexy woman, but she didn't seem aware of that fact at all.

It was a slight shock when he heard Brad White's name announced. Judging by the way the crowd applauded him, he still had the charm that had worked on everyone except Sean.

"Thank you, neighbors, right back at you!" Brad applauded the crowd. *What a fake.* "I know you'll all be happy to hear that the campaign is going great, and chances are good that Jupiter Point will have its first hometown representative in Sacramento!"

Big cheers answered that.

What the fuck? Was Brad White seriously running for office? Didn't anyone here know what he'd done?

Sean looked at Evie. All the color in her face had leeched away.

He glanced at the girl sitting next to her, the redhead he

vaguely remembered as Evie's best friend. She was clapping for Brad too. Either she didn't know or it didn't matter to her.

Disgusted, Sean pushed off the wall to head for the exit when Brad's next words stopped him cold.

"You all know and love Evie McGraw. As the new president of the Jupiter Point Business Coalition, and definitely the best-looking one," more laughter, "she's here tonight to make an important announcement on behalf of my campaign. Evie?"

As Sean watched, incredulous, Evie rose to her feet.

What the hell? Was she *working* with Brad? Had she completely forgotten what Brad did that night?

Chapter 5

Evie's heart was pounding so fast and furious, she was afraid it might trip over itself. She clenched her fists and dug her fingernails into the heels of her hands. This didn't have to be a big deal. Everyone was expecting an endorsement. The downtown business owners certainly were. Brad definitely expected it. It was safe to say the entire town considered it a done deal.

Endorsing Brad for state representative was a no-brainer. He'd give the town a higher profile. Everyone would benefit, and he might even do a good job. His family owned the biggest bank in town, so he knew finances. He knew how to schmooze. He *loved* the spotlight.

She knew he was also a manipulative, cruel slime ball, but no one else knew that.

Just do it, Evie.

She opened her mouth to release the words she'd memorized. *Happy to endorse…excited about what this means for Jupiter Point…future is bright…*

And then she made the mistake of looking in Sean's direction.

Instead of leaning against the wall, as he had been, he was standing bolt upright, staring at her with eyes that seemed to burn right through her.

Tremors ran down her body, from her scalp to the soles of her feet. Her toes curled inside her sandals and she gripped her sweaty hands together. A strange, surreal sensation took over her body, as if she was floating somewhere overhead. She dragged her gaze away from Sean's and looked over the heads of the city council members.

The voice that came out of her mouth didn't even sound like hers. "I regret to say that the Jupiter Point Business Coalition is unable to endorse Brad White for state representative at this time."

After a stunned moment of silence, a noisy surge of questions assaulted her eardrums. Her vision swam, as if she might faint.

What had she just done? She never made waves. Never, ever. It wasn't the McGraw way. She should take it back. Right now.

She opened her mouth but that wasn't what came out.

"I'm sure Brad will do just fine without our endorsement. I have to go now."

She slipped into the aisle and hurried toward the exit. The red letters blurred. Her face burned as everyone swung in their seats to watch her go.

What was wrong with her? One simple phrase—"I endorse Brad White"—and she couldn't even spit it out of her mouth.

~ ~ ~

After reaching the hallway outside the auditorium, she stopped, clutching her stomach. Oh God, she was going to throw up. Yes, she'd vomit right here on the scuffed floor. Then she could march back in and explain that she was sick. That's why she'd done such a stupid thing. Food poisoning or something.

She bent over, stomach heaving.

A warm hand settled on her back. A male voice, like molasses over gravel, resonated above her. "Are you okay, Evie?"

She straightened. Sean Marcus stood over her. This close, he was even more overwhelmingly masculine. His scent, sort of woodsy and clean, cleared her head.

"No. I'm not."

"You did the right thing. How could you even think about endorsing that guy?"

Suddenly furious, she lashed out at him—physically. Actually thrust her hand against his hard chest. "This is *your* fault."

He caught her hand by the wrist. The strength of his grip made her catch her breath. He seemed more amused than upset, which for some reason got her even more riled up. "How do you figure that?"

"I was *fine* before you showed up. The right words were on the tip of my tongue. I was about to say them but you were staring at me with that look."

"Look?"

"Like I'm some kind of sellout. A coward." She ripped her hand away from his and stalked down the hallway. "This is ridiculous. You don't know anything, and why would you care anyway?" She had to get out of here and try to regain some kind of composure. She felt almost as if she'd just stripped naked in front of all of Jupiter Point.

Everyone was going to be talking now. Everyone would want

to know why in God's name was she "unable" to endorse Jupiter Point's own candidate for state representative.

And she couldn't explain, not unless she wanted to get even more naked. Metaphorically speaking.

Sean Marcus was still pacing next to her, all sexy and rugged and confident. Just inside the big double doors that led to the front steps of the high school, she whirled on him. "Why did you even come back here?"

He leaned one hand on the door over her head. To open it? Keep her from opening it? Hard to tell. "Why shouldn't I? I'm a good firefighter. You might need me one of these days."

The wicked gleam in his eye gave her the shivers. "I won't. I mean, I suppose the town might need you, if there's a fire, but I don't. I mean, for anything other than a fire."

Apparently she'd temporarily lost all control over her own utterances. He was looking at her closely, as if he could see inside and see every little butterfly careening around her belly. "You're worried I might say something. About that night."

"I'm not a coward," she blurted out. "I have reasons. Lots of reason. My mother's been ill, she doesn't handle stress well, and you know what my family's like—" She pressed her lips together to stop the flow of words.

Enough was enough. No more blurting out things that should just stay locked in the past. Sean Marcus wouldn't understand anyway. He was the embodiment of confidence. You might even say arrogance. He didn't worry about what people said about him. He didn't care about keeping the peace.

In fact he *disrupted* the peace. He was disrupting hers right now.

"Look, Evie." The sound of her name on his lips sent an odd thrill through her. "I'm not here to make trouble, but I don't mind trouble either. Hell, I'm used to it. If you need me to—"

The door of the auditorium opened and Mrs. Murphy stepped out. She scanned the hallway avidly then homed in on Evie and Sean.

"Uh oh," Evie whispered. "That's the entire Jupiter Point grapevine coming at us right now."

"Go," ordered Sean. "I'll head her off."

She nodded gratefully and pushed open the door.

"And Evie," he called after her. "If you want some tips on keeping your head in a firestorm, come on out to the base. Happy to help."

Without another glance at him, she ran across the dark parking lot. Screw Sean Marcus. Screw Brad White. This was exactly why she avoided men completely. She was going nowhere near that base, not a chance.

~ ~ ~

The drive back to the base was one nonstop interrogation. Josh started in as soon as the door closed behind him.

"Who is that chick? Old girlfriend?"

"No."

"New girlfriend?"

"For cripes' sake, Marsh. Give it a rest. She's the little sister of a friend of mine, Hunter. I lived with her family before I left Jupiter

Point." Truth to tell, he barely remembered that time. His head had been shrouded in a fog of shock.

"You lived with her? Was she already a babe back then?"

"Christ, she was maybe fourteen. I had other things to think about."

"See, that's the difference between me and you. No matter what else is happening, I always take time to appreciate the women in my life. Note the plural."

Sean rolled his eyes. "Do I need to lock you up at the base to keep you away from Jupiter Point? My reputation's on the line here."

"What are you so worried about? Were you really such a bad seed? We call you Magneto because you look like him, not because you're a villain."

"Depends who you ask." Sean steered onto the two-lane road that led to the base, which sat at the edge of a wilderness area. "I didn't have a record or anything. I fought with my father a lot. I had a lot of anger and found creative ways to let off steam."

"Hmm. I get it, you were the town bad boy. And that girl. What's her name?"

"Evie McGraw." Saying her name brought up an image of her face, and all the emotions churning behind her silvery eyes during that brief conversation at the high school. She fascinated him.

"Definitely more the town sweetheart type. This should be interesting." Josh squinted into the distance, imagining God knew what.

"Nothing to see here. Move along."

"Uh-huh. First he marries a stripper, then he goes for the town sweetheart."

"Are you ever going to let that go? I was twenty-two and drunk off my ass."

"Which is why I'm never, ever going to let it go."

The old Army base—Sean still couldn't think of it as a "fire and rescue compound"--seemed even more quiet and empty when Sean and Josh finally got back. It was a small outpost of modest, low-lying buildings painted standard beige on the outside, standard Army white inside. Standard being the theme. After the nearest ranger station had burned down, several state and federal agencies had joined together to take over the decommissioned base. They'd relocated the rangers and fire dispatch, set aside space for the hotshots, and planned to add a search and rescue crew. During the day the ranger station got a certain amount of traffic.

But for now, the compound was still mostly empty at night.

In the room they'd designated as a common area, Josh kicked back on a pile of blankets and cued up a Netflix movie on his laptop. The cots were due to arrive tomorrow. Until then, they were making do with sleeping bags and blankets.

Sean skipped the flick and went for a night run.

Never mind that he'd jogged five miles up and down hills just that morning. Running always cleared his thoughts and gave him energy. He chose a trail that wound around the outer perimeter of the base.

As he ran, filling his lungs with the crisp early March air, he kept looking up at the wide-open, star-studded sky above. He'd forgotten what the stars were like here. Jupiter Point prided itself on its magnificent stargazing. The way the air currents swirled around the promontory kept the smog at bay. City ordinances dictated that street lights be kept low, and most residents followed the same rules. The town even had a motto—"Remember to Look Up at the Stars."

Sean made a mental note to make sure the hotshots respected the regulations. Just another detail he should be nailing down.

Instead, he couldn't stop thinking about Evie McGraw.

And that night.

He'd come back from basketball practice and spotted movement inside Brad's old beater Chevy. He'd never liked Brad— why was someone his age hanging around a fourteen-year-old? So he peered in the window and saw Evie's terrified eyes flashing silver. Yanked the door open. Socked Brad in the face. While Brad moaned in agony and grabbed for his phone, Sean helped Evie inside the house. She was shaking so hard she could barely talk, but she made him promise not to say a word.

He left the house to make sure Brad was gone—but he wasn't. Blood dripping down his face, he was busy telling a bunch of lies to a police officer. The officer started asking Sean some bullshit questions—wanted him to take a drug test, and asked if he was selling pot, as Brad had apparently accused. And just like that—Sean lost his head completely. Everything he'd been through over the past half year boiled over. He took a swing at the officer—landed a left hook on his jaw.

The officer's partner, who had been questioning the neighbor who called them, came charging down the street. So Sean let loose on him too. He was so enraged it took both of them to get him in the police car and into the town lockup.

Not his best moment. Even now, he winced just thinking about it.

The next day, Evie's father bailed him out and said the charges would be dropped if he attended counseling sessions. But Sean couldn't take the disappointed, *concerned* look on his face. His whole world had fallen apart. He was teetering on the edge of an emotional cliff; he didn't want to take anyone down with him.

So he left Jupiter Point that night. He didn't see Evie again before he took off. But he did track down Brad at Barstow's, where he was boasting about his brush with the law--like the tool he was. He warned him to stay the fuck away from Evie from now on.

Then he left, and it was a relief to put Jupiter Point behind him. After the crash, everyone kept giving him those horrible, sympathetic "you poor baby" looks. He couldn't stand that. Even worse were the suspicious looks. The ones that said, *we know how much you fought with your pothead hippie father. We know the police think Jesse Marcus bought the flightseeing business to smuggle marijuana. We know the cause of the crash was never determined. We know something wasn't right. Where there's smoke there's fire.*

When he'd almost finished his starlight run, his phone rang in the pocket of his running shorts. The crazy thought that it might be Evie flitted through his mind. "Sean Marcus."

"It's Rollo."

"Holy crap, Rollo Wareham the Third, it's good to hear your

voice. How's the leg?" Rollo's leg had been broken by a falling log during the burnover. He had screws in his knee and a metal plate in his femur.

"Perfect. I'm like Iron Man. And I want on your crew."

"*What?*" He'd figured Rollo was done with firefighting after such a serious injury. He slowed to a jog to let his heart rate decrease slowly. "Why would you want that?"

"I'm getting a metric ton of pressure to join the family biz."

"CPA, right? Like you said during the burnover?"

"Uh, not exactly. It's a hedge fund kind of thing, office job. Suit and tie. I can't do it, Magneto."

Rollo didn't talk much about his family, but Sean knew they came from big money. Old money. Rollo was a big-hearted, generous, live-life-to-the-fullest kind of guy who hated social bullshit. Sean would love to have him on the crew. The brotherhood of the burnover reunited.

He dropped his pace to a walk. The night air cooled the sweat on the back of his neck. "Are you sure this would be the right move for you? Maybe you should find yourself a nice debutante back east and settle down."

"Did my family pay you to say that?"

Sean laughed. "I wish. Give them my number."

"Look, Sean. I don't feel like myself, you know? I've been working my ass off in PT. I want to get back into action. You can put me on probation, trial basis, whatever you want. You'll see. I'm completely ready to go. Better than before."

Sean wiped sweat off his forehead with the back of his hand

and glanced up at the thick, glowing carpet of stars overhead. "If I say yes, will you promise not to make me call you Iron Man?"

"No. It's a helluva good nickname, and I want it."

Sean laughed. God, it felt good to banter with Rollo again. For a while, after the burnover, he'd feared for his crewmate's mental state.

"Fine. Come for an interview. Give it a few weeks though. I have a list of candidates I can choose from, but they're giving me some discretion. Anyway, it's barebones here. We don't even have cots here yet. I'm sleeping on the hard floor in a sleeping bag."

"No friendly Jupiter Point girls willing to give the famous Magneto a place to sleep? You're losing your touch, man."

"You have no idea," Sean mumbled before hanging up. Less than one full day in town and he'd already sent one woman running the opposite direction.

And that wasn't right. First opportunity, he was going to find Evie and fix things. He'd upset her by reappearing out of the blue. Maybe he should have warned her. The decent thing to do would be to apologize, right? In person, if possible.

He tilted his head back to look up at the stars. His gaze went right to the planet Jupiter.

"It's community outreach," he told the distant planet—as if it cared. "That's all."

Chapter 6

The aftershocks of Evie's non-endorsement hit as soon as she walked into her parents' house the next morning. She always stopped in before work to kiss her mother and see what help her father needed that day.

"Good morning, Mama." She crouched next to her mother's recliner, where she spent most of her time since her diagnosis. Molly McGraw offered her a crooked but still radiant smile, set off by her white cotton-candy fluff of hair. The Parkinson's had been like a slow-moving earthquake in their lives. They'd adjusted to it in stages—special retrofitted shower, portable wheelchair, adaptive silverware, bars next to the toilet. The changes still came, making "normal" a moving target.

"Well, well, you look like the same daughter, despite what the town is saying." Her father walked in carrying a glass of water and a handful of pills. Everyone in town still called him the Dean even though he'd retired several years ago. Even Evie had gotten into that habit. Evie raised the recliner so her mother could take the medication more easily.

"Still me."

"I don't understand, Evie. You've known Brad your whole life."

Exactly, she wanted to say. *I know him.* But she'd never said one word to her parents about that night and didn't want to start now. "I can't talk about it right now. I have to get to work. Do you want me to do the grocery shopping or would you rather have me watch Mom while you take a break?"

Luckily, the Dean was a McGraw, and didn't like difficult conversations any more than she did. "You take care of the shopping. All this talk is bad for my digestion."

Ouch. Now she was giving her father gastrointestinal issues as well. The guilt…the guilt… "Text me a grocery list." She rose to her feet. "I'll stop by the store after work."

"Jim White's been calling me. I don't know quite what to say to him."

"Tell him I've lost my marbles," she snapped. "I'm sure that's what he thinks anyway. Have I lost my marbles, Mama?"

She made a whirling-finger "crazy" sign next to her temple. Her mother's lips lifted in an expression of delight.

"Don't do that," the Dean said sternly. "She's upset enough as it is. She slept very badly last night. Stress isn't good for her."

"Sorry." More guilt. She rested her cheek on the top of her mother's head. Her soft hair felt like comfort itself. The Parkinson's had progressed shockingly fast and she didn't speak much anymore. Talking exhausted her. Honestly, Evie didn't think something like Brad's endorsement would even register on her mother's list of worries.

But arguing with the Dean wasn't an option. They were McGraws, after all. Confrontation was not part of their DNA.

~ ~ ~

She spent the rest of the week fielding calls and visits from the other downtown business owners. Luckily Jack Drummond, the previous president and owner of the Rings of Saturn Jewelers, saved her butt.

"I've been telling everyone not to get their panties in a twist. You're holding out for more concrete promises, aren't you? Smart woman." He downed his espresso in one shot.

"I am?"

"Make him sweat. Brilliant move. He's running as a pro-business candidate. Just think how it's going to look if his own hometown business association doesn't endorse him. He'll promise us anything to get our support. I'll make sure the others understand your strategy here. Nice work, Evie."

"Um, thanks." Yup, it was all part of her master plan. The one that didn't exist and was bound to blow up in her face.

"Maybe I'll stop in at the bookstore and explain the situation to Mrs. Murphy."

"Sure. Okay." As soon as Jack left, she let out a lungful of air. This was getting so out of hand. Over the last few days, Brad had already called twice and left voice mails requesting a meeting with her. She should call him back and deliver the endorsement right now. Except that, try as she might, her fingers refused to hit the dial button.

At lunch, she turned her sign to "Moon," fled to her office, and made herself a peanut butter sandwich. Lunch of champions—or cowards hiding out in their back offices. The thought of meeting with Brad made her sandwich hard to swallow. She hadn't been alone with him since that night. But this was different. They were grown-ups. Professionals. They'd have the meeting in a public place. It would be fine. He couldn't hurt her anymore. He didn't *want* to hurt her. All he wanted was his endorsement.

Someone knocked on the front door. She ignored the intruder—couldn't they see that the gallery was closed?

After a few moments, the same knocking came at the back door, the one that opened onto her office. Exasperated, she wiped peanut butter off her fingers and flung it open.

Sean Marcus stood there, tall and wide-shouldered and mouthwatering. He wore a Dallas Cowboys t-shirt that adhered to every hard muscle of his chest. The heather-gray color emphasized his black hair and made his smoky eyes stand out like dark jade.

Her heart slammed against her chest. Not from nerves, but from something she wasn't used to feeling. Anticipation. A sort of buzz, as if something exciting was about to happen.

She ruthlessly ignored it. She had no business getting fluttery over Sean Marcus. "I'm closed," she told him.

"I noticed." He strolled in as if the information meant nothing to him.

"That closed sign applies to hotshots too."

"It doesn't apply to old friends, does it?"

She screwed up her face. "I can't say that I ever thought of you that way." Giving in, she closed the door behind him. She followed him as he prowled into her domain, struggling to keep her gaze off his killer rear-end.

"Really? That sounds almost flirtatious."

"Well, it wasn't," she told him firmly. "I never flirt. I wouldn't even know how to."

In the midst of surveying her office, he paused and examined her intently. "Why not? Does a woman like you not need to?"

"A woman like me? What does that mean?"

He raised an eyebrow and looked her up and down, quick and scorching. "Come on, Evie. You don't need *me* to tell you you're a knockout."

She honestly hated it when anyone made reference to her appearance. She definitely didn't see what everyone else seemed to. "Eye of the beholder," she muttered, shrugging off his compliment, if that's what it was. "What are you doing here, Sean?"

"I talked to Hunter. He told me you started this gallery a few years ago. Said you like to show it off."

"I *love* to show it off during regular business hours." She brushed crumbs off her skirt, an A-line number in a lovely shade of putty.

"All right, point taken. But this is the only time I could make it. Come on, I came to apologize. Give a guy a break."

Oh, that sneaky groove in his cheek—it ought to be abolished. It took his face from rugged to devastating.

"Fine, I'll give you a tour, but let's make it quick. This is my only break and the entire town's been driving me crazy all day."

"I bet. Even I've been hearing about it."

"Really?" She pulled a face as she led the way out of the back office onto the main gallery floor. She'd painted the walls a creamy white and installed a cherry wood floor that she was still paying off. The new espresso bar took up the far corner, and a big bay window overlooked Constellation Way. The space was clean and understated, but she wondered if it looked maybe a little dull.

"Gas station, coffee shop, you name it. You're the talk of the town. They say what you did was very out of character for the virgin saint of Jupiter Point."

"The *what*?"

"They didn't use those words," he added quickly. "It was more of an overall impression. People say you're kind and caring, sweet, accommodating."

Accommodating, my ass. "Were you always this aggravating or have you been working on this side of your personality?" She moved around the counter to the espresso machine. Caffeine might improve this encounter.

"Truth?"

She batted her eyelashes at him. "Only if you sugarcoat it for the virgin saint."

He smiled broadly. "Touché. By the way, yes, I'd love an espresso."

She ground her teeth. She hadn't even invited him here, and now she was giving him a tour and making him coffee? The nerve. "That'll be ten dollars."

"A ten-dollar espresso?"

"The price goes up when I'm closed."

He laughed. "I'd pay a lot more than that to have coffee with you."

Again that excitement surged into her throat. She put a hand to her neck as if to push it back down. She went behind the counter and pulled two shots of espresso, but in truth, she barely knew what she was doing. Sean had all her attention. Goose bumps rippled up and down her skin as his deep voice washed over her.

"Truth is—since you asked—I'm going out of my way to irritate you because I like that look you get in your eye."

"You mean that bloody-murder look?"

"That's it. Exactly. It suits you."

She pushed the demitasse of espresso across the counter. A bit of coffee sloshed into the saucer. "Didn't you mention something about an apology?"

"Right." The grin vanished from his face and he looked at her seriously. "I upset you after the meeting. I felt bad about it."

"I wasn't upset because of you. Well, not originally, anyway. It was just…" She trailed off. "I wasn't really mad at you. I was mad at myself for doing something so crazy."

He picked up the tiny cup. She was fascinated by how big his hands looked compared to the cup. A scar ran across his knuckles and a raised burn mark marred his thumb. "You said what was real. You didn't want to support that asshole. What's so crazy about that?"

"My personal feelings have nothing to do with it. And I don't want to talk about this anymore. Please. I've been bombarded all week."

"As milady commands." He lifted the cup to her and tossed back the shot. "Can I ask one more question?"

She rested her elbows on the counter and propped her chin in her cupped hand. "Could I possibly stop you?"

"Of course you could. But why would you want to? We're old friends, remember?"

A smile quivered at the corners of her lips. She remembered how much Sean Marcus used to fight with his father. "A handful," he'd been described as back then. Not much had changed, apparently. "What's your question?"

But now that he had her permission, he didn't seem to want to ask his question. He got to his feet and prowled close to the display of photographs taken through the infrared telescope at the Jupiter Point Observatory. Solar flares in vivid purples and oranges, a close up of the Tarantula Nebula, a view of Mercury during its transit across the sun.

"Did you take any of these?" he asked abruptly.

"Of course not. Those are from the Observatory telescope. I'm just an amateur." What would it be like to photograph Sean? Spectacular, most likely. Those turbulent eyes, slashing cheekbones, jaw brushed with stubble. She'd pose him straight on, staring right into the camera, daring the viewer to pass judgment. The background would be dark, with a shaft of sunlight illuminating him.

"You used to talk about backpacking around Europe or Southeast Asia with your camera. Did you ever do that?"

She hadn't thought about that idea in years. "No."

He looked at her inscrutably. "College?"

"Sure." She lifted her chin. "Jupiter Point Community. My father was the Dean there, remember? What about you?"

"Sort of. After I left here, I got my BA in fire science and took a bunch of extra training courses. I have the equivalent of an advanced degree. But it's all in fire science."

"Why firefighting?"

He shrugged. "I wanted to keep busy. I thought about the military, but you remember my dad. The ultimate anti-government hippie. The whole 'question authority' thing was drilled into me pretty hard. Of course, he hated it when that included him. Anyway, I decided I wouldn't be a good fit as a soldier."

Back when Sean had lived with them, her mother used to try to draw him out on the subject of his parents. But he never bit, not once. And now he was bringing the topic up on his own. Intending to comfort, she put a hand on his forearm.

The shock of the contact felt like a current of voltage passing through her. Quickly, she snatched her hand away.

He gave her a funny look, as if he wanted to say something but wasn't sure he should.

"What?" She clasped both hands behind her back and tried to steady them.

"You should go out to dinner with me."

"*What?*"

Nothing he said could have shocked her more. Not that dinner invitations were unusual. She received more than her share, and definitely more than she ever thought about accepting. Sometimes she thought asking her to dinner and getting rejected must be a rite of passage for the men of Jupiter Point. Like getting drunk at Barstow's Brews or skinny-dipping at Stargazer Beach.

"Does that seem like a strange idea?"

"Well…" She trailed off. He hadn't exactly *asked* her to dinner. He'd just told her she should. "I don't date."

"Ever?"

"I mean, I go on dates, of course. But…" She bit her lip, embarrassed to complete the thought.

"But…" he repeated. When she didn't answer, he folded his arms across his chest. "I'm not leaving until you answer," he warned her. "You can't just leave that 'but' hanging out there. Isn't there a grammar rule about that?"

She scowled at him. "You're aggravating me again."

"Yes, I can tell. Your eyes are all lit up like a backyard bonfire. It's turning me on."

"Fires turn you on?"

"No. That's all you, sweetness."

She wanted to run. She wanted to tackle him and kiss him. She wanted to scream. All at the same time—which made no sense at all. "I don't date because of this. Exactly this." She gave him a little mock-shove. Which would have worked except that she felt the warmth of his body and the solid curve of muscle under his t-shirt. And then she couldn't pull her hand away. And *then*—he was holding her hand in place, nice and secure, right against his hard chest.

"Because of what, exactly?" His voice was low, intimate, and did devastating things to her insides. "You'll have to be more specific."

"Because of men. Because men are men. Like you. Being a man." Oh, the babbling…but it was impossible to keep her head when he smelled so good and felt so strong.

"Guilty as charged. I'm feeling especially man-like at the moment."

She swallowed hard. That tingling sensation racing through her made it so hard to concentrate. "I occasionally go on dates, but only out of obligation. I have much better things to do with my time."

A muscle ticked in his jaw, and for an instant, awareness flashed in his eyes. *He understood*, she realized. He knew it was because of Brad. That panicked her more than anything else.

But as quickly as it came, the look vanished, replaced by something more smoldering. "If you go to dinner with me, I promise it'll be the best possible use of your time."

She pulled herself from his grip. It felt like fighting against quicksand, or gravity.

"Sorry," she told him coolly. "I'm far too busy these days. I have a town scandal to deal with. And don't you have a hotshot base to open?"

He tilted his head, as if granting her the victory—temporarily. "Fine. The offer's still on the table if you change your mind. Thank you for the coffee." Whistling softly, he headed for the door.

On his way out, he flipped her sign to "open."

"You're welcome," he called as he disappeared down the

street.

The *nerve* of the man.

Chapter 7

"Margaritas," declared Brianna when she breezed into the gallery shortly before closing.

"Count me in," Evie said right away. Brianna darted into the back office, where she kept a change of clothes. The sound of water splashing told Evie that her friend was rinsing off the soil accumulated from her day of tending gardens around Jupiter Point. Ever since they used to build fairy houses in the woods as children, Brianna had wanted to design gardens, and she was brilliant at it.

Evie finished tallying up the day's receipts just as Brianna reappeared. Her hair clung in damp curls around her face and she wore a flowered sundress.

Evie raised her eyebrows in surprise at her tomboy friend's transformation. "Are we celebrating something?"

"Yes. We survived week one of the Brad-apocalypse. These brain cells need a reward. And you look like you could use some tequila in your system. Merry has a booth waiting at the Orbit. Come on!"

They strolled down Constellation Way, past the Fifth Book

from the Sun and the Goodnight Moon B&B, with its courtyard draped with jasmine and star twinkle lights. Jupiter Point's downtown businesses catered to tourists, especially honeymooners. Honeymooners didn't mind spending money on a once-in-a-lifetime experience. Their little town had more B&Bs and romantic restaurants per capita than any other town in California. If you honeymooned in Jupiter Point, you could enjoy a catered night picnic in a bungalow on the beach, a romantic sunset sailboat cruise, maybe a private tour of the Observatory with a chance to name your own star.

As the president of the JPBC, it was Evie's job to make sure business continued to grow.

Great job so far.

They joined Merry Warren at the most popular hangout in town, the Orbit Lounge and Grill, with its glow-in-the-dark stars scattered across the ceiling. Evie had become good friends with Merry after she'd written a piece in the *Mercury News-Gazette* about the gallery opening. Merry had moved to Jupiter Point from Louisiana to advance her journalism career. Evie loved her fiery spirit and her passion for facts and details. Even though some locals had been wary of an outside reporter—of mixed race—she'd proved herself right away.

Merry rose to her feet and gave Evie a long hug and a whispered, "Hang in there."

"In case you're wondering," she added as they sat down, "I'm off the clock and everything said tonight is in the vault. So feel free to vent."

Evie took a long swallow of the watermelon margarita already waiting for her. "I'm fine, really. I'll say one thing. Becoming the talk of the town is good for business. This was the busiest day for the gallery so far. I even managed to guilt a few people into buying pieces."

"Come for the gossip, stay for the art?" Brianna grinned as she picked up her usual neon-green melon margarita.

"Whatever it takes." With a weary smile, Evie sucked down another inch of her margarita. In fact, after Sean had asked her to dinner, the rest of the day had sailed by as if it were a dream. Not even Mrs. Murphy's afternoon interrogation had bothered her.

"Sean asked me out," she said casually, straw still between her teeth.

"*What?*" Brianna spluttered in the midst of swallowing.

"That's what's known as burying the lead, girl." Merry gave her a little flick on the arm.

"Ow."

"When did this happen?" Brianna bounced up and down on the black pleather seat. "This is fantastic! He's so hot, I can barely stand it. Are you going to go out with him?"

"Of course not."

"*What?*" Both of her friends stared at her as if she'd turned into a cactus.

"I don't like dating. Everyone knows that."

"Yes, but…this is Sean Marcus." Brianna enunciated the name carefully, emphasizing every syllable. "He's a fireman." She ticked off the items on her fingers. "He's brutally hot. He has money. You knew that, right? He inherited everything after the plane crash. He's got that bad boy thing going on. Didn't he spend a night in jail?"

"Really?" Merry perked up, her eyes bright with interest. "No one mentioned that to me when I did my profile on him for the paper."

Evie hurried the conversation past that topic. "I'm not interested in going out with Sean."

"I call B.S. on that," said Brianna. "I saw you looking at him during the meeting. And I also saw him looking at you. No no, Evie, this is great news. I'm not letting you off the hook on this one."

"Excuse me? I can make this decision for myself." The waiter dropped off a bowl of guacamole and chips, then hurried away again. The place was starting to fill up, as it always did during happy hour.

"Nope, I'm making it for you." Brianna pointed a tortilla chip at her. "You need to go out with him. Actually, no you don't. You hate dating, and why wouldn't you? Dating sucks. You don't need to date him. You just need to fuck him."

Evie choked on a mouthful of margarita, while Merry whooped and high-fived Brianna.

"I'm tired of this ice queen act you've been working on. You've convinced yourself that you don't need a man. But I know that's not true. Maybe you don't *need* a man. But you *want* a man."

"You don't know what I want."

"Merry, help me out here. Does or doesn't Evie want Sean Marcus's hot body?"

Merry gave Evie an apologetic smirk. "Based on my

observations as a reporter, I'd have to say that's a yes."

"You're attracted to him, right, Evie? Come on. This booth is a zone of complete privacy. And we're your friends so you can tell us anything."

When Brianna got that look in her eye, Evie knew she wouldn't quit. "I admit I'm attracted to him. That doesn't mean anything."

"It means *everything.* Evie, I'm tired of you locking yourself away like, like, Sleeping Beauty or something. You have so much more to offer someone. I know you're not happy. I've known you my whole life. I know Happy Evie, and this isn't it—I mean, you."

Stung, Evie lashed back. "I'm not locking myself away. I'm a semi-successful businesswoman. I'm the head of the Jupiter Point Business Coalition. I'm always there for my mom. I'm a good friend."

"You're an amazing friend," Brianna agreed.

Merry nodded and put her hand to her own heart. "You are a fantastic friend. I'd still be an outsider here if you hadn't befriended me."

Brianna continued, almost as if she were putting Evie on trial. "And you're an amazing daughter. You stayed in Jupiter Point so you could help take care of her. You're always kind, always calm, amazing, perfect Evie, like…like…Venus shining from the sky."

None of this sounded like praise. "I never said I was perfect." Tears sprang to her eyes, then overflowed.

"Oh no, I made you cry. I didn't mean to make you cry! I know you didn't say you were perfect. Evie, you know I love you."

Brianna was sitting next to her, but she scooted closer and wrapped her arms around Evie and leaned her head against her shoulder. "You're my best friend. I adore you. But you need to break out of this rut you're in. And if you're attracted to Sean, that's your body telling you you're still alive. That Happy Evie is still in there."

Evie endured Brianna's hug, wishing she could explain. Evie had never told her what happened with Brad, how ever since then, she froze up when she got within kissing distance of a man.

Except...she hadn't frozen up with Sean. And he'd definitely been within kissing distance. He'd been so close to her body. She'd felt his heat, his solid physique, the ridges of tendon and muscle. She hadn't freaked out. She'd gotten excited. Turned on.

Wow. Maybe Brianna was right.

"You okay, Evie?" Merry asked softly. One of the things Evie loved about Merry was her perceptiveness. Not that Brianna wasn't perceptive...well, she wasn't, actually. She was more of a bull in a china shop, knocking things down every time she turned around. She was forthright—okay, maybe tactless—but her heart was always in the right place and no one was more loyal. Brianna always had her back.

She should tell her friends what had happened with Brad. Before she lost her nerve, she opened her mouth to do so.

Then snapped it shut as she caught sight of Brad and two of his campaign workers walking into the Orbit. In shirtsleeves, with his suit jacket slung over his shoulder, his tie loosened, he could have walked out of a men's magazine article on up-and-coming politicians.

He scanned the guests, waving to some, winking at others. Then his gaze lighted on her and his smile dropped for a fast second. He beckoned to his two followers and the group headed toward their booth. She felt like a rabbit hypnotized by a snake.

"Evie McGraw, I've been trying to reach you."

"Hi Brad." *Keep your cool, keep your cool.*

She felt Brianna take her hand and squeezed back, grateful for the grounding effect of her warmth.

"I was hoping we could have dinner sometime to discuss this situation." Even though Brad was smiling, his gray eyes held a frigid fury. It was hard to believe she used to moon over him. "Word has it you're playing hardball, and I'm willing to play along for the good of the town. Controversies aren't good for the honeymoon business."

Ugh, he knew her soft spots so well. She didn't want to hurt Jupiter Point. She loved her hometown, and she loved peace and harmony as much as she hated controversy. Now she was stuck in the middle.

She glanced around and saw that everyone in the Orbit was aware of their conversation. Some customers were openly staring; others were more surreptitious.

Brianna spoke up. "If Evie doesn't want to, she shouldn't have to—"

Evie cut her off. As much as she loved Brianna, she had to fight her own battles. "That's fine, Brad. We can discuss the situation over dinner."

"I'll have someone call you and set it up." Brad nodded to one of his lackeys, who made a note in his smartphone. He beamed one of his fake smiles at her, forcing her to respond with one of her own.

Great, now everyone in the place had seen them smiling at each other. Point to Brad.

As soon as Brad's group had settled in at their own table, Evie slumped against the back of the booth. She gripped her hands together to stop them from shaking. "Did I really just agree to dinner with him?"

"Yes." Brianna drained her margarita. "Two dinner invitations in one day, and you say yes to Brad's. I have to say, between Sean and Brad, I'd pick Sean any day. Between Brad *Pitt* and Sean, I'd pick Sean."

The waiter swung by their booth with a tray of margaritas. "Courtesy of Brad White," he informed them. Evie wanted to throw them on the floor, but instead she smiled politely.

God, she was tired of smiling politely.

"What about that other hotshot?" Merry posed the question. "What are we thinking about him?"

Evie withdrew into herself as Merry and Brianna began playing the "Who Would You Rather" game. The violent revulsion she felt around Brad still echoed through her nervous system. Her heart was galloping, nausea clutched at her throat. He had such a powerful effect on her, even after all these years. How was she going to survive an entire dinner with him? She might throw up.

This was exactly why she always avoided him. Why she avoided all—

A lightning bolt of understanding flashed through her.

Brad White had stolen her sexuality.

She'd never thought of it that way before. She knew she avoided men because they made her anxious. The Incident had been too traumatic, too unexpected, and too completely suppressed. The one time she'd spoken about it, to Aunt Desiree, she'd been warned to keep her mouth shut. The memory sat there like a big, ugly, silent toad, tainting everything. As if Brad had put a spell on her.

Brad had stolen her sexual side. No—she'd *let* him steal it. Or at least bury it so deep that she'd turned down an invitation from a very attractive, very appealing man, someone who made her feel alive.

Brianna was right. Maybe she didn't need a man, but she wanted one—the one who'd been in her gallery earlier. Her sexual side still existed. Her reaction to Sean proved that.

Maybe she'd responded so strongly to Sean because she didn't have to hide anything from him. He knew what had happened. Or maybe it was just that he was so irresistibly sexy. Whatever the reason, maybe this was the perfect opportunity to reclaim what Brad had stolen.

"Evie, did you hear what I said?"

"What?" She shook her head, tuning back into their conversation.

"If you don't want to take my advice and go to bed with Sean, I have another idea. Just give it a chance. Try one kiss with him."

"One kiss?"

"Yes. One kiss. If you feel enough sparks to take it further, then you can. If you don't, you can let it go."

"What if *he* doesn't let it go?" The nightmare with Brad had started with an innocent kiss.

"You mean if he falls hopelessly in love with you? Which is pretty likely given what a great person you are?"

Evie's face heated. Sean didn't look like the type of man who would fall hopelessly in love. "That's not what I mean."

"Look, a kiss is a kiss. That's all it has to be. People kiss all the time. In fact, Jupiter Point probably has more kisses per hour than anywhere else, thanks to all the honeymooners. It's just a kiss. Just give it a shot, Evie. Promise?"

She closed her eyes and pictured Sean's rugged face lowering over hers, the firm curves of his lips brushing against her own. Would his kiss be gentle or intense? Deep or tender? She could use her imagination…or she could use her courage. "Okay."

Chapter 8

Sean threw himself into the task of getting the crew geared up. Their crew buggies arrived—two green box-like trucks fitted with storage cupboards and space for hotshots to pile in and drive wherever they needed to. The freshly painted black lettering "Jupiter Point Hotshots" gave him a special thrill. Once the fire season started, they'd be practically living in those things.

In the meantime, the barracks would be the home for all non-local members of the crew. As soon as the cots arrived he and Josh spent half a day setting them up. He ordered gear from the nearest fire cache, and almost every day, a truck arrived with a delivery. Chainsaws, spare chains, gloves, helmets, gear duffels, line bags, canteens, boot grease, bug dope, sleeping bags, tent, everything that the hotshot crew would bring with them to a fire.

All the hard work kept Sean from thinking too much about Evie, and about all the ghosts of his past that lived here in Jupiter Point. He focused only on the task at hand. But that ended when a police car drove onto the base a couple of weeks after the city council meeting.

Sean put down the box of gloves he was unloading and watched, hands on hips, as a six-foot-seven-inch-tall black man unfurled himself from the car. Sean remembered him all too well. He was the arresting officer Sean had slugged that fateful night. Looking at the man now, it was hard to believe he'd had the balls to lash out at someone so intimidating.

He strode toward him, hand outstretched. "Officer Brady Becker."

"Chief Becker now. Been police chief for five years."

"Congratulations." They shook hands and eyed each other with mutual wariness. Josh strolled over from the supply cache to join them.

"Josh Marshall, Chief Becker." Sean watched as they shook hands. He mentally skimmed through all his recent actions. Had he broken any laws? He didn't think so.

"You're really whipping this place into shape." Becker cast a dubious glance at the boxes of supplies littering the pavement.

"We're getting there. Bit by bit. What can I help you with, Chief?"

"Can I talk to you in private?"

"Is it necessary? Josh is my assistant and needs to be in the loop on everything."

"Up to you." Becker clasped his hands behind his back, and readied himself to speak.

But before the chief could say anything, Sean decided to get something off his chest. He heaved in some air, then went for it in a rush. "I need to apologize for losing my temper that night. I shouldn't have gone after you guys the way I did. It was wrong."

Becker lifted his eyebrows. "Accepted. I gotta say I was surprised to see you back in Jupiter Point, considering how things went down."

The chief's tone of voice made Sean feel like a troublesome teenager again instead of a fully-grown adult, and he didn't like it one bit. "All that's in the past. I'm here to do a job, that's it."

"You had a job, didn't you? You left the Fighting Scorpions to come here."

"This is a better job."

Becker continued. "I remember you in that holding cell, raging at the entire world. You swore you'd never come back to this piece of shit town. That's a direct quote."

Sean winced at the reminder. That night, all his grief and anger had exploded. He barely remembered half the shit he'd said. It was probably a really good thing he'd been behind bars. "I was seventeen, and I was a little fucked up at that point."

Becker raised his eyebrow again in that silent, maddening way.

"Okay, a lot fucked up. But that was then, this is now. Why are you here, Chief?"

He heard the edge in his own voice, and saw Josh give him a 'cool it' gesture. Good idea—the last thing he needed was a repeat performance of that night.

"Can I ask what brought you back, besides the job?" Even though his tone was pleasant enough, the look on his face said otherwise. Sean felt a familiar anger build inside. Back in high school, he'd gotten that look a lot—that suspicious, "you're up to no good" look. It drove him nuts.

But he'd come a long way since then. He was much better at channeling his emotions in a good direction. "I'm not sure you have the right to ask that," he said evenly.

Becker considered him for a long moment. They stood in a sort of standoff, High Noon style.

Josh stepped into the tense silence. "I have to interrupt for a second. Sean is here because he's the best possible man for this job. I can vouch for that. You guys in Jupiter Point are lucky to have him."

Sean reminded himself to buy Josh a beer or two. It felt damn good to have someone stand up for him. Really damn good. But he knew some of the townspeople had to be worried about him being back. Was the chief here on their behalf?

Becker scrutinized them both. When he spoke again, his tone had shifted.

"Look, Marcus. I cut you a few breaks back then. You used to do some wild, reckless dumbass shit. How many times did you sneak into Barstow's?"

"Barstow's?" Josh perked up. "Is that the place with the two-dollar drafts on weeknights?"

Becker ignored him. "You had more energy than you could handle. But you got a tough hand dealt to you, I knew that. I always saw you as someone who could turn his life around. Looks like you did, and I'm glad to see it. Mind if I ask where you went after you took off?"

Sean let out the breath he'd been holding. Since Becker was no longer addressing him like a rebellious teen, he didn't mind answering a few questions. "Would that put your mind at ease?"

"It might," Becker said. "I had a responsibility, and it always bothered me that you just disappeared after the Dean came and got you." He actually offered up a smile, a wry twist of his lips.

"Chief…" Something struck Sean in that moment. "Were you actually worried about me?"

"Of course I was. I knew you were hurting."

And that, more than anything else Becker could have said, made Sean relax and answer the question. "I went camping after I left. I bought myself a tent and went into the Sierra Nevadas and hiked until my boots fell apart. Pretty nefarious, huh?"

Becker tilted his head, listening closely, so Sean went on. "When I got my head together, I went to Colorado, where my aunt lived, and got a degree in fire science. I didn't intend to come back here, but…" He shrugged. "I had to. And that's all I'm going to say."

"All right, then. Fair enough." Becker tucked his thumbs in his belt loops. "There's one more thing you can do for me, Marcus. I'm following up on a threat you made to Brad White before you left town."

"Are you kidding me? That was thirteen years ago."

"And yet he was in my office the other day reminding me of it."

Goddamn—the nerve of that guy. He must be completely sure that Sean would never say *why* he'd issued that threat. Actually, Sean would call it more of a warning than a threat. But if he kept up this bullshit, Sean might go for a threat after all.

As if he knew the direction of Sean's thoughts, Becker said in a challenging tone, "Do you promise to stay away from Brad White?"

Sean's jaw clenched so tightly it hurt. "I have so far."

"And Evie McGraw?"

"Excuse me?"

"There were three kids there that night. You, Brad and Evie. I don't know what happened, and I guess I don't need to. But my job is to keep the peace. So I'm hoping you'll keep a safe distance."

Even though Evie was keeping her distance just fine all on her own, Becker's request rankled. Sean had asked Evie to dinner, and he still hoped she'd come around. No way was he going to promise to stay away from Evie.

"You're out of line, Chief."

He threw up his hands. "You're right, you're right. Look. If you want to make a good impression around here, don't mess with Evie. She's had it rough herself, with her mother's diagnosis."

Diagnosis? Molly McGraw, the sweet, kind woman who'd invited him to live with them, had been diagnosed with something? Evie hadn't mentioned anything about that. He wanted to ask for more details, but Becker was still talking.

"There's something about Evie that makes people want to protect her. Half of my force is in love with her. One of my guys even put it into a poem. So my advice is, keep your distance."

Josh pounced on that little detail like a cat on a mouse. "A policeman poet? Now I've heard it all."

Becker swung a glare his direction. "It's a beautiful piece of work. Mentions her luminous eyes and skin like pearls. Damn literary."

"Okay then." Josh was turning red from trying to restrain his mirth.

"Word to the wise, that's all." Becker shook both of their hands, then strode back to his unit. "Let's keep things cool around here. Good luck with your boxes."

As he drove away, Sean scrubbed a hand through his hair.

"That's got to be a first." Josh finally let his laughter burst out. "A warning and a poem, all in the same conversation. I like this town."

All of a sudden, Sean felt the urge to be alone, to get away from this place, from Josh's laughter. "I'm out. Back in a few."

"Stay away from Evie," Josh called after him as he strode toward the truck.

~ ~ ~

Sean drove to the place where the ghosts lived.

Jesse Marcus had dragged his family to Jupiter Point because of an airstrip he'd seen for sale in a flight magazine. He'd purchased two small, fixed-wing planes and set up Marcus Flight Tours. Sean always suspected he intended to smuggle drugs through the flightseeing service, but Jesse never copped to it.

After the crash, no one had stepped forward to purchase the business, and it had been liquidated. The lawyers had sold the planes, but Sean had kept the property. He'd never missed a tax payment, even though they were pretty hefty. He'd turned down a few purchase offers. He wasn't sure why it was important to him, since he'd never intended to return. He had no clue what to do with an old airstrip.

But it was a little piece of Jupiter Point, and it was all he had left of his family. He hadn't wanted to let it go.

The airstrip was located outside of town, at the end of a long, barely maintained gravel road. It was only half a mile from the ocean, and beach grass grew wild to the edge of the runway. Sean parked next to the entrance, which was chained off. "No Trespassing" signs were posted every twenty feet or so—the estate lawyers' idea. A light wind rustled the knee-high grass and bright California poppies grew wild alongside the tarmac.

The property didn't have much to offer—one ramshackle hangar, a small office building that doubled as a waiting room. But the view was pretty amazing. The blue Pacific shimmered off to the west, and the stunning bulk of Jupiter Point rose to the east. The scent of salt air and sweet grass, and the faintest ghost of airplane fuel, brought back a rush of memories.

Ugly memories.

The time he'd been so angry at Jesse that he'd jumped out of the cockpit while the plane was still moving.

The time Jesse had locked him in the hangar until he'd finished the maintenance chores he'd been assigned.

He could practically hear the voices from all those battles floating in the air.

"This is the stupidest thing you've ever gotten us into, Jesse! Even stupider than that peony farm!"

"Your adolescent rebellion is getting old, man. It doesn't matter what I pick, you'll hate it. It's an adventure, that's what life is for."

"How is some Podunk nowhere town an adventure? Smoke some more weed, why don't you?"

"You should try it. A little more mellow would do you good."

"I should call the cops on you. You're offering a controlled substance to a minor."

"Department of Empty Threats, you have a caller."

"I'm going to file for emancipation as soon as I can."

"I don't know why you haven't already. You afraid?"

"Yes! Afraid you'll do something really stupid and land Mom in jail!"

Sean shook his head violently to chase away those voices. All those fights with his father and nothing had ever been resolved. And it never would be. One freak accident and it was over. No more fighting. No more words at all.

For months after the crash, the words Sean wanted to say ran through his mind on a nonstop loop. The stuff in his head had more reality than anything around him. He was barely aware of the McGraws. He zoned out during school. He hardly spoke to Hunter, even though they shared the upper floor of the house.

It wasn't until he'd spotted Evie's panicked face squished under Brad White that he'd snapped out of his stupor. Then during that night in jail, he realized it was time to stop thinking and act. Pick a path and take some sort of step forward. Ever since then, he'd kept moving. He'd been driven to succeed, to prove himself. To triumph over every impossible situation.

So why had he come back to Jupiter Point? *Good question, Chief Becker.* Why the fuck would he come back to the place where people saw him as nothing but trouble? The place where he was known as that hippie Jesse Marcus's no-good son?

Maybe he wanted to prove he was more than that. Maybe he wanted to prove everyone wrong.

Chapter 9

As he drove back to the base, he got a text from Josh. "TROUBLE. Going for a run. Make wise choices."

Ah, hell. Was he ever going to get a moment's peace in this town?

An unfamiliar white car was parked in the visitor lot. A cute little Jetta—girl car. How much trouble could that mean?

He strode into the reception area, braced for the worst.

Evie spun around at the sound of his footsteps, causing him to stop in his tracks. Hot damn. She looked incredible and…different. Her hair was loose over her bare shoulders. She wore a sleeveless dress the color of pink roses.

The richness of the pink suited her. It put color in her cheeks and brought out her sexiness. Those long, tan legs…he gave a silent wolf whistle as his cock tightened. He hoped her effect on him wasn't too obvious.

"Welcome to the Jupiter Point Hotshots," he said easily, shoving his hands in his pockets. Maybe that would help mask his reaction. "What can I help you with?"

She pulled her bottom lip between her teeth and stared at him. He had no clue how to interpret her expression. She looked as if she was about to jump off a cliff or something.

A sudden thought struck him. "Is your mother okay? Chief Becker mentioned that she was sick. Hunter never told me, or I would have said something. She was always very sweet to me and—"

He broke off, because she was now walking toward him with an air of firm determination. "Evie?"

"Yes?"

"What are you—"

And then she was pressed against him. She stood on tiptoe and brushed her mouth against his. For a moment he stood frozen to the floor while the sweet sensation of her soft lips sent shockwaves through him.

Evie McGraw was kissing him.

This was real. And spectacular. And it might never happen again. *Don't blow it.* He restrained his natural reaction, which was to haul her against him and ravage her mouth. He stood immobile, letting her take the lead. One wrong move might make her come to her senses.

She kissed him with gentle curiosity, as if she was testing something. Experimenting. Sliding her tongue across his upper lip, into his mouth. Nibbling. It felt so fresh, so new and fascinating, like the beginning of a story he hadn't heard before. Her scent surrounded him, not just the sweet rose petal fragrance of shampoo, but the deeper, wilder scent of *her*.

Was that the real Evie hiding behind the cool, calm exterior?

Unable to keep his arms still any longer, he brought them around her back and stroked the sleek length of her spine. Her breath hitched. That soft sound sent blood pounding into his cock. He moved his hips backward because he didn't want her to feel how hard she made him. Something told him it might freak her out.

"Sean," she whispered against his lips. "Will you do something for me?"

"Yes," he said promptly, not caring what it was.

"Will you kiss me for real?"

His hands spanned her lower back. The urge to yank her against him was strong, so strong, but he fought it. "We *are* kissing, thanks to you."

"I know we are. Believe me. But I want *you* to kiss *me.* The full-on, full-throttle, Full Monty version. Like a movie kiss."

"A movie kiss. You got it." He pulled her snug against him, allowing her to feel his hard-on. Hey, she had mentioned "Full Monty." Her eyes widened in awareness. He plunged his hands into her rich fall of hair, enjoying the silky slide against his fingers. Slowly, firmly, he tilted her head back. He hovered his mouth over hers, enjoying the quickening of her breath, taking in every close-up detail of her silvery-green eyes, her long lashes, the little scar near her cheekbone.

Finally, when he couldn't wait anymore, he swept his tongue across the seam of her lips. She opened for him eagerly. With long, deep strokes, he explored the succulent wetness of her mouth. Lust churned inside him. He imagined her full lips around his cock, the innocent way she'd take him deep into her throat. He pictured her spread open before him, flushed with pleasure as he drove his cock balls-deep.

Oh *fuck*.

He muttered words against her swollen lips, hot things off the top of his head—*I want to throw you down...I want to lick your nipples...I want to take you deep*—he barely knew what he was saying. She pressed against him, her nipples pebble-hard, the sensation sending new jolts of lust through him.

When she pulled away, it was such a shock he actually got disoriented. He yanked his hands away from her and interlaced them behind his head. She was too tempting. He wanted to touch her too badly. "You okay?"

She stared at him, looking just as disoriented as he was. One hand came up to touch her lips. Color came and went under her creamy skin. He couldn't read her expression—aroused, yes, that much he could figure out. But what else? Upset? Excited? Angry?

"Well," she finally said in a breathless voice. "I guess that answers that."

"Answers what?"

"The question I had."

He lowered his hands and shifted his jeans so they didn't press against his engorged cock quite so much. "That's pretty mysterious."

"Sorry. You're right. I just...I have to think about this."

"Think about what? The fact that we just kissed in the reception area of the Jupiter Point Hotshots? By the way, I have twenty cots back there just waiting to get broken in."

That brought a smile to her kiss-swollen lips. "That's very romantic."

"That's me. One hundred percent romance. What brought you here, Evie?"

She blinked at him. "I wanted to kiss you."

"That's it? Mission accomplished?"

"Well, there's…there might be something more." She laced her fingers together. "I came here for a reason, you're right, and…I did want to…um, propose something. Suggest something. But we should probably talk more first."

Hot color flooded her face. God, she was adorable. He wanted to scoop her up and lick her all over, turn her boneless and happy and blissed-out.

"Okay," he agreed. "You busy tonight?"

Her face fell, all that lovely sparkle evaporating. "I can't tonight. I have a dinner meeting. It's not something I want to do, but I said I would."

Her frowned. That sounded ominous. "Who's your meeting with?"

"I have to have dinner with Brad."

"*What?*" He gripped her upper arms. "No way. You can't do that."

"Of course I can." She tugged against his grasp. "I have to. It's all arranged. I'm the current head of the business coalition and this is part of my job."

"Then I'm going too."

"No. That's not a good idea."

Even though Chief Becker had told him the exact same thing earlier in the day, Sean didn't care.

"Please, Evie. I know what he is. You can't trust him. I won't get in the middle of anything. He won't know I'm there. Just tell me where you're going to be and I'll sit in a car outside."

"With binoculars and a fake mustache?"

Great, now she was making a joke out of it. His jaw tightened and he drew her a little closer. If only he could kiss some sense into her. "Whatever it takes. I saw his face when you refused to endorse him. He's furious. You shouldn't be alone with him."

"He's not violent, Sean. We live in the same town, our families are close. His father grew up with mine."

"Weren't all those same things true when you were fourteen? Don't tell me he was just a kid then. He was my age, and he knew exactly what he was doing."

She bit her lip and looked down at the floor. He felt bad, being this forceful, but in his opinion, she wasn't taking this seriously enough.

"Fine," she finally said, looking up. "But don't let him see you. That might piss him off even more."

"I won't. I promise. Hand me your phone, I'll put my number in. Keep it pulled up, ready to dial. I'll be less than a minute away."

After she drove off, Sean thought again about Chief Becker's request. He wanted Sean to avoid Brad and Evie. Now he was going to be in the same place as both of them. At the same time.

Well, he'd always had trouble doing as he was told.

~ ~ ~

Even though Evie thought Sean was being an alarmist, it helped knowing he was nearby. That fact made the prospect of dinner with Brad less excruciating. Not *un*-excruciating. Just less so.

Or maybe it was the fact that kissing Sean had lit something inside her. Warmth and happiness still radiated through her being, like a secret she held close to her heart. It almost felt like a shield, as if Sean had woven a net of protection around her that not even Brad could penetrate.

He didn't even try, at first. She met him at one of Jupiter Point's most popular spots, the Seaview Inn. It was situated halfway up the second-highest hill in the area, the first being Jupiter Point, where the observatory was located. It boasted a stunning view of the ocean and the observatory. It was always crowded, which was both good and bad. Good because Brad wouldn't do anything inappropriate surrounded by so many people. Bad because before the night was out, everyone in town would know they'd had dinner.

They ordered appetizers and drinks—lager for Brad and seltzer for Evie. She wasn't going to chance alcohol tonight; she had to keep her cool.

At first, Brad was nothing but charm. He'd been perfecting his public persona ever since he'd become the face of the family bank, White Savings and Loan, after college. Every time the bank gave money to a charitable cause, Brad appeared to represent the family. She'd seen his act from afar—speeches, handshakes, the trademark boyish grin—but this was her first up-close experience with Brad White, political candidate.

He asked about her family. He talked about running for office and what it was like being on TV and having strangers recognize him in other cities in their district. He mentioned some of his plans if he won the election, and what the latest polls were saying. So far, the race was neck and neck.

All that chitchat got them through the main course. Evie was just starting to relax when he got to the point.

"I think you're going to be very grateful to me, Evie."

"Excuse me?"

"You've created an embarrassing situation for yourself, and I'm offering a solution."

She darted a glance around the room, with its white leather banquettes and orchid arrangements. The novelty of seeing Evie and Brad all cozy by the fireplace must have worn off, because no one was paying any attention to them. "Are you sure it's not more embarrassing for you?"

His hand tightened around his glass of lager. "I'm not going to lie. You did embarrass me, which I assume was your purpose. So that's done now. We can move on. I'm giving you an out, little Evie. I'm willing to play your game."

She stared at him, that "little Evie" still echoing in her ears. He'd used that nickname because he was four years her senior. It didn't sound endearing anymore.

"Come up with something that you want," he continued. "Something the business coalition can get behind. I'll announce that I'm including whatever it is in my campaign platform. And you'll come out smelling like roses."

Jack Drummond had suggested exactly the same thing. "Is that how it works?"

"That's how it works. You've successfully played the game—if you accept this offer. If you don't accept..." He paused.

"What?"

"Well, you'll come off as the town kook. It's not like you have a legitimate reason for withholding your endorsement. The other business owners are going to want to know why."

An impulse surged within her, something volcanic, something she had no control over. "*You know why*," she said in a low voice.

Her nerves jumped as soon as the words hit the air. Never, not once, never had she referred to that night around Brad or to Brad. She'd kept her silence absolute, like a nun who'd made a vow. Those three words hung between them like little grenades.

Except to Brad, apparently they weren't grenades. They were more like jelly beans. He gave her a smile that was more like a pat on the head.

"You'll have to be more specific."

She got the feeling that she was a step behind in this conversation. "You seriously want me to be more specific?"

He tore off a piece of bread and popped it into his mouth. His casual manner seemed designed to tell her how little she frightened him.

"Let's just say that I'm calling your bluff. I know you, Evie. You won't ever say anything. You never have and you never will, because that's not who you are. You're the classic peacemaker. You don't like to make waves or upset anyone."

He made her sound like a complete wimp. She felt all her

confidence drain away, same as it always did around him.

"It's a nice quality, and I know your family appreciates it. So does the community. You're the sweetheart of Jupiter Point. Everyone loves you. But no one likes a troublemaker, do they? Right now, you're making trouble by withholding your endorsement."

Evie's blackened trout suddenly looked disgusting to her. She pushed her plate away.

"See? Even this conversation is making you uncomfortable, isn't it?"

Of course it was. He wanted it to be uncomfortable. That was why he'd arranged this entire thing. He wanted her to be so uncomfortable that she would crawl back into her gallery, curl up in a ball and never bother him again.

She swallowed hard over the lump in her throat. Everything in her screamed to get away from this man.

He scanned her face intently, but she kept her expression blank. Until she made a public announcement of some sort, let him sweat. "Do we have an understanding?"

No. She'd never understand someone like him. Someone who pushed people around just so he could get what he wanted.

He leaned over the table. She caught a whiff of his aftershave. Nausea threatened, but she clenched her fists tight and refused to back away.

"You know, Evie, I'd be a pretty good congressman, did you ever think of that? I have everything it takes. I have the funding, I have the charisma. I know the issues. I can do good things for Jupiter Point. I can introduce a bill to add a lane to Route 78. That would bring more traffic to town. There's no end to how much I can help you. We can make a deal right now that will be very, very good for you and the business coalition. How about new downtown Christmas decorations? That rec center you've been talking about? A community garden that Brianna can run? My press guy can write something up and we can announce it first thing in the morning. Better yet, call your friend Merry and we'll give her an exclusive."

He sat back and pushed up the sleeves of his shirt. A man of action, ready to dig in and get to work. She stared at his newly exposed forearms, at his golden hair and a scattering of freckles, the thick wristband of his platinum-rimmed watch. Then she made herself look at his hands. Felt them pushing her down against the mangy sheepskin cloth that covered his passenger seat. Felt it physically, as if it was happening right that moment instead of thirteen years ago.

She jumped to her feet. "I'll…" She cleared her throat. "I'll let you know what I decide."

Surprise flashed across his square-cut face. That was some satisfaction, anyway. Obviously he thought she'd follow the script he'd provided.

"Don't wait too long, little Evie. I have a few other ways I can go."

Turning on her heel, she walked out of the inn with as much dignity as she could manage. As soon as she reached the lobby, she ran.

Chapter 10

Outside, she filled her lungs with crisp night air. Sean was somewhere in the parking lot waiting for her to come out, but she couldn't face him yet. She felt too humiliated, too small. Instead, she headed down the wide steps that led to a terrace with a view of the ocean. Even though a brisk wind came off the ocean, a few hardy guests sat drinking their after-dinner coffee at the ironwork tables behind the balustrades.

Too many people.

Evie had spent a few days helping Brianna landscape the Seaview's grounds, so she knew all its secret spots. She veered toward the little-used back road that wound up the hill. It was the quickest way to town, and she'd driven up it with truckloads of mulch for Brianna. There was a spot she remembered…yes, there it was. A path that meandered out to a breathtaking overlook. Brianna had created a bed of moss there and installed a little loveseat shaped like a toadstool—a fairy tale touch for the honeymoon crowd.

And right now, for the disgusted single crowd.

Evie slipped off her shoes and dug her feet into the soft,

spongy padding of moss, which felt cool and slightly moist. She needed to feel something *real*. She wanted to feast her eyes on beauty, on the moon lighting a path across the ocean. If she could dive off this spot, into that dark water, and surface as a moonlit mermaid, that would be perfect. She'd never have to face Brad again, or the business coalition. People could say what they wanted about her, and since she'd be gone, it wouldn't matter.

She buried her face in her hands and let out a long, shaky whoosh of air. Her entire body felt slimy. Brad hadn't touched her once, but still she felt his scent on her, his gaze, his presence. The way you might feel if you walked through cobwebs and got them stuck in your hair. She wriggled her entire body, hoping to get rid of the sensation. It actually helped, so she worked her shoulders, jumped from one foot to the other, then pogo-sticked up and down.

On the last jump, she landed a little askew and realized someone was standing about three feet away, someone tall and broad-shouldered. She let out a surprised yelp.

"It's just me," the man said quickly.

Sean. Of course. Now that her eyes were adjusting to the shadows in the overlook, she could make out his solid, powerful frame. And of course she'd recognize his deep molasses-gravel voice anywhere. "Hi."

"I saw you come out of the restaurant. I wanted to make sure you were okay. Then you came here and started performing some kind of weird moonlight ritual dance."

She laughed. "It's called the get-that-man-out-of-my-hair dance."

He stepped closer, frowning. Moonlight slid across his wide shoulders. "Did he do something? Do I need to get my left jab warmed up again?"

"God no. Please, that's all I need. Do you promise not to go caveman on me?"

One corner of his mouth lifted in a rueful smile. "I'm not seventeen anymore. I can control myself."

Those words, in his sexy voice, inspired all kinds of flutters inside her. Which was amazing, considering how queasy she'd been just a few moments ago. Sean really…just really did something to her, she realized with a sense of wonder. He made her feel safe and strong and sexy. Three things she wasn't used to feeling at all.

"Brad said he's calling my bluff," she blurted. "He thinks I'll never say anything about that night. I never have, not to anyone. I didn't tell my parents, I didn't tell my friends. I kept thinking, it wasn't so bad. He didn't…rape me or anything. Not exactly." She lowered her voice for that last part. It felt so shocking to even say the word aloud. Not even Sean knew the entire story.

"I know he traumatized you," Sean said gently. "I can vouch for that. You were shaking so hard you could barely walk or talk. I had to help you inside."

He'd been so kind to her that night. Rough, intimidating, notorious Sean Marcus had gently lifted her from the Chevy and set her on her feet. She could still remember how she'd dug her nails into the muscles of his forearm as they moved down the sidewalk. That must have hurt so much, but he hadn't even winced.

"I let you down, Sean. I should have told the police why you punched Brad. I should have stood up for you. You stopped him from doing something worse, and then I just let you take the rap for the whole thing. I'm so sorry." She looked at the moss under her feet, feeling overwhelmed with shame. "I kept thinking how upset everyone was going to be, and how my mother would cry and my father would be so disappointed in me. McGraws don't get into situations like that. They just don't." She attempted a smile. "When I first saw you at the council meeting, I thought you might hate me. I wouldn't blame you if you did."

He took another step closer. She caught the scent of wood smoke that always seemed to follow him. So different from Brad's pricy aftershave. "Are you picking up a 'hate' vibe from me?"

Excitement welled within her, as it always did around him. "Not really, no."

"That's good. You were a fourteen-year-old kid and you'd just gone through something shocking. I didn't blame you for any of it. I blame the asshole who was in the car with you. And at dinner with you. That guy. I do blame him."

He was so solid and sure, so fearless, his feet braced on the path as if Brianna had planted him along with the hydrangeas and rosebushes. His strength shone from every pore of his body. Being with him filled her with courage.

"You know something? I should have ditched Brad and had dinner with you instead."

"Of course you should have. As it happens, I still haven't eaten. I was on a stakeout tonight. Without the steak."

She laughed. "I would have brought you a doggy bag but I

barely even remembered my purse."

"Want to go grab something in town?"

The thought of walking into another of Jupiter Point's gossipy restaurants made her heart sink. She could imagine what everyone would be saying the next day. *Is Evie McGraw double-booking dates now? Did you hear, first Brad White, then Sean Marcus?*

But the thought of spending more time with Sean, yes, that part she definitely liked. "I have a better idea. I remember you used to love my mom's mac and cheese."

Even in the moonlight, she caught the flash of his grin. "Your mom's mac and cheese was incredible. It was the best thing I ever tasted in my life. I've actually told stories about it during campouts. She had a secret recipe that she never told anyone."

"Yeah, well, I'm her daughter. Who else is she going to tell? I have it written down in three places *and* stored on my computer. Not only that, but I happen to have some already made, just sitting in my fridge."

"Then what are we doing here with all this moonlight and flowers and shit? Mac and cheese, now you're talking. Let's go, lady. Don't you know firemen are always hungry?"

A well of laughter bubbled inside her. Sean had a way of making her smile no matter what the situation. He made her feel light and safe and ready to take on the world.

It wasn't until she was driving down the hill that it really sank in. He was going to be inside her house. *With her*. Being all sexy and irresistible.

Chapter 11

Sean followed Evie's little white Jetta down the hill to a Craftsman-style bungalow not far from the McGraw home. Evie had him tied up in knots. First that out-of-left-field kiss had blown him away. Then her moonlight apology had just about ripped his heart out. And now she'd invited him into her home.

Something told him things like this didn't happen very often. From what he'd seen, Evie had some pretty solid self-protective walls in place. She'd shot down his earlier dinner invitation pretty hard. But he couldn't help imagining all the things that could happen between them. More of that kissing, for instance. Or the things that came after kissing.

At the base, when he'd made that crack about the cots, she hadn't gotten offended or kneed him in the balls. But since she'd just come from an encounter with Asshole Brad, it probably hadn't been the best time to try another kiss.

He vowed to keep his hands to himself now, too, no matter how tempting his attraction to Evie McGraw.

As he followed her up the curving path to her front door,

tracking the sway of her hips every step of the way, that vow seemed like the stupidest idea he'd ever had. He tried not to watch as that shapely rear-end twitched back and forth. She'd worn a classic little black dress to her dinner with Brad—nothing overtly sexy. But she exuded sensuality and the hell of it was, she didn't even seem to know it.

She glanced over her shoulder as she unlocked her front door. The innocent worry in her eyes told him he was the only one with all these naughty thoughts.

"It might be a little messy in there." She pulled a face. "I don't have a lot of guests who aren't friends, and they're used to me. I'm not home a lot, that's my only excuse."

"I'm used to sleeping bags in the woods. I think I can handle it." He followed her into her living room. She switched on a light and he stopped dead. "Whoa."

"I warned you."

It looked as if a washing machine had exploded in her living room. A giant pile of clean laundry filled her couch. He spotted pink thong panties in an erotic tangle with a black bra and averted his eyes.

"Yikes, it's even worse than I remembered." She kicked off her black high-heeled sandals and dashed barefoot across the room. She grabbed a throw blanket from an armchair and draped it over the pile. "Just pretend I don't have a couch."

"Sure." He glanced at the rest of the furniture. Random piles of clothes seemed to be a theme. A pair of yoga pants had been tossed over the back of the armchair, along with one balled-up striped sock.

"Does Jupiter Point know you're this messy? No one mentions that when they talk about sweet Evie McGraw."

"I wish they wouldn't talk about me at all. I sound like a caricature." She darted from one armchair to another until she had an armful of sweaters, sports bras, yoga pants and a black leather jacket. She lifted the throw blanket off the clean laundry pile and shoved the new collection of items on top of the others. "I'm always at the gallery or with my mom. I haven't had a chance to clean up in a while."

"Hey." He lifted a hand to stop her explanation. "No judging. Honestly, I'm just surprised. You always look so...put together."

"Yeah, well, looks can be deceiving." She made a face at the stack of mail that covered half the coffee table. "I only look cool on the outside. Inside, different story."

She swept the mail into her arms. A photography magazine slithered out of her grasp and landed splayed open on the hardwood floor. Sean bent to pick it up.

"You probably remember my parents' house." He realized that she was nervous. "It was always immaculate. My mother trained me better than this, believe me. When my parents come over, you should see this place. Not a single speck of a mess. But when it's just me..."

"Evie, relax. I don't care how messy your place is. My ex used to pile dirty dishes in the bathtub when we ran out of space."

Oops. That information had slipped out without any forethought whatsoever.

"Ex?" She froze as he handed her the magazine. "Ex-what?"

"Ex-wife, though the wife part only lasted three months.

Drunken Vegas mistake," he added. "We both fixed it as soon as we could, no harm done."

She still stood staring at him, more magazines and envelopes slipping from her hold. "You were married?"

He had to laugh at her surprise. "Is that really so strange? I know I'm no catch, what with the risky career path and being gone most of the summer, but some girls actually like that. We got divorced about nine years ago. Is…uh…everything okay?"

"Yes." She nodded, as if trying to convince herself. "Everything's okay." Still holding her mail, she walked through a pass-through and turned on a light. Kitchen, he saw, craning his neck. He was just about to follow her when she poked her head back out. "Actually, it's not okay."

His gut tightened. "You're upset because I'm divorced?" Damn, had he just managed to ruin his chances with Evie completely? Some people were conservative about divorce. His own parents had never married, but even so, he'd felt bad about getting divorced. Especially at such a young age.

But he was what he was. No sense in hiding it. "The divorce was the least of it."

"The least of it?" She withdrew her head, then popped it out again. This time she held a corkscrew poised over a bottle of wine. "Do I need alcohol for this story?"

"There's plenty of alcohol already in it," he said drily. "But whatever you need."

She withdrew her head again, and he heard the sound of a cork popping. Great. He was driving her to drink. Might as well get this over with.

"After I left Jupiter Point, I avoided alcohol. It got me into too much trouble when I was growing up." He spoke to the now-empty pass-through. "But once a year, I used to get wasted. When I was twenty-one, I got completely blitzed at a strip club in Las Vegas. My buddies bought me a lap dance. That was how I met Mandy. I was so drunk I asked her to marry me during the lap dance. She thought I was cute, I guess, and we ended up drinking some more after her shift and next thing we knew, we were married."

He heard the glug-glug of wine being poured. Hopefully Evie was pouring it into a glass and not down her throat. An appliance beeped and a delicious, cheesy aroma drifted from the room. His mouth watered.

"Then what happened?" she called.

"We were both equally horrified the next day, but I had a few weeks before I had to report to my first smoke-jumping gig. So we decided to give it a shot. A few months later, we got divorced."

Evie emerged with two plates piled high with steaming macaroni and cheese. "I gave up on the wine, since you said you don't usually drink. Could you just clear a space on that little table?"

He followed her gaze to a little round table in the far corner. Since it was overflowing with art books and accordion files, he hadn't noticed it at first. He pushed aside a laptop, a book on digital photography and a Pez dispenser shaped like a Minion.

She set down the two plates and went back into the kitchen. Sean found two chairs and dragged them to the table. He wondered if it would be rude just to bury his face in the food, silverware be damned. Now that he'd smelled the mouthwatering, familiar mac and cheese aroma, he was ravenous. Evie came back with two forks, but instead of putting them on the table, she gripped them in her fist and gestured with them.

"Here's why I'm upset, in case you're wondering."

"I get it, Evie, I'm not proud of it either—"

"No." She held up her fist, with the forks sprouting from it like metal-pronged flowers. "It's not you. I'm upset with myself. You left Jupiter Point and did...life stuff."

"Life stuff?"

"Marriage, divorce, strippers, drunken nights in Vegas. Whatever came up. You *lived*. Whereas I stayed here in this little pocket of the world and let the time float by. Did I get married? Did I even come close? Do you know how many men I've kissed over the last thirteen years?"

That seemed like an extremely dangerous question to try to answer. "At least one," he said gravely, deciding to stick with facts.

She rolled her eyes. "Before you. Don't worry, it's not a trick question. I've kissed six men before you. I even slept with one of them. We were really good friends, and I thought that would make it easier. It didn't work out that way."

"I'm sorry." Sean really wasn't sure how to handle this conversation. She was going somewhere with it, obviously, but discussing her sexual experiences with other men wasn't all that appealing to him. In fact, he felt...face it, jealous. He had no standing to be jealous of someone else touching Evie, kissing those sensual lips, stroking her silky skin...

Suddenly he wished he had that glass of wine after all.

"It didn't work out because he was gay," she said. Then she held up a finger. "Hang on." She dropped the forks on the table and ran back into the kitchen. She came back with the wine but no glasses. She sat one hip on the arm of the couch and tipped the bottle to her lips.

"Actually, that's not the only reason why. Also, Brad."

Sean nodded slowly. So that's where this was headed. He put out his hand for the bottle and she handed it to him. He took a sip, wondering if he should push her to talk more about that night. He knew the rough outline of what had happened with Brad, but not the details. There was probably much more to her story.

"Something like that can really mess with you. Have you ever talked to anyone about it?"

"Sort of. I kind of said something to my aunt, Suzanne's mom, but I didn't use his name. I don't know if you remember Aunt Desiree, but she's a lot younger than my parents and worked as a model and seemed to know all about boys. She told me to keep quiet because people would blame me. She said girls always end up with their reputations ruined."

Sean vaguely remembered a bubbly Betty Boop lookalike— who apparently gave very bad advice.

"What about a counselor, someone like that?"

"No." She snorted. "You know what Jupiter Point is like. It's so small, and there are only two therapists in town. Everyone would find out, and my parents would want to know what was wrong with me. I wouldn't be able to keep it a secret."

He handed the bottle back to her. "There's nothing wrong with counseling."

She took another swallow then wiped a droplet of wine off her bottom lip. He tracked the motion of her little pink tongue. "You're a big tough fireman. Aren't you supposed to laugh at the whole concept of needing help?"

He shook his head at her and reclaimed the bottle. Instead of drinking from it, he stashed it behind him. "That's a load of bull. Want to know why I got drunk in Vegas and nearly messed up my life and Mandy's?"

She raised her eyebrows. "Why?"

"Because it was the anniversary of my parents' death. I didn't know how else to deal with it, so I got drunk. After the divorce, I saw a counselor. I'm not embarrassed by that. In the fire service, we see a lot of bad shit. Sometimes you have to talk about it or it'll take you down. That doesn't make me less of a man, believe me. If you want proof, I'm happy to provide it."

She licked her lower lip, chasing a runaway drop of wine.

Okay, that was the last straw. He had to touch her. He reached out and stroked a finger down her smooth cheek. "And I'm pretty sure you'll still be a sexy, desirable, incredibly gorgeous woman even if you talk to a counselor."

She tilted her face into his palm. "I could do that, I suppose. Or..."

"Or?"

"We could do something else." She peered at him from under her eyelashes.

Man, she was buzzed.

His lips twitched, but he held back his laughter. "You're a lightweight, aren't you? A few sips of wine and you're gone."

"They were really, really long sips," she pointed out.

"That is true."

"And I'm not really drunk. For instance, I'm not drunk enough to give you a lap dance and then marry you."

He ran his thumb across the exquisite arch of her cheekbone. "I get it. I spill my guts and you use my sordid past against me."

Her eyelids lowered and she practically purred as he caressed her skin. "It's all part of my master plan."

"You have a master plan?"

"I do." Her eyes opened fully, and he lost himself for a moment in their shimmering, silvery-green depths. She was reeling him in, moment by moment. He couldn't resist her, and wasn't sure he should try. "My plan is that I'm going to speak up more. How am I ever supposed to get what I want if I never even say it out loud? Brad thinks I'm going to just follow some script written by his press agent. But I'm not going to do that."

"Good. I support that decision."

"No, no, that's not the important part. The important part is me." She took a step away from him and put a hand over her heart, then trailed it down her body. "This. My sexuality."

His heart nearly stopped. Just how buzzed was she?

"I am a woman," she said firmly. "I'm pretty sure that I would like sex if it wasn't with a secretly gay man. You're not—"

"No," he said quickly. "Pretty solid on where I stand on the

Kinsey scale."

"You know what's the best way I can fight back against Brad and what he did to me?"

Rhetorical question, he assumed, and didn't answer. He held his breath, captivated by every move she made, every dip of her eyelashes, every quiver of her lips.

"The best way I can fight back is to have sex with you. Hot, passionate, steamy, naked, fabulous sex. With orgasms and everything."

All the blood left his head and zoomed right for the part of his body in charge of orgasms. Since he was standing right in front of her in snug-fitting jeans, she noticed that fact. He knew she noticed because her gaze dropped to his crotch. His erection noticed that she noticed, and swelled even bigger. It was quite the feedback loop, and his better judgement wasn't part of it at all.

"So?" All of a sudden, Evie's chutzpah vanished and she bit her lip, looking vulnerable and almost painfully beautiful. "What do you think about that idea?"

Take it easy, big guy. He wrestled his libido into submission. He needed to approach this situation carefully. "Couple questions," he finally managed. "Are you trying to get back at Brad somehow by having sex with me?"

"No. Absolutely not. This is about me. I want to reclaim my sexual side. With a man. You, specifically."

"So this wouldn't be a...relationship? I'm not good at those. You can ask Mandy, she'll tell you. I'll be gone most of the summer, on call or out in the field. It's dangerous work, the families worry a lot, you probably wouldn't like that—"

"I'm just talking about sex, Sean. But if you're not interested, just say so. We'll pretend we never had this conversation." She started to spin away from him, but he snagged her before she got too far.

"I'm interested. Very interested. I've been wanting you ever since I saw you at the town meeting. I've had at least a half-chub most of the time I've spent with you."

"A half-chub?" She looked fascinated.

"Curious?" She nodded, and he took her hand and rested it on his crotch. The soft pressure made him see stars. "That's more than half, but you get the picture."

"You want me," she whispered.

"Yes. Like crazy. And that kiss today…" He whistled. "You rocked my world with that kiss." Her palm pressed against the front of his jeans. There was something so tentative and innocent about her touch. He focused on that and tried to block out the arousal she was generating with her light caresses.

This wasn't a good idea. Obviously, Evie still carried the emotional scars from that incident with Brad. Even if she was ready to move on and "reclaim her sexuality," she might be more vulnerable than she realized. He didn't want to hurt her. He'd never forgive himself if that happened.

"So, are you in or out?" Her throaty voice made his cock pulse. "Because if you're not, then I'm going to have to find someone else."

"What?" He gripped her wrist, stilling her so he could focus on something other than his raging hard-on. "Who?"

"You may not know this, but I get asked out a lot. I'll just wait until one of those people who ask is someone I have some chemistry with. There must be someone out there."

He pulled her against him, catching just a glimpse of her smug smile before they were front-to-front. "Bullshit. You're bluffing."

"Sean Marcus. Do you really think I'm going to give up the whole idea of having sex just because you said no? Seriously?" She coughed, burying the word "arrogant" inside the sound.

When she put it that way…hmm, maybe she wasn't bluffing. She could end up with anyone. She'd be an easy target for some unscrupulous jerk because she hadn't been out there learning the ropes. Too naive, that's what she was. There were so many ways she could get into trouble.

It was practically his duty as a first responder to take her to bed.

God, when his dick did the talking, logic got twisted like a pretzel.

"We'll take it slow." He cupped her ass, filling his palms with her curves. "So I know you're okay."

"Slow?" She bit his neck gently. "Not too slow, I hope."

"Slow is good, sweetheart. Slow is when the magic happens. But we can move up from slow. Hard, fast, slow, it's all good."

"Okay." Her voice sounded higher, almost squeaky. "I trust you."

He wasn't sure that was such a wise move. Why should she trust a wildfire specialist whose longest relationship had been with a stripper he didn't remember marrying? But he'd warned her. He'd been completely upfront about his shortcomings. He'd told her a relationship wasn't in the cards. That wasn't what she wanted, anyway.

She wanted sex. And damn it, he could do that. Sex, he could definitely provide.

He nuzzled his nose into her soft neck and breathed in the fragrance of some exotic combination of flowers that must have been designed to make a man lose every last shred of common sense.

That was it. That was the best he could do for Evie. He'd help her rediscover her sexual side and make sure she was as safe as possible in the process. After all, he trusted himself with Evie more than he trusted any other man. He actually cared about her. She'd opened up to him about how that night had affected her. That meant he knew her in a way most people didn't.

Someone else might want to use her or count her as an especially gorgeous notch on his belt. He, on the other hand, would devote himself one hundred percent to making this the best experience possible.

Even though he couldn't offer her stability, a family, permanence, or any of the other things girls usually wanted, he could do one important thing for her.

He could take care of her in bed.

Chapter 12

In her dream, Sean was braced over her, kissing her, every
stroke of his tongue setting her on fire. She moaned against his
mouth, "I want you, I want to be naked with you." She arched her
back and pressed her nipples against his hard chest, and suddenly she
realized she *was* naked. So was Sean. Naked and breathtaking. His
chest rippled with muscle as he bent his dark head to her breasts. He
swiped his tongue in delicious circles around her nipples. Teasing,
tugging. The pleasure was so intense she actually heard bells ring.

They rang again. And again.

Evie's eyes popped open. Her phone was ringing. She lay face
down on her bed, in a tangled mess of her favorite goose down
comforter, alone. Unfortunately, she remembered every detail of
what had happened the night before.

She'd thrown herself at Sean and he'd nearly rejected her. But
then he'd changed his mind and said yes to her
request…offer…proposal…whatever you wanted to call it. But not
last night. Apparently trading a bottle of wine back and forth had
triggered his protective male impulses. He'd carried her into bed,

tucked her in and left. Now he was probably calling to check on her—that protective male thing again.

Not that she minded.

She snatched up the phone and answered. "Begging for another chance?"

"Oooh, that sounds juicy!" Merry answered her, not Sean. "My reporter's Spidey sense is going off. Who wants another chance? At what? Why and when?"

Evie rolled onto her back. "It's way too early for an interrogation. What time is it?"

"Time to face the world, chickie. I'm calling on the down-low to give you a heads-up on something."

For a blissful moment, Evie had forgotten about the rest of her evening. Now it all came back. Brad. Their dinner. The way she'd fled from the Seaview Inn. "Does this have anything to do with Brad White?"

"Yup. I don't know the details, but apparently he's going to write an op-ed that will appear in tomorrow's paper."

The *Mercury News-Gazette* came out once a week, on Thursdays. Everyone in town read it, either in its paper or online version. The *Gazette* had already given its endorsement to Brad's candidacy. Then again, so had everyone else in town.

Everyone except Evie, whose stomach was now tying itself into knots. "What does the op-ed say?"

"I don't know that. But it's definitely about his campaign, and I heard a rumor that he's going to mention you. I just thought you might want to know."

"Thanks, Merry." Evie swung her legs out of bed. That dream had been so real. And so wonderful. If only she could stay in that world.

But she couldn't. She had to get dressed and get to work. Face the fallout from her disastrous dinner with Brad.

"You know," Merry was saying, "you could do the same thing that Brad's doing."

"What do you mean?"

"Look, girl. Something's going on here. Brad's an ambitious man and right now you're standing in his way. That just isn't like you."

Wow, did everyone in town see her as such a pushover?

"I admit that conflict is not my comfort zone." Feeling slightly queasy, she carried the phone to her closet and scanned her selection of blouses. And really, why were all her clothes cream or slate or shades of beige? Her head pounded. "But what are you suggesting?"

"I feel like you should fight back or you're going to get buried. You can write an opinion piece about why you haven't endorsed Brad. You could tell your side of the story. Opposing opinion pieces always get attention. The deadline is three o'clock, so you have plenty of time to get it done."

*Tell her story…opposing opinion pieces…*oh God. Everything would be out in the open. Nausea suddenly hit her hard. She ran to the bathroom and bent over the toilet, stomach heaving. Wine definitely didn't combine well with anxiety.

"Evie? You okay?" She heard Merry still talking on the other end of the phone.

"Yeah. Sorry. I had a little too much wine last night, I think."

"Hot shower, plenty of water, and my special hangover cure. Horseradish by the spoonful," said Merry kindly.

She almost retched again at the sound of that. "That's the most disgusting thing I can imagine eating right now."

"That's from my grandmama down in Louisiana. So, what do you think, Evie? If you don't want to do an op-ed, maybe I can just interview you. You're going to have to say something sometime."

"I know. I know." Evie put the phone down on the bathroom counter and splashed water on her face. "God, this is crazy. I don't know how I got into this mess."

"I want to help, Evie. I really do."

She opened her medicine cabinet and fumbled for a bottle of aspirin. No way was she going to talk about Brad with a hangover. "Let's see what he writes in his article. Maybe it has nothing to do with me. I'm sure he has other things to worry about besides the JPBC endorsement."

"Have it your way," Merry said dubiously. "But I'm here if you need me. Either as a friend or as a reporter. Whatever you need. I'll stop by the gallery later."

"Thank you, Merry."

Evie clicked off the phone. She went back to her closet and stared at her array of boring blouses. She thought about the rumors flying, the talk gathering. Mrs. Murphy was probably already hovering outside the gallery ready to pounce. Jack Drummond would be next, demanding to know what her plan was.

Screw it. She was calling in sick. The gallery could live

without her for a day.

Her phone rang again. This time it was Sean—protective male impulses and all.

"How are you feeling?" The immediacy of his molasses-over-gravel voice made it seem as if was in the room with her. Goosebumps rose on her skin.

"Oh, nothing a little horseradish can't cure."

He coughed. "I'm not even going to ask."

She smiled, feeling better than she had since she'd been dragged out of her dream. She was starting to think Sean had that effect on her, as if he turned up the light in any given room. "What are you doing today?" she asked on impulse.

"I'm interviewing some local applicants for the crew. Two people are coming in this morning. Why?"

"Well…I'm taking the day off from work. I thought you might want to do something."

"Something?" His tone was the verbal equivalent of a raised eyebrow.

"Yeah, *something*. Don't make it sound so nefarious."

"I was aiming for lascivious."

She laughed…actually laughed, even though half an hour ago she'd been on the verge of throwing up. It was amazing how Sean made her feel alive and sort of fizzy—even over the phone.

"Speaking of which…" He dropped his voice into a lower register that made her stomach clench with desire. "How…uh…how are you feeling about last night?"

She drew in a deep breath. If she wanted to back out, this

would be the best time. She could pretend she didn't remember, or blame it all on the wine. That would definitely be the best thing to do, because getting involved with Sean Marcus was such a bad, terrible, crazy idea. He'd told her so himself. He was a bad bet for a relationship.

"If you're asking if I remember it, yes, I do," she said.

"And?"

"If you're asking if I regret it, no, I don't."

"Just to be clear, you still want to—"

"Yes," she said quickly. No need to say it out loud. "I still feel the same way. If you do, I mean. Scratch that. I still feel the same way and I hope you do too."

Silence followed. Evie died a thousand deaths during those few moments. "Sean?"

"Sorry." He came back on the line, sounding rushed. "My first interview is here. What about when I'm done? If you're still free later, do you want to go reclaim your—"

"No! Yes!" Beet red, she dug the heel of her hand into her forehead. Then she heard Sean's soft chuckle. He was probably trying to relax her, to get rid of her nerves. "You're an idiot."

"An idiot, but a lucky one. I'm glad you haven't changed your mind, Evie. I'll pick you up when I'm done with my interviews."

When she hung up, Evie felt as if she'd downed an entire pot of coffee and her head didn't hurt at all. How did Sean do that? He must have magical powers. He was better than horseradish.

~ ~ ~

When Sean asked Josh to hold down the fort while he "took

care of some details in town," the other firefighter laughed in his face. "Do these details have the initials E.M.? Are these details the ones you're supposed to stay the hell away from?"

"Leave it alone, Marsh." Sean tried to step past him, but Josh blocked his path to the truck.

"The thing is, I can't. How many times does a thirty-one-year-old guy get to be superintendent in charge of setting up a new crew? Evie's cool, but she's a distraction. I don't want you to blow this."

"I can handle my own shit."

"I'm just looking out for you, man. Think of it like this. She's the fire, and I'm the one cutting line to keep you from getting burned."

"Would you get out of my way? I'm not going to do anything stupid."

Josh reluctantly backed away, and Sean spent the drive into town telling himself his friend was right and he should rethink this thing with Evie.

His willpower vanished the instant he laid eyes on her. Before he could exit his car, she came running down the steps wearing denim shorts and a blue-and-white-striped shirt. She was barefoot, but a pair of hiking shoes tied together by their laces hung from her backpack. Her hair bounced over her shoulders and her wide smile was brighter than the afternoon sunshine.

If Josh was right, and Evie was the wildfire—bring it on.

"You look like you have a plan," he said, eyeing her backpack as she slipped into the passenger seat.

"Yes, I actually have kind of a special request for you. Unless you have something else in mind?"

"Nope. Whatever you command, milady."

"You said that before. That word 'milady.' I have to say that it totally works for me."

"Good to know."

She shot him a look. "Are you okay?"

"Yup. A-okay." God, that sounded fake. He wasn't really okay. He was wondering what the fuck was wrong with him and why he had no willpower around her. "So where are we going?"

She placed her backpack on her lap and stretched out her legs. Her long, shapely, smooth-skinned legs. He dragged his gaze away and turned the key in the ignition. Driving While Ogling—not a good plan.

Well…" She hesitated, giving him a cautious glance. "It's for my mother."

"Evie, why would you even hesitate? I'll do anything your mother needs. I wasn't sure if I'd be welcome, after the way I left. But I'd like to visit her."

"Really?" The way her face lit up made him feel like an ass. He should have paid a visit as soon as he got to town. "She'd like that. But she's…well, she has a pretty advanced case of Parkinson's. She doesn't like to go out anymore. So I take photos of her favorite places. That way she can see what flowers are blooming and if any swallows are nesting yet and what kind of pie Mary Lou is serving today. That sort of thing."

His heart gave a weird little skip. He remembered how she used to chatter on about photographing the Himalayas and Bali and places like that. Instead, she'd stayed in Jupiter Point to take photos for her mother. That was Evie in a nutshell.

After a short moment to control his emotion, he cleared his throat. "So what's the special request? What do you need from me?"

She hesitated, fiddling with the strap of her backpack, as the tidy little houses of Jupiter Point flashed past. "Her favorite place of all is the old airfield," she finally admitted. "She used to go out there to sketch when your parents owned it. She said the view is one of the nicest in town. But now it has 'no trespassing' signs all over it. I've stayed away, but now that you're here, and I can request access in person…" She offered him a smile that was half-apology, half-plea. "But I understand if you'd rather go somewhere else."

He looked at her curiously as he turned the pickup toward the road that led to the airstrip. "Of course I don't mind. Why would you think that? Are you worried I couldn't handle going back there?"

"I wasn't sure." Air from the open window whipped strands of her silky hair against her cheek. She tried to tuck them behind her ear, but they kept rebelling. "I mean, come on. You're talking to the woman who practically had a nervous breakdown at the thought of dinner with Brad. I'm not exactly a pro when it comes to facing difficult things. I mean, look at me. I'm playing hooky so I don't have to face all the questions everyone has. I suck at confronting things."

He laughed. "The first step is admitting it."

"Fine. I admit it. There." She pursed her lips, which made him want to kiss her right then and there. "Maybe I'm hoping a little of your fearlessness will rub off on me."

"You think I'm fearless?"

"Yes, look at you." She waved a hand in his direction. "You're strong and fearless. You confront things all the time. Wildfires, for instance. You confronted Brad. You confronted the whole world after you left Jupiter Point."

They'd reached the outskirts of town, where houses gave way to the first gentle slopes of the foothills. Through the open window, he smelled the salt-wildflower-pine combination that always made him think of Jupiter Point. "I wouldn't put it that way."

"Really?" She shifted her position, propping her back against the door so she could look at him directly. "What did you do when you left? We were never sure."

He nearly laughed out loud. After thirteen years of never thinking about that time, he'd been asked about it twice in just a few days. "Funny, Chief Becker was asking me the same thing the other day. I went camping in the mountains."

Strangely, Evie didn't seem surprised. "Hunter thought you might have done that. He wanted to go after you, but the Dean said no. How long did you camp out?"

"Until winter."

"Until *winter*? That must have been over a month. Were you terribly lonely?"

"No. I had a lot of shit to work out. I figured it was better if I did it without people around. I did a lot of staring up at the stars and crying and ranting at my father and fate and everything else. I stayed away from campgrounds. I didn't want to be around anyone."

She touched his forearm in comfort, and he felt his muscles

tense at her touch. Talking about that time brought back visceral memories. The burn in his thighs from running up mountain trails. The icy streams he dove into for relief. The spookiness of moonless nights. The profound peace he experienced while watching a white-tailed deer graze in a clearing.

"Honestly, the Sierras might have saved my sanity. When I came back out, I felt like I could breathe again."

"Wow," she said softly. "That's an incredible story."

"I guess so, until I woke up one morning to a foot of snow outside my tent." He laughed at the memory of that moment. A foot of snow, boots falling apart. He'd even run out of the beef jerky he'd been living on. Yet another impossible situation.

"What did you do then?" The fascination in Evie's voice made him wonder why he didn't tell this story more often. Normally he didn't talk much about himself. He liked action, not talk. But with Evie, everything was different.

"I hiked down to a lower elevation and found a campground that had fire pits. But my matches were all wet and I'd lost my lighter. I went around the campground looking for someone to borrow matches from. I ran into a bunch of guys grilling trout they'd caught in the river. They turned out to be a crew of smokejumpers on an end-of-season campout. They pulled up a camp chair for me and let me dry my stuff by their fire. I hung out with them the rest of the week and listened to all their smoke-jumping stories." He shook his head. "Damn, Evie, you really know how to get a guy talking."

"Don't stop yet! I want to hear what happened next. 'Whatever you command, milady.' remember?"

"You, milady," he told her, "are big trouble."

"Yes, but didn't you say you don't mind trouble? Now keep going, please. Is that why you became a firefighter, because of those smokejumpers?"

"Yup. They were cool guys. They all had different lives during the off season. One was a documentary filmmaker, another was training for an Iron Man race. One of them traveled someplace different every winter. But they all came back to the smoke-jumping job every summer because they loved it and it paid well. By the time they'd packed up to head home, I knew I wanted to be one of them."

Evie laughed. "It's funny how things work out, isn't it? You ran into exactly the right people at the right time. What if they'd been accountants or encyclopedia salesmen? Oh, look!" She pointed up ahead, to where the ocean shimmered just beyond the airstrip. "There's your place."

Chapter 13

Time spent with Sean passed differently than time spent with other people. It zipped by so fast, Evie barely noticed. She'd been so caught up in his story that before she knew it, they were bumping down a back road shortcut to the airstrip. Every time she looked at Sean, with his dark hair all tumbled and sexy, the planes of his face so ruggedly appealing, her heart skipped a few beats. His broad shoulders kept brushing against hers. His energy was so dynamically masculine. Really, he made every other man seem kind of…boring.

He pulled over at a spot that had a slightly higher elevation than the airstrip. From there, they had a panoramic view of the ocean, the old tarmac, the hangar and other buildings. "How's this?"

"Perfect." She looked around, noticing the high grass bending before the wind. Her mother loved the sound of the wind. Pulling out her camera, she set it to record video. "This is really nice of you, Sean."

He jumped out of the truck and stood with his hands interlaced behind his neck, stretching from the drive. "It's not a problem. Do your thing, milady. I'll be over here enjoying the view."

She stepped out of the truck. The wind lifted her hair and rustled through the grass. She hit the record button on her camera and aimed it at the grass. That was what her mother loved. The swishing, whispering susurration. That was the word her mother used for it. She'd made Evie look it up once. *Susurrus*. Whispering, murmuring or rustle.

When she'd recorded enough audio, she framed some close-ups of California poppies and wild strawberries. Molly McGraw used to scoff at Evie's obsession with photography. She'd always told Evie that no photo could show as much as a sketch could. Losing her ability to draw might have been one of the toughest effects of her Parkinson's. Not that she'd ever complained. No, McGraws simply didn't do that sort of thing.

Evie let out a sigh as she straightened up and put the lens cap back on her camera. Sean had closed his eyes and tilted his head back so the mid-March sun could warm his face. The wind molded his t-shirt against the musculature of his chest. She treated herself to a moment of shameless ogling. Her photographer's eye appreciated the perfect vee between his wide shoulders and narrow hips. His well-worn jeans hugged his rear-end just right. His pose read as confident but not threatening. Strong but not a bully.

Her heart did a few slow flips and she let out an involuntary sigh.

His eyes opened and he glanced over at her. Her appreciation must have been written all over her face, because he grinned and raised an eyebrow. "I'd say penny for your thoughts, but I'm betting they're worth a lot more than that."

"Were you always this sexy?" she asked, walking toward him. She put her camera on the hood of the truck as she passed it. "Was I too young to notice when you lived with us?"

He laughed and swung her against him. "You're crushing my self-esteem now. You didn't notice that badass jacket I used to wear all the time? Skull on the back, black leather?"

"That's right! I did forget. That was part of your 'bad boy' wardrobe."

"I was told that chicks dig the bad boys."

"Yes, we do," she assured him. "We really do, especially when they're the kind that put out fires."

He looped his arms around her and brushed his mouth across hers, causing an instant riot of tingles. "I'm thinking more about starting one right now," he murmured against her lips. "And since I'm trained, you're perfectly safe."

"Maybe I'm tired of safe."

"Whatever you say, milady."

She smiled as he worked his hands under her shirt and ran his thumbs across her lower back. The skin there was surprisingly sensitive. No one had ever touched her there, so she hadn't known. He did that for quite some time. The slow, patient sweeps of those calloused thumbs made her melt against him. She wanted to feel him too, so she dragged his t-shirt up. Her fingers traced the long, lean muscles along his spine. Every flex and jump of his muscles sent desire flowing through her.

"I think you should take this off," she whispered.

She pulled his shirt higher, tugging it over the broad expanse of his shoulders. He ducked his head so she could work it all the way off. When he stood bare-chested before her, she stared at him in awe. Every muscle had the sort of definition she'd only ever seen in ads or magazines. He was absolutely cut, ripped, whatever the word was. A tattoo wrapped around his rib cage—a single flame that spiraled in two directions, heart and back. Outlined in black, filled in with shades of crimson and persimmon-orange, it looked almost alive thanks to his rapid breathing.

"How do you look like this?" she asked, pressing her hand against the firm surface of his abdomen. "Do you spend hours and hours at the gym?"

"Not really. My thing is running up mountains. Sometimes I bike up mountains too. Or carry heavy backpacks up mountains."

She could picture him powering his way up a steep trail—bare-chested, of course. Sweating. Pumping. Oh Lord.

"Which mountains? Where were you living before you took the job here?"

"I have a house in Boulder, Colorado. That's where I'll go when the fire season ends."

For a moment, her heart sank. Of course he wasn't going to stay in Jupiter Point. Why would he? He'd had a whole life before he came back. She told herself it didn't matter anyway. She wasn't interested in a relationship. She was interested in S.E.X. And that was pretty much a first for her, so she'd better not mess it up with other emotions.

She bent her head to swirl her tongue across his nipple. He let out a hiss of breath but stayed stock still while she explored his musculature with hands and lips and even teeth. The texture of his flesh was so firm and springy. It fascinated her. And when she nibbled on the tiny pebble of his nipple, she loved the way it hardened.

To have this tough, strong man at the mercy of her tongue filled her with a sense of power.

"How about you lose *your* shirt and I try that on you?" Sean asked in a strained, raspy voice that sent shivers through her. She remembered her dream and the way he swirled his tongue in circles around the peak. "Come on. Show me your boobs."

"What?" She straightened, laughing in surprise.

"Please? Come on, I'm busy restraining every primitive impulse in my body. And believe me, I have a lot of those. You're licking on me and stroking me and my dick is as hard as a gear shift. Don't I deserve something here?"

"You make some valid points." She took her hands away from his chest and lifted her shirt in a quick flash. At the expression on his face, she burst out laughing.

"No fair. I blinked at the wrong moment. And you're wearing a bra."

"If you blinked, how do you know I'm wearing a bra?"

"Damn it, why do you have to be so smart and all? Do it again. For the fire service. For the guy who's going to keep your precious town from burning down."

She rolled her eyes. "Drama queen." Again, she yanked her shirt up, but this time he snagged her wrist before she could cover herself. She closed her eyes under his long scrutiny.

"I think you might be the most beautiful thing I've ever seen," he said softly.

A feather-light touch traveled across the upper slope of her breast, then dipped into the valley between them. Her skin rippled with reaction. Her breath sped up until it came in quick little pants. She closed her eyes so she could give herself fully to the sensation. The rustling wind, the faraway crash of waves on the shoreline, even the distant honk of a car on the highway, all of it became part of the experience. As if the boundaries between her and the world around her were dissolving.

The pad of his finger had a rough grain to it, but the way he touched her was so gentle. The contradiction was delicious. He tugged down the edge of her bra and cupped her breast in his warm hand. His thumb glanced across her nipple almost casually. She jerked at the electric sensation.

"You know I think you're gorgeous, right?" he murmured.

"You said that, yes." She felt her gut tighten, as she always did when people spoke about her appearance. It always felt like something outside her, something alien.

"And feel this." He put her hand on the front of his jeans so she felt the swell of his erection. "That's not because of how you look. It's because of how you respond to me. I bet you're as wet as that ocean right now."

She froze. Words from the past—Brad's words—buzzed in her ears. *That's not supposed to happen. I bet there's something wrong with you. Do your parents know what you're really like?*

Trembling, she jerked out of his arms and yanked down her

top. "What did you say?"

Looking bewildered, he raised his hands in a defensive gesture. "Hey, that wasn't an insult. I said it was a turn-on. I'm not complaining about it."

She turned away and buried her head in her hands. No matter what she did, she couldn't make Brad shut up. *I'll tell everyone what a nympho you are...*

"I can't do this," she gasped. "This is a mistake."

"Sweetheart, we don't have to do anything you don't want to do. But come on, talk to me." She finally managed to raise her eyes to his. She didn't see a hint of mockery in his smoked-green eyes, just pure concern and bewilderment. He didn't step away, didn't throw up his hands in disgust. He just stood patiently, waiting for what she would say next.

"I'm sorry," she finally managed. "I—" She had to tell Sean. She wanted to tell him. The shame from that night pressed against her heart until she thought it might burst. But how could she talk about something shameful without feeling the shame all over again? "With Brad, in that car that night, it wasn't exactly what you think."

His jaw flexed at her mention of Brad. "Okay."

God, this was hard. No wonder the McGraws never talked about anything difficult. Because it was freaking difficult! She clenched her fists—*do it, Evie, grow some lady balls*—and took in a deep breath.

Her phone buzzed loudly. With a sense of relief, she dug it out of her back pocket. It was a text from Merry. *Sending you Brad's op-ed. Brace yourself.*

Her face must have showed her fear, because Sean was at her side in an instant. "What is it?"

"Give me a second. I have to read this."

She opened the PDF and scanned through it.

"It's a shame, in this day and age, that personal issues are allowed to interfere with the forward progress of our community. Those business leaders who are unable to put aside their own feelings of rejection should step aside for the good of Jupiter Point. I represent unity and success for all. But when our leaders make decisions on the basis of emotion instead of logic, how are we supposed to come together to advance our mutual interests? Already my opponent is making political points from the failure of my own hometown to support me. This is a shameful moment in Jupiter Point history."

"Oh my God," she whispered. "He didn't."

"Let me see."

She thrust the phone at him. Everyone in town was about to read it anyway. "He's throwing out innuendo about emotions and rejection, like I'm some kind of spurned lover trying to get revenge. No matter what I say now, I'll look bad."

He scanned the article, then handed the phone back. "Tell him to fuck off. Make a statement. Tell everyone what he did, why you can't support him."

Heat rushed into her face. "I can't do that."

"Why the hell not? Do you need a witness? I was there, Evie. I can back you up. We can't let him pull this crap."

She worried at her bottom lip with her teeth. "It's not that simple. My mother doesn't respond well to stress. The last thing I want is a controversy."

"Honey." He cupped her face in his hands. "There's already controversy. If you want it to go away, you'll have to do what he says and step down."

She studied his face. "You think that's what I should do?"

"No, I think you should punch the dude in the face. Worked for me."

Burying her face in her palms, she let out a low moan. "I hate that he's trying to push me around, but how do I fight back without upsetting my family? This is an impossible situation."

He drew her close, and she felt his hands running up and down her back. "Take it from me, sweetness. That's the best kind."

She sighed against his chest. This afternoon had not gone the way she'd wanted at all. "Can I get a rain check on this conversation? And the rest of it? I should call Merry and check in with my parents."

For a moment, he didn't answer. "Sure, I'll let you off the hook. For now."

Chapter 14

Mrs. Murphy didn't waste a second barging into the Sky View Gallery the next morning.

"You should hear some of the things people are saying out there." She heaved her rear onto a stool and fanned her face. She was wearing a red cape and an old-fashioned bonnet—her "story time" outfit, which seemed appropriate to Evie. "I've heard people say you've been in love with Brad White since you were kids. They say you've been pining after him all these years. You never told me that."

"Because it's ridiculous." Evie sorted through the mail that had come into the gallery during her spontaneous day off. She'd decided to take the high road in response to Brad's op-ed, mostly because she didn't see another option she could stomach. "I have absolutely zero interest in Brad White."

"But you used to go with him, didn't you? Jess over at the Milky Way says she remembers Brad bringing you in for ice cream a couple of times."

"That was a very, very long time ago. There is nothing

between me and Brad, and there never will be."

"Well, that's all well and good." Mrs. Murphy pulled a copy of the *Mercury News-Gazette* from the inside pocket of her cape. "But it was in the paper, hon."

Evie snatched it from her hand and gave a quick glance at the op-ed, which featured a posed photo of Brad's slick, smiling face. "He can say what he wants, but it doesn't make it true. You notice how he never called me by name?"

She handed the paper back. Mrs. Murphy took it, though she looked disappointed that Evie didn't have anything more to say about the article.

"Anyway, I heard you were with Sean Marcus yesterday, and you were looking pretty cozy."

Evie pretended to be fascinated with a framing catalogue. She should have seen that coming. She contemplated the pros and cons of word getting out about her and Sean's…thing, whatever it was. The upside was that people might abandon the topic of her and Brad. The downside was that her private life would be the subject of conversation.

Then again, it already was.

"Well, everyone knows we're old friends," she said. "He used to live with us, remember? He was good friends with Hunter. We're just reconnecting."

"Reconnecting." Mrs. Murphy's eyes lit up. "That's exactly what I thought. I always thought he was a good boy, just a little misunderstood. And that father of his, what a disaster. But I must say, he's grown up right."

Evie couldn't agree more. She indulged in a moment of reverie over the feel of his skin stretched over his firm muscles. The rippling topography of his torso. The strength in his wide shoulders and smoky-green eyes.

She blinked and focused back on her catalogue. *Gilt corner frames. Matte backing. Work. Reality.*

"Believe me, Mrs. Murphy, I'm entirely focused on work right now. Work and my mother, that's it. No time for much socializing."

Just then, with her usual perfect timing, Suzanne waltzed into the gallery like a brisk ocean breeze. "Cuz, you are holding out on me. Is it true you and Brad used to be engaged, but he broke it off because you didn't want to be a political wife?"

"Of course not." Evie snapped shut the framing catalogue and moved on to the electric bill. "Don't you think you would know if I'd ever been engaged?"

"Evie has a new man," Mrs. Murphy informed Suzanne. "That hunky fireman, Sean Marcus."

"That's it. Cousin privileges revoked." Suzanne folded her arms and tapped her foot. "When you start seeing a man as fine as Sean Marcus, you are bound by the cousin code to share the news."

"Sean and I spent one afternoon together." Evie scowled at her long-limbed cousin. "We took photos for Mom. And there is no cousin code."

"An afternoon? You spent an afternoon together?"

"Yes. So what? And don't I have a right to some privacy?"

Suzanne ignored that rhetorical question, since in her mind clearly it didn't apply. "That means it's serious. I know your usual

M.O. when you're on a date. It involves an hour and a half of stilted conversation that ends right after your last spoonful of chocolate mousse. An afternoon, now, that's completely different."

Even though Suzanne was two years younger than Evie, she loved to play the role of relationship expert. After all, she actually had an active love life and was currently *this close* to getting engaged. Her current boyfriend was on the verge of graduating from law school and kept dropping hints about a proposal coming soon. Evie hoped he knew what he was getting into. Suzanne was a wild card, completely fun and unpredictable, with an edge that could sneak up on you.

"That's right. It *was* different. It wasn't a date. It was a photography project." Evie tossed the electric bill in the trash, then bent to retrieve it while Suzanne hooted.

"Oh, how can I resist the ten million naughty jokes that just popped into my brain?"

"Well, that's probably my cue. I should get going." Mrs. Murphy slid off the stool. As usual, Suzanne twitched the older woman's dress back down over her butt. "I've told you a million times, Evie," the older woman sighed. "These stools are the bane of my life."

Maybe she should raise them even higher, Evie thought uncharitably as the front door closed behind Mrs. Murphy. Or take them out entirely.

Luckily, she didn't have to face any more questions from Suzanne. Unfortunately, that was because everyone in Jupiter Point seemed to find a reason to stop by the Sky View Gallery over the next couple of days. Thank goodness, a steady flow of tourists who knew nothing about Brad White or Sean Marcus kept her busy. She helped a pair of honeymooners from Japan select a photo of the Andromeda galaxy. She did a portrait photo of a young couple from Long Beach who had just gotten engaged.

Then the hammer fell.

Benito Marquez from the Goodnight Moon B&B stopped in to inform her that Jack Drummond, the previous president, had called an informal meeting of the Jupiter Point Business Coalition for later in the week. "If you want to keep your position, you must come," he told her. "Very important. Most people think you've been doing a good job, Evie, until now. You must explain to us what you're doing. I voted for you, but now I have doubts. Our town is drawing the wrong kind of attention."

"I understand."

"If you decide to step down—"

"No." She didn't even need a second to think about it. "I'm not considering that."

"But this must be difficult for you, no?"

"I'm not stepping down," she said firmly as she showed Benito to the door.

Stepping down would be the same thing as letting Brad win. That's why he was making such a public spectacle—because he liked the spotlight and she didn't. He knew she'd do anything to avoid being the center of attention. He was playing her like a harp.

And he was so good at that sort of thing. He'd been honing his public relations skills for years, while she...

She'd been turning her sign to "moon."

~ ~ ~

Sean had interviews booked solid over the next few days, but it was hard to concentrate on the eager local candidates when all he could think about was Evie McGraw and the way she'd pulled away from him and told him it was all a mistake. The woman was driving him nuts. If he was smart, he'd walk away right now.

But he didn't want to. He wanted more kissing, more touching, more of her smile. And he wanted to find out what had her so twisted up inside.

That night…it wasn't exactly what you think.

He could drive himself crazy wondering what she meant by that. He couldn't read her mind. At some point, she was going to have to tell him what these land mines were all about. Otherwise, he'd keep tripping over them and unintentionally blowing up their relationship.

Not that they had a "relationship," per se. But they had a thing. Or did they? Was she pulling the plug completely?

"Sir?" The candidate in the Folding Chair of Death squirmed. Sean realized he'd been scowling at him as if he was responsible for the way Evie was confusing him. "Did you have any more questions?"

"Yes." He glanced at the sheet in front of him, which listed the basics about the candidate, Tim Peavy. Josh had done a thorough job of checking into his background. A military vet with two years of deployment in Iraq under his belt, he'd recently gotten his red card. One of Sean's mandates was to increase the number of veterans on the crew. "You've been taking extra fire science courses, you said?"

"Yes, fire science and EMT."

"Good, good. And you've been getting into shape for the physical tests?"

"Yes."

"Drop down and give me some pushups. One minute. Fast as you can."

The kid did as told—that military training paid off—and launched into a rapid series of pushups.

Josh, who was leaning his chair against the wall, kept the time while Sean counted. "Stop," Josh called after a minute.

Tim sat up, face red but grinning. "How many was that?"

"Twenty-seven."

"Awesome!"

"You'll need to do at least thirty in sixty seconds," Sean told him. "Forty-five sit-ups in a minute, and seven pull-ups, all performed consecutively. Hotshots have to show up fit at the start of the season, so get to the gym, the dojo, the track, whatever you do."

Tim's grimace drew a laugh from Josh. "If you think that's tough, guess how many pushups Sean here does?"

"How many?"

"What's your record, Sean? Forty-three in sixty?"

"Never mind that." Sean gestured for Tim to sit back down. "I'm sure you can get into shape in no time. I like that you have military experience and that you've been educating yourself about fire science. That's all great. Let me ask you one more question before you go. It's going to be a tough one. When's the last time you lied? I want you to tell me about that."

"*What?*"

"Standard question."

"Yup," Josh agreed. "Important question too."

Tim glanced from one to the other. Slowly his face fell. "I used to lie a lot before I joined the Army. I was into drugs. I got busted for underage drinking. I lied all the time."

Sean nodded encouragingly. "And now?"

"It's behind me. I don't want that life. That's why I joined up. I needed to stay out of trouble."

Sean glanced at the sheet of paper before him. Based on what Josh had found in his background check, everything the guy said was true.

"I'm not that person anymore," Tim said. "I'm married. We're trying for a kid. I want to make something good out of my life."

Sean nodded, knowing exactly what he meant. He'd been in that exact spot about thirteen years ago. He loved hiring guys like this—guys who'd had a rough start in life but wanted something better.

"I get it," Sean told him. "I just wanted to hear what you had to say. I'm looking for men—and women—with character, not just skills. It's not easy to be honest about your faults or your past. But on a crew like this, we have to trust each other. And that means telling the truth. To yourself and to the other guys. That's what makes us a team, not just a bunch of people working together. You understand?"

He nodded eagerly. "I do. I do. That's what I want. I want to be part of a team doing something good."

"It's some of the hardest work you'll ever do," Sean warned. "Can you handle sixteen-hour days?"

"For two weeks straight?" Josh added.

"Uh…"

"Cutting paths in the dirt? It ain't all that glamorous. You're scraping the line down to mineral so there's nothing there to burn. You do that over and over again, hour after hour, until your back aches and your hands feel like claws. And then there's always the chance that the fire you're trying to stop will jump that line."

"You ever been chased by a three-hundred-foot tall, half-a-million acre monster?" Josh asked.

"Well, I was in the Army, so…"

They all laughed. Sean's phone vibrated with an incoming text. He glanced at it briefly to make sure it wasn't one of the higher-ups with something urgent.

The text was from Evie. *I finally showed my mom the photos from the airstrip. They'd like to invite you to dinner tonight. Will you come? Please?*

She wasn't pulling the plug. Their "whatever it was"—still was. When Sean looked up, his changed expression must have shocked the wannabe hotshot.

"I'm in. I'm in, aren't I?" Tim looked over at Josh for confirmation. "He's smiling. Am I hired?"

Sean grinned. Why not? "Subject to final approval, welcome to the Jupiter Point Hotshots."

~ ~ ~

After the last interview, as Sean and Josh unloaded a shipment of tents, Josh said, "I got a call from Finn. He wants to fly us out to LA so the screenwriters can interview us."

"No."

"Come on, Magneto. Free trip to Hollywood. Models, actresses, Kardashians. We could take a side trip out to San Gabriel. I have friends in the fire department there."

"I don't have time for a vacation in LaLa Land. The fire season's only a few weeks away. That's if it doesn't start early, which most people are saying it will." He tossed a box to Josh, who caught it easily and swung it onto the shelf.

"Which is why it's a perfect time for a break. Once summer hits, it'll be nonstop."

Sean squinted at his friend. "Why are you so into this movie thing?"

"For the chicks," Josh said promptly. With a bandanna tied around his head to keep his shaggy mop of hair away from his face, he looked like a pirate.

"Bullshit." Sean knew perfectly well that Josh's "player" facade was mostly an act. "Can I ask you something? During the burnover, did anything come into your mind about what you wanted to do afterward?"

"Sure. Emma Watson. I told you guys."

"Something not related to women. Like for me, I knew I had to come back to Jupiter Point." Sean checked the back of the van, saw no more boxes, and closed the doors with a slam.

"But you came back for a woman."

Sean's jaw dropped. "The hell I did. I came back to prove them all wrong. Show them I wasn't a punk kid anymore."

Josh was watching him closely. "Prove it to who? The McGraws?"

"No. Well, yes, them. And everyone else."

He scrubbed a hand across the back of his neck, suddenly nervous at the thought of seeing the McGraws for the first time since he'd left. He could probably use some moral support. He pulled out his phone and sent a quick text to Evie.

"Josh, what are you doing tonight? Feel like a home-cooked meal?"

Chapter 15

Between the drama of Sean's disappearance thirteen years ago
and the even more exciting drama of his return, Evie worried all day
long about what dinner would be like. Suzanne agreed to come as an
extra buffer, and when Sean asked if Josh could come along, she
jumped at the chance for more distraction.

But she shouldn't have worried. One huge advantage of
growing up in the McGraw family was that politeness always ruled.
In classic McGraw fashion, the Dean greeted Sean and Josh with
distant courtesy, as if the events of thirteen years ago were simply
too uncouth to mention.

Her brother Hunter would be laughing his ass off.

Molly McGraw was having one of her good days and
remembered Sean right away. She even teased him about his
macaroni and cheese obsession. Even though Sean seemed
uncomfortable at first—maybe unsure of his welcome—he relaxed
as soon as he realized no one was going to bring up the past.

Nope, not in this household.

After the Dean said grace, Evie cut up her mother's meatloaf into manageable pieces and tried to think of a neutral topic. Nothing at all came to mind. Not the gallery, not the JPBC, nothing to do with Jupiter Point at all.

She shot a pleading glance at Suzanne, who looked especially sunny in a daisy-printed sundress. "You owe me," she mouthed, then turned to the Dean.

"Uncle Fred, I was wondering what you thought about the new partnership between the community college and the observatory? It has amazing potential, don't you think?"

Evie's jaw dropped. Every time she dismissed Suzanne as a boy-crazy social butterfly, her cousin surprised her.

"I'm very hopeful," the Dean answered. "I've told them they can count on my help."

That was another classic McGraw trait. Her family might not be great with conflict, but when it came to community service and doing their duty, no one could find fault with them.

She'd tried her entire life to do that. But what if there was something inside her, something stubborn that she'd never be able to completely control? Something that was keeping her from delivering the endorsement everyone expected?

Every time she looked over at Sean, that wild part of her howled like a wolf in the wilderness. Everything about him called to her. His messy dark hair, the insane delineation of his physique, the polite way he listened to her father, the secret glance from those deep-green eyes.

When the community college topic petered out, Josh Marshall stepped into the silence. He told a funny story about the first time he'd tried to run with his pack on during training. He had no problem with the run, and in fact felt lighter at the end than when he'd started out. That was when he realized he'd left it unzipped and all his gear had fallen out along the way.

Everyone laughed except Suzanne, who had apparently decided to look at Josh as some kind of wayward child. "I hope you picked everything up."

Josh fixed laughing gray eyes on her. "Of course not, that's what the hose honeys are for."

"The *what*?"

"He's teasing." Evie jumped in before Suzanne could explode from outrage. "From what I've seen, he does that a lot."

"Yup," Josh agreed. "Never take anything I say seriously, unless there's a fire. Then you should do exactly what I say, without question. Actually, maybe you should always—"

"Where is Hunter these days?" Sean interrupted, addressing his question to the Dean.

"Hunter has been working in Los Angeles." Evie's father adjusted his spectacles on his nose. "He works for a record company. I looked it up on the Google and apparently it's one of the top companies in that field. He's planning to move back this summer, happily. This family could use some good news."

Evie winced at that little dig. Her family might not like conflict, but it had a way of sneaking up on them anyway. When an awkward silence stretched on, she jumped in herself. "I can't wait for Hunter to come home. And I'm really excited to meet his new girlfriend. She's a famous pop star. Starly Minx, have you heard of her?"

Sean and Josh both looked impressed, but the Dean pinched the bridge of his nose, a familiar gesture that told Evie he wasn't happy with something. Starly's fame or profession, most likely. But being a McGraw, he just changed the subject and addressed Evie. "By the way, have you seen this week's *Gazette* around? What's the point of paying extra for home delivery when they keep neglecting to deliver it?"

Oh *crap*. Evie had confiscated her parents' paper because of Brad's op-ed. Sure, it was a cowardly thing to do, and pointless too. They were going to find out sooner or later; she preferred later.

"I don't know why you even bother with home delivery anymore, Uncle Fred." Suzanne poured herself another glass of lemonade. "Most papers are online and—" Halfway through that sentence, Evie tried to kick her but couldn't quite reach. She mouthed a panicked plea for help to Josh. He elbowed Suzanne in the side. "Ow!" She broke off and glared at Josh. "That was my rib you almost cracked."

"Sorry. Old firefighting injury. My arm spasms sometimes."

Suzanne narrowed her eyes at him suspiciously. "Don't you work with a chainsaw?"

"Yes. It's a real problem. Especially in the shower."

Sean, in the midst of swallowing, covered his mouth. He looked awfully close to bursting into laughter and spewing lemonade across the table.

Oh Lord…this dinner was totally going off the rails. On the bright side, Molly McGraw wore the biggest smile Evie had seen in while.

Suzanne pointedly shook her head at Josh and turned back to the Dean. "As I was saying about reading the news online—"

Evie shot to her feet. "Anyone want dessert? I made a shortcake. Suzanne, want to help me?"

"I'll help." Sean rose to his feet and, despite her very obvious efforts to get Suzanne's attention instead, he followed her into the kitchen.

"What are you doing?" she hissed at him. "I don't want Suzanne telling the Dean about the online edition. He's lived without it so far."

"I know what you're doing." He cupped her elbows and drew her closer. "You're trying to keep your father from finding out about Brad's op-ed. Do you seriously think that's going to work? He's going to find out, one way or another. Wouldn't it make more sense for you to just tell him about it?"

"No." She tried to tug away, but he clasped her even closer.

"Hey. I'm not the enemy here."

"I know. I know. I just…what if he starts asking questions? And he will. Not that he *wants* to. If he wanted to, he would have done it by now. He'd much rather avoid the topic, of course. But once he hears what everyone's saying, he's going to want to know more."

The closeness of Sean's body made it hard to stay upset. In his white dress shirt and gray trousers, he looked so handsome she wanted to eat him up. He'd probably dressed nicely in deference to her parents, not to make her panties fall off, but she couldn't help her reaction to him.

"Honey, did you ever think that you're maybe going about this wrong?"

"What do you mean?"

"That the more you keep something secret, the more it can hurt you?"

He ran his hands up and down her back. She inhaled his scent, pine woods and freedom. What would it be like to be that free? "It's not that simple. I don't want to hurt my *parents*. It's about them, not me."

"Sweetheart, what are you so afraid of? Do you think anyone's going to blame you for what happened with Brad? You were fourteen." They were talking in urgent whispers now, aware that anyone could come in from the dining room at any moment.

"You don't understand." She pressed the heel of her hand into her forehead. "It was my fault too. Maybe it was *all* my fault. I don't know. At the time, he said that it was. Aunt Desiree thought so too. Maybe he was right and I'm not being fair to him now. I'm keeping him hanging just like I did before, and—"

A surprise sob hiccupped from her mouth. This was more than she'd said to anyone. Ever.

"Hey. Hey, hey." He wrapped his arms around her and cradled the back of her head against his chest. "Come on now. What is this crap you're telling yourself? How did you keep him hanging? I feel like I'm in the dark here. I don't know how to help you."

"Evie? We're waiting," her father called.

She tore herself from the circle of his arms. "I can't talk about this here." She grabbed the strawberry shortcake off the kitchen counter. "Can you grab the whipped cream from the fridge?"

"This is a McGraw family habit, isn't it? Just when things get interesting, you run for cover." He opened the refrigerator and retrieved the whipped cream. "I'm going to take Josh home and then I'm coming back to get you. We're going to talk. Tonight." Sean brandished the can of Reddi-Wip in her direction.

His firm tone gave her a little thrill. More than a little, actually. "You're kind of bossy."

He took a long stride closer so he loomed over her, eyes gleaming. "If you *really* want to see me bossy, come to bed with me." His face lowered, his mouth hovered over hers, and she swayed toward him, her body drawn to his like a flower to the sun.

"Hey!" Suzanne whispered from the door. "Nothing naughty in the McGraw kitchen."

Josh's head popped up behind hers. "Not even with whipped cream? Spoilsport."

Suzanne shoved her elbow back into his ribs. "Do you ever stop?"

"Only one way to find out."

Evie made a face at both of them and ducked under Sean's arm. Just before vanishing out the doorway, she looked back and met his eyes.

Tonight, Sean mouthed.

She nodded. Tonight. It was time.

Chapter 16

Sean drove Josh back to the base, with Josh pestering him the entire time.

"Let's go hit the bars, man. Let off some steam. Evie's just one girl, the town's full of them. I got a list of the best drinking spots from Suzanne. There's only two, so that keeps it simple."

"Count me out. You go ahead. Take one of the rigs."

"What's up your butt? You haven't gone out once since we got here."

Even though Sean didn't drink much anymore, he usually went out with the crew just for the company. But tonight, he was anxious to get back to Evie. "I spent enough time in those bars with my fake ID back in the day. I don't want the town seeing me that way."

Josh threw his head back and laughed. "You're old before your time, bro. Take one step inside the city limits of Jupiter Point and you turn into an old lady. They'll have you teaching Sunday school soon."

That actually got under Sean's skin a little. Was his desire for Evie changing him? Never before had he felt so protective of a girl.

Protective of her *feelings*. He'd lived by the mottos "enjoy yourself to the fullest," and "if it's not working out, move on." But none of that kind of thinking seemed to apply when it came to Evie.

Sean pulled up at the entrance of the base and gestured for Josh to get out. "I'm…uh, going back out."

Josh swung his long legs out of the car and smirked. "Say hi to Evie. Again. Better hope the Dean doesn't catch on that you have your eye on his little girl."

"She's twenty-seven years old."

"Also, if you see Suzanne, tell her I'm all alone out here. Sad, lonely, horny, whatever you come up with."

"Forget about Suzanne. She's practically engaged."

"You know me. I like lost causes. And challenges."

With a last salute, Josh jogged toward the barracks. Sean swung the wheel and headed back into town. Luckily, Evie had told him to pick her up at her place instead of her parents'. Being back in that house had made him twitchy. Its familiar suffocating atmosphere—always quiet, always orderly and serene—made him want to scream. He remembered how it had felt back then, when his entire world had just been knocked out from under him.

Life with the McGraws had felt like a lie.

As if the McGraws were lying to themselves about what the real world was like. Reality wasn't nice and peaceful and caring. Fuck no. It was chaotic and terrible.

Evie was waiting on her front stoop, her backpack next to her. Her arms were wrapped around her shins and she was gazing up at the starry night sky. He'd barely pulled up to the curb when she jumped up and ran to the passenger side.

"Let's go to the Point," she said breathlessly. "I can see Mars and Jupiter from here on my porch. It should be amazing from there."

Riiiight. The local obsession with stargazing? He put his truck in gear and headed in the direction of the high promontory locals called the Point. "What is it about this town? Haven't you guys figured out that watching a good movie is a lot more fun than watching the stars?"

"We have movies here. The movie theater added two screens, did you hear? Who says we can't change with the times?" She tossed him a saucy look. "I heard we're even getting a new shipload of firemen. That's a lot of testosterone for a tiny little town like ours."

"You have no idea," he muttered. "I've been trying to pick some of the less good-looking guys, but it hasn't worked out that way."

"Why would you do that?"

"This is a peaceful place. Are you sure you're ready for twenty-plus rough-and-rowdy, adrenaline-junkie hotshots?"

"As a matter of fact, we've been wondering about a calendar. Good promotion for the town, all proceeds could go to the pet shelter—"

"Hell no." He'd been approached about posing for calendars before, but had always refused flat-out. Firemen were supposed to put out fires, not take their shirts off for the camera. Josh, of course, felt the opposite. He'd already posed for three calendars, representing March, August, and December. He claimed to be aiming for the whole twelve-month cycle.

"Oh come on. Since you're the superintendent, we could put you on the cover. I'd buy that in a flash."

"I'll give you a private pose. Anytime you want."

"Honestly, Sean, I never would have guessed you'd be so shy. Do you have something to hide?"

"You'll find out soon enough." He grinned at her shiver of anticipation. As he drove, he kept treating himself to little sidelong glances at her. She'd changed since dinner, and now wore a short, fuzzy sweater that skimmed the waistband of her loose cotton skirt. Her hair was twisted in a careless knot at the back of her head, revealing the elegant curve of her neck. He wanted to drop kisses all along that soft, exposed skin.

He stepped on the accelerator and hugged the curves that switchbacked up the hill. It had guardrails all the way up, but the only illumination came from the reflectors embedded in the road. No streetlights were allowed here since they were so close to the Observatory.

Evie directed him to a spot he'd never been before, a pullout past the turnoff for the Observatory. Even though there were enough parking spaces for four vehicles, they had the place to themselves.

Sean shouldered Evie's backpack and followed her down the barest trace of a footpath until they reached a flat piece of ground covered with fragrant creeping thyme. The bulk of the hill was at their backs and the ocean stretched before them like a vast secret world. Up above, starlight rained down from countless vibrant points.

It was breathtaking—literally. "Wow," he finally said.

"Oh, I don't know. I think we can still catch the last showing of *Jackass 8*."

"Touché." He gave her a little salute as he swung the backpack to the ground.

She crouched down and pulled out a soft fleece blanket. He caught one edge to help her, since the wind wanted to play with it too, and they spread it on the ground. Evie pinned one corner with her backpack and Sean took off his boots to do the same with the opposite side.

He stood with his hands on his hips, taking big lungfuls of the ocean-cooled breeze. Pure exhilaration. Almost as good as the rush of beating back a fire.

"I brought fortifications," Evie announced as she pulled a flask from the backpack. "Hot chocolate with a kick. It's mostly for me, but you're welcome to share it."

"Fortifications? That sounds like you're getting ready for war."

"I'm *in* a war, haven't you noticed? Brad and his supporters want to take me down. The coalition's meeting this week. I wouldn't be surprised if they voted me out."

He settled onto the blanket and stretched out, arms interlaced behind his head. The stars were so incredibly bright and alive, vibrating like tiny, busy chatterboxes. "What's the worst that could happen? You get voted out, then what?"

She settled cross-legged next to him and unscrewed the cap of the flask. "I go back to minding my own business. Gallery, photography, same old, same old. Brad gets his endorsement. Brad wins a seat in Sacramento. Jupiter Point becomes known as the home of State Representative White. It's just a stepping stone for him. He wants to go to Washington, probably within a few years. We watch in amazement as the hometown hero becomes famous nationwide."

"But what about you?"

"What about me? I told you. Gallery. Photography. My mother will need more care. Those are the things that matter most, right? Brad can go ahead and reach for the stars, and I'll—" She broke off, pressing her lips together. "I'll be right here."

He reached a lazy arm toward her and rubbed her back as she tipped the flask to her mouth. "Maybe here isn't so bad."

"Here is great. It's wonderful. It's so beautiful it makes me want to cry."

"Then are you fine with losing your position?"

She was quiet for a long moment. "I should be. It's not as if it's a lifelong dream. I ran because…I don't know, I wanted to try something new. And the business owners are a pain in the ass sometimes. Everyone has an opinion, they get into feuds over the silliest things. But when I think of stepping down, or getting voted out, I get…" She tipped the flask to her mouth again. "I get kind of angry."

"*Kind of* angry?"

"Yeah. Kind of." She looked almost alarmed at that admission. He wanted to laugh but stopped himself. The hot, heady realm of anger was so familiar to him, like a childhood sandbox. To her, apparently, it was a whole new world.

"Come on, Evie. Let it out, girl. You can do better than that."

"I can?"

"Hey, there's no one here except for me and the stars. And Jupiter." He gestured toward the bright planet shining down on them. "Jupiter won't mind if you let out a few curse words."

"I don't curse."

"Maybe that's your problem right there. Try it. A little one."

"Like…crap?" She practically whispered it.

"Well, that barely qualifies, honestly. Crap is one of those words you say when you don't want to say something worse. How about "screw Brad." How does that feel?"

"Screw Brad," she repeated, as if she was testing the words in her mouth. "Screw Brad for trying to shut me up."

"There you go." He gave her an encouraging pat on the knee.

"Screw Brad for manipulating me. Screw Brad for trampling over my life so he can get what he wants." She gained steam, breathing hard.

"Say it like it is, Evie."

"Screw him for even *thinking* about going out with a fourteen-year-old!"

"Amen."

She waved the flask in the air. "Why did my parents even allow that? Why? Screw him for fooling everyone."

"He's such a fucking asshole."

"Hey, I'm the one doing the swearing here."

"Sorry," he said immediately. "My bad."

"Screw him for making me feel like, like…" She seemed to

teeter on the edge of something big, something almost too much to say out loud. He held his tongue while she took another swallow from her flask. Then it came out in a tumble of nearly indistinguishable words. "Like some kind of disgusting, embarrassing nympho slut whose parents would disown her if they had any idea what she was really like."

"*What?*" Sean sat up in shock.

She buried her head in her hands, except that she still held the flask and it bonked against her forehead.

Gently he took it from her fingers and screwed the top back on. "What are you talking about?"

"He…God, this is so embarrassing." With her fingers, she wiped tears away from the corners of her eyes. "I can't believe I'm telling you. Seriously, I think the only reason I am is that you don't live here anymore."

For some reason, that comment made his heart kick. "You know I won't say anything."

"I know. You didn't say anything when it happened, even though you had to spend a night in jail. So I guess I can trust you, huh?"

He shrugged. "Actions speak louder than words."

She let out a long breath of air, then lay down on the blanket on her back and stared up at the night sky. "I can't look at you while I tell this story. Nothing personal."

"Got it. No offense taken."

"You know how I was raised. You've seen my family, you lived in our house. Sunday school. Duty. Responsibility. I was taught about abstinence. I was taught that you should wait until you really loved someone. Not necessarily for marriage, my family isn't that strict. But I remember lots of lectures about being cautious around boys. The girl had to put on the brakes because boys wouldn't. They would take things as far as you'd let them. I knew all that. Intellectually, I knew exactly what I was supposed to do. But they left one thing out. One really big thing."

"What was that?" He took her hand in his and felt her cling to it.

"No one ever told me how good it would feel. I thought I loved Brad. When he touched me, I forgot everything about how I was supposed to behave. Even if it was just my arm, like this."

She picked up his hand and drew her finger along the inside of his forearm. "Just something like that would put me into a trance. I loved it when he touched me."

Sean fought hard to put a lid on his jealous reaction. This had nothing to do with him, this was Evie's story.

"It only happened a few times because I was still in middle school. We weren't 'dating.' But sometimes I would see him after school or he would come over with his father and we'd sneak into the garage or something."

"So what happened the night I saw you guys?"

"That night…Brad had recently gotten his own car. His family had come over for dinner and we ran out of ice cream. Brad volunteered to drive to the store and pick some up, and the Dean let me go with him. Instead, we drove halfway down the block, out of sight, and he was all over me all of a sudden. It scared me at first, because he seemed so different. Sort of mean and pushing me around. When he saw I was kind of freaked out, he calmed down. Then he started doing the stuff he knew I liked. And I relaxed too, enough so I enjoyed it. He put his hand down my pants, and then I started to resist because I knew that wasn't a good idea. I kind of struggled a little, but he kept saying it was going to be okay and he wouldn't cross the line. That I should trust him because I'd known him forever."

Evie's hand was gripping his so tightly that he knew he'd have marks the next day.

"Then he touched my…well, clitoris. And it felt so good I couldn't believe it. I'd never even touched *myself* there. And—I came. He said that meant that he should be able to come too, and started undoing his pants. I said 'no,' I didn't want to have sex, he'd promised we wouldn't do that. He said, *What are you, a cocktease? Fine, then give me a blow job. You should do something for me, you little nympho slut.* That's what he said, and I was so shocked I started crying. He pushed me down and put his penis against my mouth, and the whole time he was saying the same kinds of things, that I was a slut because I'd let him touch me, and a nymphomaniac because I'd orgasmed, and that my parents would be so disappointed in me if they knew, and that if I didn't do what he wanted, he was going to tell his friends all about me and everyone in town would know what I really was."

Chapter 17

Sean wrapped his arms around her to calm her violent shaking. He gave her time to catch her breath, then asked gently, "Is that when I showed up?"

"Yes. As soon as you knocked on the window, he pulled away. Then you opened the door and dragged him out and…I guess you know the rest."

From the way she refused to meet his eyes, he knew how embarrassed she was. He knew he had to choose his words carefully—not his forte. Punching Brad again would be so much easier. "Evie, if a young girl came to you and told you that story, what would you tell her? That it was her fault? That an orgasm makes her a nymphomaniac? That she shouldn't have trusted a friend of the family? I'm just curious, because I know what I'd tell her."

"What?" she whispered.

"That she got conned by a fucking *asshole*." Out came his anger, fiery and swift. "He said whatever it took so you wouldn't tell. He intended to rape you. It doesn't matter how many times he got you off. He still didn't have the right to make you give him a blow job if you didn't want to."

"Yes but…" She shook her head fiercely, clamping down on her bottom lip with her teeth. "That means I was being a cocktease. I know he told his friends something like that, because I used to hear that word if I walked past the gym when they were shooting hoops."

"Which makes him double the asshole. You were *fourteen*. I remember you then. You were a kid, Evie. I liked girls—a lot—but I never once thought of you as a girl I would shag."

She sat upright, then shifted onto her knees. "You're saying I'm not shag-worthy?"

"You're very shag-worthy. *Now*. He had no business messing around with you, and I bet he did it because he knew he could shame and manipulate you. You never told anyone, right?"

"I kind of told Aunt Desiree, but not everything. She told me I was better off forgetting it ever happened." She shook her head, her silvery eyes catching light from the stars. "I was so afraid of what he'd say about me. It was safer just to avoid boys altogether. Also, it was my word against his."

Damn, he'd never thought about that. By leaving, he'd deprived her of her only witness.

"That's not your fault," she said quickly. "I begged you not to say anything. I don't blame you. And honestly, I was glad you were gone. I was so embarrassed, and I just wanted to forget the whole thing ever happened. That's what Desiree said to do, and I tried."

He rolled onto his side and propped his head on one hand. "And how'd that work out for you?"

"Not too bad, until you showed up." She laughed and gave him a little push. "And until I got elected president of the coalition just in time for Brad to run for political office."

"Yeah?" He picked up her hand and bounced it against his palm. "Let me ask you this. How many orgasms have you had—with a man—since then?"

"Kind of a personal question, don't you think?" He couldn't tell for sure in the dark, but her voice sure sounded like she was blushing.

"Hey, I'm just trying to do my job. You hand-picked me for this mission, remember? Mission Reclaim your Sexual Side? I'm pretty sure this is essential background information. And besides, remember how good I am at keeping secrets?"

"Right. Okay. Well, then. As you can probably guess, the answer is zero. I've been having my orgasms without a man."

"Ouch. I guess we *are* sort of nonessential, if you think about it." He ran his thumb across the tender skin of her wrist.

"I admit, I thought that for a long time," she said softly. "I know how to make myself feel good. And I do. But when we kissed that time at the hotshot base, and then when we made out…well, I realized that I've been cheating myself. I was afraid of being scorned and shamed if I did that with a man."

"But Evie, sweet girl, we like it when you come. I mean 'you' as in 'women,' and by 'we' I mean normal men. Not sick, manipulative bastard men. Ask any normal guy on the street how it feels to make a woman come apart in his arms, or orgasm against his tongue, or shatter when he fingers her, or drives his cock into her, and you know what he'll say?"

Her pulse was skipping in a crazy rhythm, her breath coming fast. "What?"

"He'll say it makes him feel like Superman. Like a hero. There's no better feeling in the world. Although my own orgasms come close," he admitted.

She giggled, a light and carefree sound. He took that as a good sign, that maybe her confession was helping her.

"You gave that bastard the biggest gift, and he threw it back in your face and made you feel like shit about yourself. And then you protected him."

"No." She shook her head fiercely. "I wasn't protecting *him*. I was protecting myself and my parents. I mean, there was no evidence of anything. He didn't hurt me physically. If I'd told my parents, nothing good would have come of it. There would have been drama and conflict and everything they don't like. I wasn't even sure I had the words to tell them. They would have understood something like 'he attacked me' or 'he raped me.' But 'he made me come with his hand then insulted me and tried to force me to give him a blow job'? I didn't understand it myself. I didn't understand how I could be so…different from them."

He thought about how she must have felt, so alone and confused and humiliated. "What about your friend, the girl with the freckles?"

"Brianna."

"Did you tell her?"

"Sean, you're not listening to me. Other than what I told my aunt, I never told a single person the whole story. Until now."

The importance of this moment felt as vast as the Pacific Ocean below them. "I'm honored," he said softly. "So tell me this. How does it feel now that you've told someone?"

"Weird," she admitted. "I feel nervous. I'm not sure what you think of me now."

"What do I think of *you*? I think you're beautiful and passionate and kind and exactly the same person you were before. If you want to know what I think of Brad, well, I guess you probably know that by now."

"Passionate. Is that a code word for slut?"

"Fuck." He pushed himself up into a sitting position. "No, of course it isn't." He remembered that moment between them at the airstrip, when he'd put her hand on his erection. "That's why you got so upset when I told you that you turned me on. You thought it was some kind of insult?"

She nodded reluctantly. "I know it doesn't necessarily make sense. But I've been so terrified of showing any kind of sexual…anything…since then. The funny thing is, after it happened, I went to the library and found a book about sex. I used to read it in little snatches when the librarians weren't looking. I figured out that I wasn't some abnormal freak for having an orgasm like that. I'm not uneducated or clueless. I get that it's normal. I do. But I just couldn't forget the look on Brad's face and those horrible words."

"I get it. It's hard to trust anyone after that." He was dying to touch her, to take her into his arms and wipe away the memory of that dickhead, but he didn't know if she would welcome that.

"Yes. Especially here in Jupiter Point. Everyone knows Brad, and I didn't know what he'd said to whom. I was afraid to get intimate with anyone. I figured I'd just bide my time until college then leave. Maybe start somewhere new with a clean slate. I really think I would have broken free by now if I'd left. But then my mother got diagnosed with Parkinson's and I couldn't bring myself to leave my parents on their own. So I just put on the blinders and pretended that Brad was just any other guy I'd grown up with. So…" She gave a jaunty little laugh, as if all of this was the biggest joke in the world. "There you have it. My entire sexual history. Oh wait, I left out the time I lost my virginity."

"To a gay man. I remember that much."

"Yes, he was one of my best friends. He used to work at the gallery with me. One night we decided that since we were such good friends, and we were both single, that we should try having sex. I trusted him because he didn't grow up here and didn't even know Brad. And that was all fine except for one little problem. It took him an hour to get an erection and about a second to lose it after he'd penetrated me. The next day he came to see me and said he finally understood that he was gay. And *that* brings us up to the present. Pretty pathetic, isn't it?"

"Hey." He gave her a little swat on the rear. "No putting yourself down or I'll have to spank you."

"Is this the bossy side you warned me about?"

"No, you haven't seen my bossy side yet." He bared his teeth at her. "But if you keep that up, you will."

She made a saucy face at him. *Attitude*. That's what he wanted to see. If she could keep that "screw Brad" attitude, she'd be fine.

"You left out a few bits, by the way," he said. "Like what made you decide to kiss me."

She smiled. "Maybe I'm just a nympho slut."

"Evie McGraw, did you really just make a joke out of this?" He gripped her slim shoulders and grinned so wide his face hurt. "If you can joke about it, you're halfway cured."

"Oh my God, you're right. I did make a joke." Her eyes lit with triumph. "Take that, Brad White."

"Hell yeah." He offered his hand for a high-five.

Still smiling, she tugged at his shirt until he ripped it off his own body. He loved the way her eyes went wide at the sight of his bare torso. She gave him a gentle push and urged him onto his back. He lay there, arms spread wide, as she straddled his hips.

"I bet I can guess the other half of the cure," she teased.

"Are you sure, Evie? I don't want to do anything that's going to upset you."

She reached behind her head, undid the clip fastening her knot, and shook out the waterfall of dark silk. "It won't upset me. I'm tired of holding back because of that one stupid time."

He let his fingers play across the skin of her thighs, just above her knees. When he heard her soft sigh, he explored higher, savoring the texture of her inner thighs, smooth as cream. She parted her legs farther as he reached her panties. He felt the heat already radiating from her core. Glancing up, he saw her lips part, her lovely features painted with gentle starlight.

She nestled her rear against the hardening rod between his

legs. He gritted his teeth against the sweet torture.

"I intend to make you come," he told her. "And I intend to enjoy every damn second of it. So if you have any hesitation about that, tell me now. No, scratch that. You can tell me at any point; it's okay. Whatever comes out of your mouth is fine. 'No' is fine. 'Harder' is fine. 'Sean, you're a fucking sex god' is fine. All of that works for me. Whatever comes into your head, just let it out."

Evie laughed down at him. "Why shouldn't I? That's what *you* do, right?"

"Exactly." He reached the edge of her underwear and swept aside the material to unveil her secret intimate folds. Already damp. Her clit already swollen and pouting from its delicate nest of hair. He brushed his thumb across it experimentally. She trembled and her thighs tightened around him.

"You feel so good, sweetheart. I love how your clit presses against my thumb, so thick and hot," he murmured. "Can you feel how hard I am right now?"

She wiggled from side to side, so her delicious, hot weight slid across his cock.

"And…now I'm even harder," he told her. "Thanks a lot."

She laughed. "You're welcome."

"I'm going to make you pay for that. In orgasms." He slid his finger along her wet slit. She was so juicy and primed, her intimate tissues so unbelievably soft. When he reached her clit again, he increased the pressure just slightly, all his senses tuned to her reaction. Her sounds, her squirms, her sighs. "That's all I want, sweetheart. I want you to feel good. I want you to come apart for me."

"That feels amazing, Sean." Her head tilted back. The wind flirted with the long strands of hair around her face. The pale, muscular stretch of her throat made him long for the day she would open for his cock. But not yet. Right now, he had only one job to do.

Make her come, and make her feel good about it.

Chapter 18

Every time Sean pressed her clit, Evie felt as if shooting stars were dancing through her body. She should feel awkward, but she didn't. Something about Sean's straightforward way of talking about sex made it impossible to feel embarrassed. She knew he was right there with her because he kept saying so. Every word he spoke was about how much he wanted her, how beautiful and desirable she was, how sexy. None of it made her feel self-conscious. The opposite. It made her feel free and wild and happy.

The heat of his erection filtered through his pants. She ground against it in the same rhythm he used on her clit, and oh my God, it felt amazing, so, so much better than how it felt when she used her own hand on herself. She rocked her hips forward and back, chasing the sensation hovering just out of reach.

Her breasts ached to be touched. She could do that. She could take off her top and touch herself, or lean forward for Sean to lick her nipples. But that would be wrong—kind of porny and slutty.

No. No more fear.

With a quick movement, she pulled off her top and unsnapped

her bra. Her breasts spilled into the cool air, nipples hardening instantly. She took them between her fingers and pinched lightly. An immediate jolt of pleasure shot to her sex.

"Oh yeah," said Sean, with nothing but deep, gravelly, male approval in his voice. "That is fucking hot, babe."

And that sent another swift clutch of heat to her belly. There was no need to hide anything from Sean because he liked it all.

She closed her eyes and let her head fall back. She felt as if starlight was raining down on her. Freedom whispered to her in the wind, with its edge of chill from the ocean. Wildness sang to her in the slow grind of Sean's hips, the pulse of electricity between her legs. It built and built, higher and hotter, an urgent drumbeat demanding its due…and then it burst into an explosion of sensation. Spasms of pleasure rippled through her, again and again. Every time they started to slow, Sean would change the angle of his thumb, press harder, or different, or something.

Nothing existed except the bliss pouring through her body. She reveled in it like a cat rolling in catnip, as if nothing mattered beyond the next second, the next blissful jolt.

A cry was echoing in the air, a low, erotic sound that she'd never heard before. As the convulsions of her orgasm slowed, she became aware of the awkward sound.

It was coming from her!

She snapped her mouth shut. Oh geez…so *embarrassing*. Who made sounds like that during sex? It didn't sound like any of the pornos she'd ever happened to catch on late-night cable. It sounded raw, sort of like a wounded cat.

What would Sean think now?

Cringing, she glanced his way. In the night, with her own body blocking the starlight, she couldn't read his expression. "Sorry," she gasped. "I don't know where that came from, that sound."

He sat up, shifting her so they could face each other comfortably. He looped his arms loosely around her back. "Evie, normally I wouldn't mention this fact at this particular moment, but remember how I said I married a stripper? Sex sounds don't bug me. I love 'em."

She bit her lip dubiously. Even though her lower body still vibrated from her climax, and her limbs felt boneless, her worry was casting a shadow over the whole experience.

"When people come, they make all sorts of weird noises. Mandy told me I sound like a hog during sex."

"A hog? Like how?"

"I don't know, like a grunting sort of...I don't know, I'm not sure I can recreate it. I think you might have to find out firsthand." He flashed a gleam of a smile. "If you want. When you're ready."

She saw what he was doing—making sure she knew the choice was hers. But honestly, everything about this encounter was so different from the time with Brad. With Brad, the brief pleasure had brought shame and humiliation, then fear. She searched her heart for any hint of those emotions, and didn't find a single bit of any of them.

Should she take her chances and find out if going all the way would provide another huge, monumental contrast with that other horrible time?

"You probably want to be satisfied too," she whispered. "It's not fair if it's just me."

"Look, sweetheart. I'm not going to lie. This wild thing between my legs is raring to go."

A crazy thrill shot through her. *Wild thing.* She loved those words. Her body loved those words. The secret part of her that had been asleep at the wheel loved those words.

"But, you know, he and I have a good relationship. We'll figure something out." He ran his hands up and down her back. The size and strength of his hands never ceased to amaze her—or their gentleness. "The important thing right now is you. How are you feeling?"

"Amazing," she said, after a quick check to make sure that was still the case. "That was amazing."

"Good. That's all I want to hear." He brushed her hair behind her back and combed his fingers through it. The soothing sensation made her eyes half close. The breeze cooled the sweat on her body. In another minute she'd be chilled, but for now, it was perfect.

"So…you'd be okay if we never had actual sex?"

"I might have the biggest case of blue balls on the planet, but yeah, I'd be okay. It's not like we're…well, you know. It's not a relationship. I don't expect anything."

She feathered her fingers across his chest. Hot skin, firm muscles. All man. Straight up, honest, grown-up man. He was right, this wasn't a relationship. It was a "mission"—one she'd requested of him. That was part of their agreement and that was totally okay with her. Right? Wasn't it?

"Hey," he said gently. "What just happened?"

She shook off her melancholy. *You made this bed, now lie in it.* "Sorry, I was just thinking. We're doing this because I asked you to help me find my sexual side again."

He skimmed his hand across her mound, making her breath hitch. "I think we've accomplished that, unless you have unbelievable orgasm-faking skills."

She flicked his arm in revenge for that comment. "That's one thing about satisfying yourself, you don't have to worry about faking it."

"True that." He laughed, the deep rumbling sound touching a chord deep inside her. Sean's voice had a way of arousing her all on its own.

"*Anyway*," she continued. "It seems to me that finding my sexual side ought to include the actual act of sex. You know, penetration."

She felt his erection jump against her thigh. "Keep talking," he said in a strained voice. He stroked her upper thighs under her skirt. Her skin rippled—was it more sensitive than before? It seemed so.

"Um…what about?" Hadn't she just said what she wanted to say?

"You had me at 'penetration.'"

"Right. As I was saying, I'm pretty sure my sexual reclamation project will not be complete without it."

The phrase "sexual reclamation" also inspired a reaction from his male parts. She drew her finger across the bulge in his jeans. "Does that always happen?"

"Do you mean does my cock respond to words that sound sexy? Yes. It also responds to stuff like the look you're giving it right now. And the fact that every time you shift your thigh just the tiniest bit, you pull my jeans against it. There's a seriously good chance that I'm going to come before we even get close to penetration."

"Really?" She was so fascinated by how freely he talked about sex and everything associated with it. "That would be uncomfortable, wouldn't it?"

"Yes. But also kind of a relief." He moved his hands back up her thighs, thumbs gliding along the most sensitive inner skin. When he reached the vee between her legs, she yearned for him to touch her more intimately, but instead he veered the other direction, back down the outside of her thighs. A low thrum of need vibrated through her nervous system.

"You could…I don't know…maybe bring it out. And I could stroke it. Even if we don't do anything else, that would feel good, right?"

"Fuck yes, that would feel good. But I don't want you to feel like you have to. I'm a big boy, Evie. I chose to be here with you, knowing what you're dealing with. You don't owe me anything."

"I know that." And she did, she truly, truly did. The fact was— "I want you," she admitted. "I want to see what it feels like when you're inside me. I don't think it will hurt. It didn't hurt the last time, with Pete. It just felt strange."

"Good strange?"

"Not really. Just strange."

"You know, I might be a little cocky here, but I bet I can beat 'strange.'"

"I bet you can too." Something was expanding inside her, a wild, free, warm feeling. The night air, the vibrant stars, the fresh scent of scrub grass, Sean's muscular body and slightly pained grin— it all intoxicated her more than the spiked hot chocolate. For the first time in so long, the future felt bright and wild and full of possibility.

Before she could think better of it, she unzipped his pants and touched the hot organ hiding behind his cotton boxer briefs.

He groaned. "Oh Evie, I gotta warn you, there's absolutely no chance that I can last long enough to make this good for you."

"This one's not about me." She pushed him back so he lay on the blanket.

"Evie—"

"Shhh." She reached bare skin and stroked him gently. She savored the feel of his thick ridges, soft veins, the satiny glide of skin over hard muscle. He arched his hips into her touch. His arm muscles clenched as he dug his hands into the fleece blanket underneath them.

Inspired, she bent down and touched her tongue to the hot tip of his penis.

"Jesus, Evie." His voice was thick with desire. "That feels fucking incredible."

She circled her tongue around the thick head and lapped up a tiny drop of liquid. It was all so new, so alluring. She loved the salty flavor of that firm flesh and his vulnerable position, sprawled under her. It made her feel powerful but also generous. She wanted him to enjoy himself. Wanted him to feel the kind of pleasure he'd given her. She wrapped her hand around his length again and moved it lightly up and down.

And then—suddenly—it was over. He went rigid and arched his back. Warm liquid spilled into her hand then overflowed onto his stomach.

And there it was—the hog sound.

A deep, harsh, grunting bellow that would have frightened away the birds if it hadn't been the middle of the night.

She bit her lip to keep from laughing. That wouldn't be polite, to laugh at the sound he made when he came. Would it? But it was so *funny*…

Looking utterly spent, Sean splayed his arms wide and opened his eyes a crack. "It's okay," he said wryly. "You can laugh."

Even though she still didn't want to, the laughter burst out of her in a cascade of giggles. "I'm sorry," she gasped, trying to stop the flow with her hand.

He rolled his eyes and grinned. "I told you to laugh. So laugh. Don't worry about it."

"It's just…it was so…" She tried to imitate the sound, but it came out as more of a *moo*. That made her laugh even harder.

"I do not moo after sex." A smile quivered at the corners of his mouth.

"I…I know you don't…" On and on, the laughter came. She just couldn't stop it.

He fixed her with a stern gaze. "I oink. It's different."

"Ahahahha!" A full-on gale of laughter racked her body. Tears streamed down her face. "You…don't…oink."

The word "oink" was so hilarious suddenly. *Oink*. Who came up with the word "oink?" She laughed and laughed. It felt as if years of tension leached from her body. Even if she and Sean never did anything sexual again, even if they never got around to "penetration," she'd gained something incredibly valuable. She'd learned that laughing after sex—maybe even during—made it that much more fun.

Sean lay back and listened, watching her with a smile playing over his mouth.

"It's a really good thing I don't have self-esteem issues," he told her when her spasms of hilarity started to die down. "Also, it's a good thing I heard *your* sex sound first. You have no grounds to ridicule me, woman."

"I know. And I'm not." She wiped the tears from her eyes. "I promise I'm not."

"You know something?" He cupped her face, thumb brushing her chin. Although she couldn't make out the color of his eyes without extra light, she could feel them on her. She could sense the smile in them. "If it makes you laugh like this, you can ridicule me all you want. I won't mind."

The most amazing feeling of security settled deep inside her. Maybe they weren't in a relationship. Maybe they never would be. But obviously Sean cared about her. Otherwise, why would he look at her like that? Now that he'd made her come, he knew things about her nobody else did. But she trusted him, because he honked like a hog when he came and didn't even care. She could probably get up and do the chicken dance naked and he wouldn't blink. She loved that about him.

Not that she loved him. That would be a big mistake, and wasn't going to happen.

"Hang on a second," she told him. "I have something in my pack to clean up with." She rolled off him and dug in her backpack for the toilet paper she always brought with her for photo-expedition pee emergencies. She wiped her hand, then gave him the roll and watched as he wiped himself off. He showed no signs of embarrassment as he did so. Was it even possible to embarrass Sean Marcus?

Why not ask? Why not take advantage of this feeling of freedom he inspired in her?

"Do you ever get embarrassed?" she asked as she put her bra back on, then her top.

He shot her a curious look as he finished up. "Are you thinking I should be?"

"No, I'm just wondering."

He appeared to think about it as he zipped up his jeans. "My father used to go out of his way to embarrass me. He did all kinds of shit. He once showed up to a parent conference meeting wearing a fringe jacket, short-shorts and platform shoes, like some kind of hippie drag queen."

Evie laughed incredulously. "Were you mortified?"

"I was pissed. He always had to grab the spotlight. He believed in free expression, of any fucking thing he wanted to express. When

I was little, I thought he was the most fun kind of father you could have. When I got older, I hated being yanked out of school to go harvest algae, or hunt for morels. I hated moving and starting from scratch on every sports team."

Evie searched her memory, but couldn't come up with an image of Jesse Marcus. "I don't remember meeting him, but your mother came to our house a few times. She was always so sweet, kind of shy."

His shoulders hunched, the muscles flexing as he reached for his shirt. "Yeah. She was. Jesse cheated on her, but he never called it that. He called it "engaging." People here thought he was a hippie, but that's not fair to hippies. He didn't believe in love and peace and all that. He just believed in self-gratification."

She watched him button his shirt. It was almost tragic to hide away all that magnificence. "He must have had good points too. I mean, look at you."

He shrugged. "Yeah. He did. It turned out that he was pretty good with money. He could be fun. A risk-taker. He got his pilot's license, then turned around and purchased a flightseeing service. Nothing scared him."

"That sounds familiar."

"How do you mean?"

"A fun, fearless risk-taker. Hmm, where have I met someone like that before?"

He stared at her for a long moment, then jumped to his feet and tucked in his shirt. Had she offended him with that observation? She got to her feet as well and folded the fleece blanket into a tight square to cram it into her backpack. As soon as she fastened the buckle, he held out his hand for it.

"I'll take that," he said tightly. "Hotshots and heavy packs, that's what we're all about."

She handed it over and he slung the straps over his shoulders, then headed for the path that wound up the hillside. He was moving so fast, she had to skip to catch up with him. His long legs ate up the trail in easy strides. She remembered that he'd told her running up mountains was his favorite form of exercise.

It definitely wasn't hers. "Sean. Why are you going so fast?"

When he turned to look back at her, he had a remote expression she hadn't seen before. "Sorry." He reached his hand to her and helped her over a rocky spot in the path. "I should get back to the base. I can't leave Josh alone out there for too long. He might throw a party and invite every girl in town."

When they reached the top of the trail, she saw that a few cars were parked in the main viewpoint lot. The big telescopes, the ones set into the concrete, were all in use. Her face colored as she thought about the sounds they'd made.

"Do you think anyone heard us?" she whispered as they crossed the parking lot.

"Nope. Even if they did, they probably figured there was a wounded hog and a weird ghost nearby."

"Ha-ha."

Even though he smiled faintly, his mood had shifted. All the playfulness was gone. And she had no idea what had triggered the change.

Chapter 19

Usually after sex, Sean felt on top of the world. Clear-headed, carefree, ready to launch into the next thing. But driving back to Evie's house, a whole different category of thoughts kept dive-bombing his brain.

Why did he and Evie have to get onto the topic of his family? It always made him edgy. It brought up all kinds of weird feelings. Not grief, so much. That had faded with time.

In Boulder, or any of the various hotshot or smoke-jumping bases where he'd worked, no one connected him with his family. The Marcus name meant nothing beyond what Sean gave to it. To his fellow firefighters, "Sean Marcus" meant skill, drive, intensity, good firefighter, smart risk-taker, reliable. To women, it meant short-term sex, hopefully good sex. It meant a fun time, some laughs, no strings, no expectations.

Here, in Jupiter Point, "Sean Marcus" had some other layers that kept springing at him like ghosts. "Marcus" meant fuckup, weirdo, maybe even crazy. "Sean Marcus" meant bad boy, rebel, underage drinker, hothead.

Those things didn't seem to bother Evie. Maybe she liked them. Maybe that was why she'd picked him for her "mission." Was he perfect for her "sexual reclaiming" because she didn't have to take a member of the Marcus family seriously?

Not that he wanted "serious" in terms of a relationship. But maybe he wanted to be a contender. Or at least a potential contender. He remembered how she used to pine after Brad White when she was a kid. He was just as good as that fucking guy.

Speaking of Brad…he tuned back into Evie just as she was saying the dude's name.

"What about Brad?"

Evie gave him a chiding look. "I was conveying the very important decision I just made, but if I had known you weren't even listening…"

"I'm listening now. Anything to do with Brad, I want to be in the loop."

"I don't know if you're going to like this." She twisted her long hair back into a knot. "I realized that he just doesn't matter to me at all."

"He doesn't *matter*?" The jackass had assaulted her. Sean's knuckles actually itched with the urge to knock him out *again* now that he knew the whole story. "I don't get it."

"Well, I just feel different now that I've talked about it." She aimed a sweet smile in his direction, but it didn't work on him the way her smiles usually did. "I don't have to hold on to any old grudges from the past. I can move on now. I'm free."

Sean frowned as he turned onto Constellation Way. The little downtown area was snugged up tight for the night. The low-lumen streetlights created a golden-orange glow around the tidy storefronts and hand-carved signs. They passed the Goodnight Moon Bed and Breakfast, with its little turret perched on top. Night jasmine flowed in soft clouds over the iron-work fence around the Orbit's outside patio.

Jupiter Point was a lovely little town, but that didn't mean that everything or everyone in it was equally lovely.

Brad White being the prime example of that.

"So what are you saying? You're going to endorse him?"

She nodded decisively. "I am. I'm going to endorse him. It's the best thing for the town. We don't need any controversy. Tourists don't come here for that. They come here to enjoy themselves. To pause for a moment and look up at the stars."

The infamous town motto; Sean hadn't heard that in a while. "So you're not going to mention anything about what happened that night?"

"No. Why should I? It has nothing to do with his political agenda." She must have sensed his disappointment, because she gave him a nervous glance. "The coalition decided to endorse him when the issue first came up, you know. I just couldn't make myself say the words."

"And now you can?"

"I think I can now. It no longer seems so important. I can let the past go, thanks to you." She touched his thigh, not in a sexual way but in a "thank you" way. He shifted away from her hand.

He didn't want that "thanks." Brad was going to get away with his heinous actions. He was getting everything he wanted from Evie—her silence about his deeds, her support for his campaign. None of this sat right with him.

But it was her call, not his.

He took Evie home and drove back to the base in a surprisingly foul mood, considering he'd come pretty damn close to having sex with Evie McGraw.

When he got back to the base, he found it blazing with light but all the common areas empty. "Hello?" he called into the deserted space. The sound of crashing and swearing led him to the gear cache, the crew's storage area.

There, he found Josh rubbing his head and cursing at a box of extra-large fire-resistant gloves. "I bring you into the family," Josh told the box in his best "Godfather" accent. "And this is how you betray me."

"Gloves, these days," Sean said dryly. "You can't turn your back on them for a second."

Still rubbing his head, Josh glanced up from his cross-legged position on the floor. "Hey, Casanova. How was your night?"

Sean didn't want to answer that question. "I thought you were planning to hit all the Jupiter Point hot spots tonight?"

"I did. It was a very entertaining five minutes. Then I figured all this crap still needed organizing. We need to get our act together, Magneto. Did you know the snowpack is half what it usually is? Dry summer coming up."

"I know. We're on track for May. That's what we're aiming for." He looked closely at Josh, who seemed a little jittery. "So the

Jupiter Point nightlife didn't do much for you?"

"Barstow's isn't bad. Pretty cool local hangout. A whiny alt-rock band was playing but I managed to tune that shit out. Had a couple of beers there. Then I stopped in at the Orbit. Connected with a few friends there."

"A few friends? Are you telling me you know people in Jupiter Point now?"

"Of course I know people. What do you think I do when you're wrapped up with your pretty princess? People are talking, by the way. The town sweetheart and the hotshot. The good girl and the rebel. It doesn't make sense. People keep saying things like, 'Remember when the Marcus family first came to town and held a party out at the airstrip? I think there was pot in those brownies they served.'"

Sean snorted. "Jesse knew how to make a splash."

"Must be a Marcus family trait."

Sean startled. Evie had said something similar earlier, and he hadn't liked it then either. "What are you talking about?"

Josh rose to his feet and brushed dust off his cargo shorts. He dug in his pocket and pulled out a pink message slip. The note scrawled on it said, *You're in BIG TROUBLE. Chief Becker wants to see you.* "The police chief called while you were out. He asked you to come into the station as soon as you can."

Sean stared at the ominous message. "I already talked to Becker. What else does he want?"

"I tried to get him to say, but he wouldn't. He just said it's important. Oh, and he said that next time, you should listen to his advice." Josh scratched his chin, pretending to search his memory. "Something…hmm…it's starting to come back to me…something about 'stay away from Evie McGraw'?"

Sean crumpled up the message and tossed it in the trash.

Chapter 20

Days passed before Evie saw Sean again. He sent her a text telling her he was interviewing the last candidates for the hotshot crew and would be busy until the end of the week.

She understood. That was completely fine. He was busy, she was busy. No need to read anything into it, just because he'd seemed so distant at the end. Right?

The Dean, a notorious hypochondriac, announced that he felt the flu coming on and asked Evie to stay over for a couple of days. Life slowed to a crawl as Evie helped her mother with the daily tasks of life. Getting her dressed took a good half hour. Assisting her from the bedroom to her recliner was a journey of patience. Molly had to take three pills each morning, and each morning the process seemed to take longer.

Even so, Evie basked in her mother's presence, in the affection that still beamed from her face. She knew Hunter felt guilty that he hadn't been around to help. But in Evie's view, he was missing something even more important--this precious time with their mom.

Besides, it was a relief to get a break from the gallery and all the town drama. On Friday, she'd attend the coalition meeting, announce her change of heart, and it would all be over.

But her break from the controversy didn't last long. Brianna stopped by with a basket filled with her first stalks of rhubarb and a complete report on everything Evie had missed.

"I heard the *Los Angeles Times* is doing a story on Brad's campaign."

"Is that unusual? He's running for state representative, that's news, right?"

"Yes, but they don't usually bother with hometowns and all that, unless there's something of interest happening. Like his own business coalition refusing to endorse him."

Evie buried her face in the rhubarb, inhaling the fresh tart scent that always said spring to her. "They're going to be disappointed, then. There's no more story. It's all going to be settled at the meeting tomorrow. I've already crafted my statement. I've even memorized it."

It was the right thing to do—at least, she thought it was. She'd been allowing her personal feelings to take over in the business arena. Personally, she still didn't want anything to do with Brad. But she was the president of the coalition and she couldn't think only of herself. She had a job to do.

In her statement to the coalition, she was going to say that she herself couldn't support Brad's candidacy for her own reasons, but if the coalition voted to endorse him, she wouldn't fight it. It might be hard to spit the words out, but she was pretty sure she could pull it off. Brad simply didn't matter to her anymore. She wasn't afraid of him. She had better things to think about now.

Like Sean. And their amazing night on the cliffs.

As incredible as that experience had been, she knew it barely scratched the surface of what could happen between them. With Sean, something had clicked inside her. She felt as if she was looking at everything with new eyes—including herself. What had she been doing for the past thirteen years? Had she even been alive? Had some sort of weird holographic image of Evie McGraw been playing her part all this time?

She blinked. Brianna was waving a hand in front of her face. "If that's how you plan to address the coalition, it should be an interesting meeting. "

"Oh. Sorry. Were you asking me something?"

Brianna let out one of her classic belly laughs. No one within a hundred foot radius could resist Brianna's laugh. "Does this have anything to do with a certain hunky hotshot who just moved back to town?"

Evie felt her face turn as red as the rhubarb. "I have a lot on my mind," she said with dignity. With her arms full of rhubarb stalks, she crossed to the refrigerator to put away Brianna's gift.

"I'm sure you do. Speaking of Sean, do you have any idea why he was at the station house earlier? Word has it he met with Chief Becker for about an hour yesterday and came out looking like death warmed over."

Evie's stomach did a slow, queasy roll. Chief Becker was the officer who had come to this very house on that night thirteen years ago. He'd questioned her, Sean, and Brad. Did this have anything to do with that night? "Maybe it's just routine, something he has to do for the hotshot crew."

"He didn't mention it to you?"

"No, which is probably a sure sign that it's nothing important." She shoved the rhubarb into the refrigerator and shut the door. "I don't even know why you're spreading gossip like this."

"Spreading gossip?" Brianna bristled like a ginger-haired tomcat. "I'm not spreading anything. I'm asking my best friend about her new crush's visit to the cops. Maybe I'm concerned."

"Last I heard, you were telling me to kiss Sean."

"Yes. Actually, I said you should fuck him. But not if he's going back to his old bad-boy ways. People used to tell so many Marcus family stories, remember?"

"*Brianna.*"

Her friend's vivid blue eyes widened in surprise. "You're raising your voice. You never raise your voice. What is going on with you?"

"What's going on with *you*? Why are always so tactless?"

"Excuse me?" Under normal circumstances, Brianna's wounded expression would make her switch gears right away. But she hated the thought of people dragging Sean's name through the mud. It wasn't fair.

"Those stories are over thirteen years old. Do you really think they need to be brought up again?"

"But I'm not the one who—"

"Sean Marcus is here to do a job that *protects* us. Protects our community. And you're talking about stuff that's ancient history.

Why don't you just give him a chance? Not just you, but all of Jupiter Point?"

Brianna snatched her basket off the counter and backed toward the kitchen door. "You've changed, Evie. This isn't like you."

Evie opened her mouth to apologize and beg her friend for forgiveness. Brianna didn't deserve to be yelled at like this. What *was* wrong with her?

But before she could say a word, Brianna broke into a wide grin. "It must be all that hot sex you're having with Sean Marcus."

"I'm not—who said—?"

Brianna blew her a kiss from the door. "Don't worry, Evie. I like the new version of you. You're like a tiger protecting your young. It's awesome. But this is Sean Marcus we're talking about, and I think he can take care of himself. Love you!"

"Love you, too!" Evie called after her as she waltzed out the door.

She took a deep breath and realized that she felt pretty good. It wasn't nice to call Brianna "tactless," and she would definitely apologize for that. But she'd made her point, and it was an important one.

She picked up her phone, fingers poised to dial Sean's number. She had to find out what he'd spoken to Chief Becker about. But she didn't want to bug him when he was busy. Call him or not? She went back and forth, until all the arguments on either side fell away and only one thing mattered.

Tonight she'd be back at her own place. And she wanted to see him. Desperately.

She texted quickly. *Want to come over tonight? I'm making pizza.*

What man—especially fireman—could resist pizza?

A second later he pinged her back with a big thumb's up and an emoji of a bouquet of tulips

~ ~ ~

Sean arrived with a real bouquet of tulips in one hand and a six-pack of root beer in the other. A day's worth of stubble covered his jaw and his eyes held a stormy intensity she recognized from his rebellious teenage years.

That expression vanished the second he laid eyes on her. It was replaced by one hundred percent lust. That was exactly the reaction she'd been hoping for when she put on the black slip dress that barely reached the middle of her thighs.

He dropped the bouquet on her little entryway table then set the six-pack on top of the poor tulips. Oblivious to the squished flowers, he advanced toward her like a beast arrowing in on his prey.

"Um…hi, Sean!" With every nerve in her body already on fire, she took an involuntary step back.

"Yeah," he growled, his hot gaze sweeping up and down her body. "Hi."

"Are you, um, hungry, because the pizza's hot and it's best when it's right out of the oven and—ack!" She broke off with a squeak as he swooped her into his arms and strode down the hall.

Forget the pizza.

He pushed open a door with one foot, then stopped dead at the sight of piles of boxes. "What's this?"

"Storage. If, by any chance, you're looking for the bedroom, it's across the hall." She felt giddy and silly, like a newly opened bottle of champagne releasing bubbles into the air.

Sean swung around and crossed the hall in one long stride. He pushed open the door and they moved into her bedroom, lit only by the warm glow of her bedside lamp. The next thing Evie knew, she was flat on her back on her king-size bed with a fierce-eyed warrior braced over her. "You're not wearing any underwear, are you?"

She giggled. "There's only one way to find out for sure."

"Don't have to ask me twice." He pushed the hem of her dress up her thighs. Instant liquid heat rushed to her sex. It was those damn hands of his, their size and power and gentleness. They made her melt just by landing on her skin.

He gazed down hungrily at her bare body. At the last minute, she'd taken off her panties just to see what it felt like. Right now, she was thinking that was one of the better decisions she'd ever made in her life.

"Good God, you're gorgeous," he breathed. He hooked her knees over his shoulders, making her squeak again. "I have to taste you."

"You do?" It was a good thing she was lying down. The carnal look on his face made her feel faint.

"Mmm. Look at you, already wet, and my mouth is watering." He bent his dark head to the juncture between her thighs. She dug her hands into her goose down comforter and squeezed her eyes shut. This was one more experience she'd never had, and she intended to enjoy it to the fullest.

The first touch of his tongue to her sex made her shriek. She plastered both her hands over her mouth in shock.

He chuckled, the sound vibrating her clit. She couldn't tell if he intended that or not, but it felt freaking amazing. "Don't hold back for me, sweetness. You know your sounds make me crazy."

He slowly drew the flat of his tongue across the little bundle of nerves. That kernel of pleasure felt like the source of everything good in the entire world. She moaned—or was it groaned—loudly, then grabbed a pillow and stuffed it over her face.

He reached up with one arm and pulled it away. "Don't cheat me out of your sounds, Evie. That's no way to treat a guy. Especially one with his mouth on your pussy."

Ohmigod, the dirty way he talked. It made her simultaneously mortified and aroused. The aroused part definitely took over when he began circling her clit with skillful, eager sweeps of his tongue. He seemed to know exactly how much to lick, how hard and how fast, to keep her right on the edge of orgasm. He put his hand under her ass and changed the angle, eliciting another muffled shriek from her.

Fine. Why try to hide the way he made her feel? That was something the old Evie would do. Not the new Evie.

Abandoning any attempt at dignity, she pushed herself hard against his mouth.

"Please, Sean. Please, I can't stand it! Make me come."

"That's right, tell me what you want. You want to come?"

"Yes."

He lifted his head, his eyes dark, burning pools of intensity. "I want to feel you come while I'm inside you. Are you ready for that?"

"Yes—God, yes."

"Hang on." He released her legs so she lay splayed across the bed, and dug in his pocket. He produced a wrapped condom that he clamped between his teeth.

"Wait," she said suddenly. The alarm in his expression almost made her laugh. "One tiny little thing."

He froze, chest rising and falling in rapid heaves.

"Could you take your clothes off? I want to see you. I get turned on even when you're dressed, but now I want to see everything. In the light."

He grinned. "Not a problem." Tossing the condom on the bed, he ripped off his t-shirt and jeans so fast, he looked like Quicksilver in the *X-Men* movies.

"Don't move," she begged him. "Just let me look at you for a minute."

Playing it up, he lifted his arms overhead in a victory pose.

She let out a sigh of sheer appreciation. In the soft lamplight, the definition of his muscular chest stood out in deep grooves and sleek ridges. He had barely any hair, just a silky swirl right in the middle of his chest.

"I wish I had my camera right now."

"So that's why you're into photography. For the naked men."

She gave a soft snort. "Hardly. Just you, Sean Marcus."

Her gaze lingered on his tattoo, then dropped lower. His erection pushed against the fabric of his black boxer briefs. "These are coming off," he warned her, just before he pushed them down his strong thighs.

Her heart jumped into her throat as his erection sprang forth in all its thick, eager glory. Heat rushed right to her core, a liquid rush of desire that stunned her. She couldn't take her eyes off it—she could stare at it forever…and touch it…and taste it…

But Sean was growling something, hands on his hips. "How long do you need to do this? Asking for a friend. You know, him." He indicated his shaft with a quick gesture of his head.

She waved him on, almost speechless from the overwhelming effect of so much maleness. "I'm good," she whispered in awe. "So, so good."

"Glad to hear it." Sean grabbed his condom and ripped open the wrapper, then worked it over his erection. Watching his big hands move across his own organ made her light-headed. Wild with excitement by now, she arched against him when he covered her with his body.

"I want you," she whispered, putting his hand on her sex. "Can you feel how much?"

"Right there with you, sweetness. Believe me." With deft fingers, he stroked her a few more times, stoking her arousal back to the peak where she'd been before, trembling on the edge of orgasm. Lashed by the urgent edge of desire, she twisted and moaned under his hands.

"Ready?" he whispered. Hunger shone from every tense line of his face.

She nodded.

At the first push of his thick head against her entrance, her body tensed. But he took his time, stroking her hips and inner thighs, whispering hot words that she couldn't make out. They acted more as a kind of chant more than anything else, simultaneously soothing and inflaming her.

It wasn't as if she was a virgin, after all, she told herself. She'd done this before. But Pete hadn't been quite this big, or maybe he just hadn't been this hard. He hadn't been fully aroused, whereas Sean...Sean felt enormous and so hard and stiff and...

He slid inside, filling her up completely, and a strange tingling feeling danced across her scalp. The soles of her feet felt it too. Her toes literally curled. He drew back, dragging his erection across her clit. Her eyes nearly rolled back in her head at how good it felt.

In again. Her channel expanded to receive him, sending ripples of pleasure through her body in every direction.

A stream of urgent murmurs poured from her lips. *"Oh my God, that feels incredible, oh yes, oh sweet Lord, how can it feel so good..."*

As soon as their bodies got used to each other, he set a faster rhythm, flexing his hips to drive deep. She closed her eyes against the sensations welling inside her. Watching his powerful body braced over her was too much, too overwhelming.

And then he reached between their entwined bodies and found her clit. He pressed the aching little nub with his strong fingers and just like that, the entire world was erased by pure, mind-blanking, orgasmic ecstasy.

She surrendered to it, letting anything come out of her mouth that wanted to. Cries and moans and pleas...she didn't care. Let it all come out.

Her climax triggered Sean's—he went rigid above her. She clutched at him, her sweaty hands slipping off his broad back.

Her orgasm felt like it came from somewhere deep inside her, from some endless, forever source that would never run out. It would always be there for her, like another part of herself. A vital, wild, essential part.

When they both finished, Sean collapsed next to her, one long leg draped over her upper thighs. She felt his hair brush against her cheek. With every rapid breath, she inhaled the delicious scent of his skin. This felt like heaven, right here, right now. He mumbled something she couldn't quite make out. Her eyes fell shut and she drifted into a soft, satisfied doze.

Chapter 21

First sex, then a nap, then pizza...Sean should have been totally relaxed by the time Evie posed her surprise question about his meeting with Chief Becker.

He didn't want to talk about that pile of shit. But she caught him off-guard and he tensed up right away.

"It's nothing you need to worry about."

"Come on, Sean. My imagination has been going in all kinds of crazy directions since Brianna told me. Officer Becker was the one you punched that night. If he's digging into what happened with Brad, I need to know."

"It wasn't about that. Well, it wasn't just about that."

Evie put down her slice of pizza and fixed him with a determined look he hadn't seen from her before. "Please, Sean, I'm begging you. I have this feeling that Brad is up to something. He's been awfully quiet since he wrote the op-ed piece. He knows that we're having a special coalition meeting tomorrow night. I want to know what's going on."

A muscle tightened in Sean's jaw. "I have it handled, Evie. I know Brad's type. He's a typical bully. You can't give into them. I intend to keep doing my job until my boss tells me not to."

She went slightly pale. "What do you mean about your job? Is he trying to make trouble for you with the hotshots? You have to tell me."

He made one more attempt to head her off. "I thought you McGraws didn't like facing difficult things."

"I'm breaking the mold. Come on, Sean. Whatever Brad's doing, I need to know." Her eyes blazed with silver light. This fired-up version of Evie was sexy as hell. Almost as sexy as the one who'd come apart in his arms.

Sean ripped off a big bite of pizza to buy himself a little time. The meeting with Becker had been like a sucker punch in the gut. He wished he could erase that hour from his life. But there was more crap coming his way, so he couldn't. Besides, with her history with Brad, she deserved the truth.

He swallowed his bit of pizza, then met Evie's eyes.

"Brad is publicly questioning my fitness to lead the Jupiter Point Hotshots. Not just because I got into so much trouble in high school. There's also…the crash."

He had to force the word past the sudden tightness of his throat.

"Crash." Horror dawned on her face and she pushed her plate away. "You mean your parents' plane crash? What could that possibly have to do with anything?"

"He's requesting that the police department reopen the investigation. There was never a final determination of a cause."

It felt surreal to be talking about this. Even during that terrible year after the crash, he hadn't spent much time thinking about *why* it happened. Jesse Marcus wasn't a very experienced pilot and he'd had a lot of hubris. Bad combination.

"I thought it was…well, pilot error," Evie said, almost apologetically. "That's what everyone around here said."

"It's okay, Evie. You don't have to tiptoe around it. I always refused to get into a plane with my father at the controls. No fucking way. Of course it was pilot error. He was a crap pilot. That's why he had to hire real pilots to run the tours."

He took a long swallow of root beer to wash down the pizza, and his disgust.

Evie rose to her feet and paced restlessly. She wore sleep shorts and a ribbed tank top that showed off her slim form. His mouth watered even more than it had for the pizza.

"I still don't understand why Brad would want to bring up the crash. It has nothing to do with the hotshot crew. You were a kid then. You lost both your parents. It's beyond callous. I can't imagine what he's thinking."

"He's just throwing a bunch of mud and seeing what happens."

"But *why*? Why is he going after you?"

Sean shrugged a shoulder. "My guess? He's afraid you'll finally come forward about that night, and since I'm the only witness, he has to trash me until no one listens to anything I say."

"Oh my God. I'm so sorry, Sean." She buried her face in her hands, the dark silk of her hair sliding over her shoulders. "This is all my fault. I should have endorsed him from the beginning."

"No." He shoved his plate aside and surged to his feet. "Don't blame yourself, that's ridiculous. I can handle Brad White. I'm not worried about it. It's all a bunch of smoke and mirrors anyway. So what if they reopen that investigation? All they'll do is waste a bunch of taxpayer money. Chief Becker says the department isn't happy about being pushed around. It's…just don't worry about it, please. Okay?"

She lifted her silvery-gray eyes to his, a frown pulling her delicate eyebrows together. Her beauty struck him right in the solar plexus. But it wasn't just her beauty, not really. It was the concern in her eyes, the compassion. "There's more, isn't there? I can tell you're holding something back."

Sean scrubbed a hand through his hair, needing to move, to act. Did she have to be so freaking perceptive?

But it would be in the paper soon enough; Brad would make sure of it. Better that she hear it from him than get sandbagged.

He came close to her and put his hands on her shoulders. "Yeah. There's one more thing. He says he found an investigator who says I made some mistakes in the Big Canyon burnover."

She drew in a sharp, horrified breath. *"What?"*

"It's okay. I didn't make any fucking mistakes. I don't know who he's been talking to but it won't go anywhere. Everyone knows we followed our training and that's why we survived. Evie, please."

She looked so white, he worried she might pass out.

"This is all my fault," she whispered.

"Stop it." He ran his hands along her bare arms. His intent was to soothe, but the feel of her went right to his head. "Seriously,

Evie."

At first she started to pull away from him, but then she gave in and rested her forehead on his chest. "This is such a mess. And now you're right in the middle of it. I just can't believe he's doing all this. Why? Just so he can get some stupid endorsement?"

He'd been thinking about that question since his meeting with the chief. "It's all ego. He wants everyone talking about how great he is. He can't stand it that one person isn't willing to sign on the dotted line."

He wrapped his arms around her slim form, wishing they'd never started on this topic. "Is there any chance we can go back to bed and forget about all this?"

She tilted her head back, her silky hair tickling his skin, her warm body lithe and perfect in his arms. "Using sex as an escape?"

He winked at her. "It's good for so many things."

Finally he got a faint smile from her. "I'm going to need a comprehensive list, if you don't mind."

"Not a problem. Complete demonstrations are also available."

"Sign me up, hotshot."

But no matter how much they teased each other, a shadow had fallen over the evening.

~ ~ ~

Despite the fact that they spent the rest of the evening in bed, switching between cuddling, laughing, and climaxing—all of which she loved—Evie didn't forget about the situation with Brad. The more she thought about it, the angrier she got. Political ambitions were one thing. But did they justify screwing around with someone's life and reputation?

She'd known Brad since they were both kids, long before the Incident. Maybe she could find a way to get through to the old Brad.

So before the emergency meeting of the business coalition she called Brad and asked to meet with him.

With barely concealed smugness, he invited her to his campaign headquarters, which were located in a restored office building at the edge of the historic district. He'd taken over the entire bottom floor. The glass storefront was now plastered with "Brad White for State Representative" banners. The space was bustling with campaign volunteers, many of whom she recognized. Everyone was tapping on a computer or talking into a phone.

Intimidated, she looked around for Brad but saw no sign of him. Finally a pretty young redhead in a silk blouse appeared at her elbow. Evie was pretty sure she recognized her from her volunteer work at the high school. "Evie McGraw?"

"Yes. I'm here to see—"

"Mr. White, yes, I know. He's waiting for you in his office." Mr. White? *Okay then.*

She led her through the maze of makeshift desks to a room in the back corner. Its closed door bore a sign that read, "Hope for White, White for Hope."

Seriously? She was squinting at the sign, trying to decide if it was a joke or a rejected campaign slogan, when Brad opened the door and beckoned her inside.

Evie stepped in, trying not to panic at the sound of the door closing behind her.

Brad hadn't always been an asshole, she reminded herself. She'd made sand castles with him on Stargazer Beach. They used to share ice cream sundaes at the Milky Way. If she could reach *that* Brad, she could talk some sense into him, couldn't she?

He gestured her toward the ergonomic chair facing his desk. She sat down, unnerved when it rolled a few inches under her weight. Did he do that on purpose? He wore a light blue Oxford shirt with the sleeves rolled up. A Bluetooth receiver perched on his ear. A deceptively boyish lock of sandy hair curled onto his forehead.

Don't be fooled, she reminded herself. He's not a boy. He's a politician.

"Good for you for coming in, Evie. I'm proud of you."

His condescending tone grated on her. "I'm sorry?"

Sorry? She shouldn't have said "sorry." That put her on a weak footing right away. She could feel the power slipping away from her like sand through her fingers.

He showed his teeth in a smile. "I'm just remembering the last time we met, when you ran off before we even made it to dessert." Somehow he made the word dessert sound nasty. Or maybe everything sounded nasty coming from his mouth these days.

"I didn't run." She pressed her lips together. *Don't get defensive*. This wasn't about her. It was about Sean. She stiffened her spine. "At any rate, I don't intend to run off. I want to talk to you about Sean Marcus."

His nostrils flared, just for a moment, before he hid his reaction behind a frown. "Some of us have some concerns about him. Apparently he's doing all the hiring for this new 'hotshot' crew.

How do we know he isn't going to bring in a bunch of ruffians, or worse? We all know about the Marcus family. I'm just looking out for the safety of Jupiter Point."

Evie gripped her hands together in her lap. In her everyday, peace-loving life, she wasn't used to feeling hatred. But every slimy word Brad spoke made her feel it now. "Cut the crap, Brad. This isn't about Sean. It's about *me*. You want the coalition's endorsement, right? Let me tell you right now, you will never get it if you keep up this witch hunt against Sean."

His eyebrows lifted all the way to his hairline. "Little Evie's getting feisty, is that it?"

"I'm just trying to stand up for what's right. You should leave Sean out of this. I'm sure we can work something out between the two of us."

He leaned back in his chair and drummed his fingers on his desk. Checked his watch, glanced at his laptop. He didn't look quite as relieved as she'd imagined he would. More than anything, he looked impatient. Or maybe bored. "You're here to make a deal, then let's hear it. What do you have in mind?"

"Simple. You stop dragging Sean's name through the mud and you receive the endorsement of the Jupiter Point Business Coalition."

He cocked his head and pursed his lips as if thinking it over. He picked up a pencil and flipped it end over end. "So let me get this straight. You withhold your endorsement for personal, *emotionally* based reasons that you refuse to explain. But when your new boy toy feels the heat, you fold like a house of cards."

Shock flashed through her, from her head to her toes. God, she was naïve. The Brad she'd known in childhood was gone forever. The person who had attacked her in the Chevy Nova was the *real* Brad. The *only* Brad, no matter what charming façade he put on.

He crossed one ankle over his knee and looked up at the ceiling. Mr. Casual. "Hmm, let me think this over." A brief pause, as if this was all a joke. "Sorry, babe, you had your chance. Statute of limitations has expired. The answer is no."

She struggled to keep her cool. "We had dinner less than a week ago. You said your press agent had a statement already prepared for me."

"I'm not talking about *that* statute of limitations." His slimy gaze dropped to her lips, then lower down, toward her crotch.

Her face flamed. Good Lord, was Brad referring to that night? Could he really be so obviously…horribly…blatant? "What is wrong with you?" she whispered.

"Nothing is 'wrong' with me. I want what I want. But once I don't want it anymore, I'm done. I don't want your endorsement anymore, Evie McGraw."

She stared at him as a numb feeling crept over her body. What was she missing? Had something changed? "You're lying."

"Nope. I'm sorry that your embarrassing trip here was a waste of your time. Why don't you head back to your little gallery and take some more photographs for the tourists? You'll have plenty of time for that in the very near future."

Her stomach plummeted. "What are you talking about?"

"Hi, what's up? Yeah, I'm just about done here." With a start, she realized he was talking into his Bluetooth as if she wasn't even in the room anymore. As if she didn't exist anymore. His chilly gray eyes flicked over her one more time, then dismissed her. "Yeah, I'm done. Go ahead."

Numb with shock, she rose to her feet and moved toward the door. It seemed to take forever to reach it, even though it was no more than a few steps away.

In that short stretch of time, she realized something. During the years since the Incident, she and Brad had taken completely different paths. He'd been perfecting his shark imitation, while she'd been playing ostrich.

Now that she'd retracted her head from its nest in the sand, she barely recognized the world around her. Everything had shifted. Brad had turned a corner into irrevocable, evil jerkdom. Her beloved Jupiter Point was becoming a playground for his slimy games. And Sean Marcus—troublemaker, rebel, bad boy—was the only person with whom she felt completely safe.

She had a *lot* of catching up to do. And hardly any time to do it in.

Chapter 22

After Brad's malicious hint, Evie knew he was planning something for the coalition meeting. But still, it came as a shock when she walked into the back room of Don Pedro's, their traditional meeting place, and saw everyone's sober faces. Even though she was ten minutes early, judging by the empty glasses littering the table, everyone else had been there for some time.

The Jupiter Point Business Coalition, which had just elected her president, was meeting behind her back.

She scanned the faces of the other business owners, but no one met her eyes. Mrs. Murphy looked as if she might burst into tears.

Evie cleared her throat. For the second time that day, she felt as if her voice had been stolen from her. "Why are you all meeting without me? I'm the president."

Jack Drummond, the former president, answered. "Evie, we didn't want things to pan out this way. None of us wanted it."

Belladonna, the owner of Written in the Stars Tarot and Fortune-Telling, swept to her feet and enveloped Evie in a sandalwood-scented hug. "Awful situation, sweet-pea. But we may have stumbled upon the perfect solution for everyone."

"This way, you don't have to torment yourself," said Benito, owner of the Dream Getaway. "We think it's the best decision for everyone."

Evie extracted herself from Belladonna's smothering embrace. "*What* decision?"

Mrs. Murphy bustled to her feet and shoved Belladonna. She took Evie's hands in hers. "Honey, we want you to take a temporary leave of absence to take care of your mother."

Evie's jaw fell open. They wanted to use her mother as a smokescreen? She pulled her hands free and took a step back.

Belladonna continued. "Jack has volunteered to take over until you're ready to come back. It's a perfect plan, sweet-pea. You can save face. You don't have to endorse the boy who broke your heart." Belladonna cupped Evie's face in her hands, which would have been a nice gesture except she wore rings that dug into Evie's skin. "The coalition is no longer caught in a controversy. And Brad White finally gets his endorsement. Best of all, your mother will get a little extra attention from her favorite daughter. Your family will no longer be in the spotlight. I understand that stress is very bad for her."

Evie shoved aside her automatic sense of guilt as she examined the faces around the table. Was someone in this group doing Brad's bidding? Where had this idea come from?

Belladonna continued. "It's a win-win-win-win-win…" She threw up her hands, rings catching the light from the chili pepper twinkle lights. "I can't even count the wins."

"Whose idea was this?" Evie was shocked that her voice sounded as calm as it did. No one answered. She turned to the miserable-looking bookstore owner. Mrs. Murphy never kept a secret in her life. "Mrs. Murphy?"

She blinked rapidly, clearly at war with herself. "It was Brad's," she blurted.

Brad's idea. Of course it was.

"And I guarantee it's only temporary. We want you back as soon as possible, believe me." Jack directed his booming laugh at the circle of anxious faces. "I know what a pain in the rear these jokers are. We all think you've been doing an excellent job, Evie. This has nothing to do with you personally."

Evie put a hand to her forehead, trying to contain her whirling thoughts and emotions. She'd come here ready to announce her change of heart. She'd been ready and willing to endorse Brad in order to stop him from smearing Sean. But now it didn't even matter. The choice had been taken away from her.

"If you're going to allow Brad White manipulate you like this, I can't be part of it." She turned on her heel and stalked toward the exit.

"Evie! Please don't take this the wrong way," Jack called after her. "We're on your side."

"Really?" She spun around and planted her hands on her hips. "Explain to me how you're on my side?"

"Well, you're a McGraw." He said it as if that explained everything.

"So? I don't see what you're getting at."

"Your family is respected and loved around here, you know that. But the McGraws are well-known for not courting controversy."

Evie tried to calm her racing heart and the fury that kept coming in waves. "Just so I have this straight." She cleared her throat and tried to even out her tone, like a good little McGraw. "Because you love the McGraw family, you are temporarily displacing me as president without even consulting me. Why is that? Did you think I couldn't handle it?"

The business owners exchanged glances ranging from worried to alarmed. "Why, sweet-pea, that's how Brad suggested we handle it. He said your feelings are easily wounded. He pointed to the scene at the Seaview Inn the other night. We didn't want to upset you." Belladonna clasped her hands at her chest in a prayer motion, as if begging Evie to understand.

Evie did understand. She understood perfectly well. She'd been outmaneuvered by Brad. He'd been running circles around her for the past thirteen years, in fact. This wasn't the coalition's fault. This was *her* fault because she'd stood by, silent and oblivious, while he did so.

"I resign," she announced. "Effective immediately."

"No, Evie, that's not necessary." Jack Drummond's voice rose above the protests from the rest of the group. Several business owners jumped to their feet. She held up a hand to stop them from coming closer.

"I know you all mean well, or at least I assume you do. But there's no way I can fulfill the duties of president if you don't think I can handle whatever challenges arise."

"But Evie," Mrs. Murphy clung to her hand, "you *weren't* handling it. We had to do something."

Evie opened her mouth—then closed it again. Mrs. Murphy was right. She hadn't been tending to the situation. Instead, she'd been playing nice while Brad stabbed her right in the back.

"You're right. All of you. Until I can do the job properly, I resign."

~ ~ ~

"Bro, the time has come," Josh announced. Wearing a loose leather jacket and his favorite bear-tooth thong pendant, he tossed the buggie keys in the air, then caught the key ring on his index finger. "We're going to Barstow's Brews and we're getting shitfaced."

"Can't. I have to get this email off to Boise." The National Interagency Fire Center in Idaho was responsible for sending fire crews where they were needed. With the fire season coming up fast, they'd been checking on his progress.

"No." Josh actually grabbed him by the upper arm and hauled him to his feet. "It's nine o'clock on a fucking Friday night. Boise can wait. You know what else I'd like to know? Who the hell decided Boise, Idaho, ought to be the center of the wildfire universe? Have you ever been there?"

"No." As he passed the corner of the desk, Sean snagged his phone, which he'd been checking about every ten minutes. The coalition meeting must have ended by now, but he still hadn't heard anything from Evie. "Have you?"

"Hell no. Question is, has anyone? Is Boise a real place or more of a figure of speech, like 'tarnation.' That's what my granny used to say. 'Where in tarnation did I leave my glasses?'"

"I don't even know what you're talking about half the time."

"Half the time? You're doing better than I am. I only know what I'm talking about ten percent of the time, on a good day. The rest is pretty much babble."

"Good to know."

In the parking lot, Sean blinked at the deep, nearly purple night sky. "Didn't realize it was so late."

"That's what happens when you ignore the world."

"I'm not ignoring, I'm just—" Sean sighed. Maybe he *was* ignoring the world. Between the burnover accusations, the crash reopening, and the constant bullshit of Brad White, the world wasn't much fun right now. The news that the investigation into the Marcus crash had been reopened had just hit the papers. And his old boss at the Fighting Scorpions had called, warning him that this new federal investigator was hell bent on finding some kind of wrongdoing.

Why the fuck had he come back to Jupiter Point? For a town that prided itself on its peace and quiet, it had given him nothing but trouble so far.

They loaded into the pickup and Josh steered them off the base.

"Gotta warn you," Sean told his friend, "I may not be the most popular person in Jupiter Point right now."

"Yeah, I know." Josh took a corner at about twice the speed limit. "That's why I'm dragging you out tonight. The worst thing you can do is hide out at the base. You have to get out there. Mix it up."

"I'm not hiding out. I've been working."

"I know that, but to the town, it probably looks like you don't want to show your face." Josh shrugged. "Any good politician will tell you that you have to go brass balls with this sort of thing."

"You're talking like I did something wrong. I didn't."

"And it's about time we corrected that."

"Is that why you're speeding? You think I haven't spent enough time at the police station?" Sean gripped the strap above the window and hung on through another rubber-laying curve.

"Tip of the iceberg, Magneto. We're just getting started."

"If I end up married to another stripper, I'm suing."

Josh just laughed and amped up their speed another notch. Dark pine trees and telephone poles whipped past, and Sean decided maybe he'd been working too hard. A beer wouldn't kill him.

Walking into Barstow's felt like stepping back into senior year in high school. The place felt more like home than Jupiter Point High ever did. It still had the same horseshoe-shaped bar with the brown vinyl bumper adorned with brass studs. The grooves in the floor's wide oak planks were worn even deeper by thirteen years' worth of feet. The dusty bottles of liquor behind the bar might even be the exact same ones from his last visit here. At Barstow's, customers drank beer on tap and the occasional shot of rum or tequila. It wasn't the kind of place where the glowing green Midori liqueur went very fast.

When Josh and Sean walked in, the buzz of conversation took

a brief pause. Sean saw the bartender snap to attention. The bartenders at Barstow's were always braced for trouble, which was wise. Sean had caused more than his share back in the old days.

Josh jumped into the temporary lull. "Howdy." He gave a cowboy salute to the crowd. Since he'd actually grown up on a ranch down south, he could pull it off. "We heard this is the best place to drink away your troubles."

"Come on in, hotshots," someone called out to them. Sean couldn't tell if it was supposed to be mocking or not.

As they passed through the crowd, Sean exchanged some low-fives with a few people he recognized, though couldn't name. To his relief, he didn't catch any nasty glances from anyone. Maybe they were too afraid to mess with him to his face. Maybe they didn't care about the dirt Brad was spreading. Maybe they just wanted to have a drink. Maybe Josh had been right and Sean had been hiding out at the base.

Maybe it was time for a drink, and he didn't usually say that. But if ever a man deserved to get a little buzzed, this was probably the time.

Josh ordered them both a beer and a tequila chaser. It went down so easy that Sean ordered the next round. Once they were nice and loosened up, they found themselves in a game of darts against members of the local fire department.

"See, here's the thing," one of the firemen kept drunkenly telling Sean as he put holes in the wall next to the dartboard. "We gotta work together. Fires don't care what kind of firefighter you are, know what I mean? Forest fire comes, you call us. We need help, we call you. We're all firefighters under here." He pounded his chest, then wagged his finger at Sean. "And we gotta stick together against the cops, am I right?"

The firefighters roared and slapped Sean and Josh on the back. Sean and Josh grinned at each other and tossed back more shots. Nothing bonded a group of firefighters like ragging on the local police department. Considering that he'd spent an hour with Chief Becker feeling like a delinquent facing the school principal, Sean went with it.

After the game of darts, they played pool with a couple of nurses from the urgent care clinic. One of them flirted madly with Josh, but sadly, it was one of the males in the group. Always good-natured, Josh played along. The other nurse, a striking redhead in her forties, kept excusing herself to smoke, which Sean always found strange in a medical professional.

They ordered another round, and things started getting fuzzy. The firefighters joined the pool game and started telling Sean Marcus stories.

"Didn't you run through here naked once?"

"Yeah, it was a dare," the one called Rabbit chimed in. "You and Hunter dared each other. You did so much crazy shit. Remember when you raced down Constellation on pogo sticks?"

"Or when you rigged the water fountain at school so the water came out red?"

Josh doubled over with laughter. "Man, I wish I'd known you back then, Magneto."

Sean just laughed and hid behind his beer. Yeah, he'd had

some fun back then. But mostly he'd been releasing energy in whatever way he could.

The next time she went for a smoke, the redheaded nurse dragged him out back with her. "Just gotta tell you, we're not getting married," he warned her, slurring the words. "Bad track record on that."

"Dream on, buddy. I got a twenty-year-old kid."

"That's cool. Really cool."

She dragged on her cigarette, then launched into a long, confusing story about her daughter and the callous older man who had broken her heart. Sean tried to focus on it, but he was worried about her lit cigarette and the scrub grass behind Barstow's.

"The most fucked-up part is that she volunteers at his office." The nurse dropped the cigarette into the grass. Sean jumped on it and ground it out with his boot heel. "She doesn't care what I say."

"Kids. They never listen." Sean knew from experience, since he never had.

"Well, the thing is, he has money. And he's got the looks. He's going places, for sure. Every time I see one of his bumper stickers, I want to rear end someone."

Sean squinted at her. Bumper stickers? He started to ask her who the man was, but Josh pushed open the door just then and yanked him back inside.

"Emergency," he hissed.

"What's going on? Streaker? Tequila shortage?"

"No. Much worse. Suzanne's here. Evie's cousin. We have to talk to her and she scares me."

Sean allowed his friend to drag him back to the bar area. Someone had put a country song on the jukebox and a line dance was forming. How could so many drunken people manage to boot kick in unison? Suzanne, her hair as bright as lemon sorbet, stood near the bar chatting with two other girls.

She lit up at the sight of them. "Sean Marcus, back where it all started. Barstow's is like your native habitat, right? I've heard all the stories, and then some. You're planning something big and crazy, aren't you?"

"See what I mean?" Josh whispered to Sean. "She makes me nervous."

"Say something," Sean whispered back. "I'm blanking."

Josh rolled his eyes and turned to Suzanne. "Not so much, Evie's cousin. We're just letting off some steam."

"Steam?" She waved her hand in front of her face. "More like fumes, Sean's friend."

"Well, this is a bar, last I checked." Josh tucked his thumbs in his front pockets. "Where do you hang out, the Tight-Ass Saloon?"

Sean snorted, which earned him a betrayed look from Suzanne. "How's Evie doing?" she asked him.

"Evie's...uh, busy. She's at a meeting."

"You haven't heard? The meeting's over. Those jerks wanted to fire her."

Sean shook his head to clear it. It didn't work. "She's the president. Presidents don't get fired."

"Nixon did," Josh said wisely. "Clinton nearly did."

"No," Suzanne corrected him. "Nixon resigned. Don't firemen

have to study American history?"

Josh shoved his hands in his pockets and scowled at her. "He only resigned because he was about to—"

"Can we get back to Evie here?" Sean felt like his head was about to explode. Suzanne and Josh seemed to really like needling each other. "What happened at the meeting?"

"She walked in and they told her to take a hike, but not in those exact words. So she told them to shove it, again, not in those exact words. She used McGraw language, you know. I understand the language, being related to them, but I'm not a McGraw myself and therefore have avoided the McGraw family communication problems."

"Too bad," said Josh with a smirk. "A little less communication goes a long way sometimes."

Suzanne stamped her foot at him. "Look, Mr. Hotshot, I don't know who gave you the right to make comments about—"

"Give me the keys, Josh," Sean interrupted. "Gotta go find Evie."

Josh put a hand on his shoulder. "Bro, no way are you driving."

"Of course you're not driving," Suzanne said. "In this *one* instance, Josh is right."

"I'll drive," Josh announced, digging in his pocket.

"You will not!" Suzanne lunged for the truck keys, which snagged on the edge of his jeans pocket, half in, half out. She tugged at them, trying to free them.

"Why, you little minx." Josh spread open his arms in a "come and get me" move. "I didn't know you were interested. All you had to do is say so."

"*Moron*," she hissed, abandoning her quest to grab the keys. Instead, she whipped her phone from her pocket. "Fine, drive if you want. I'm calling the cops right now and telling them there's a drunken fireman on the road. I bet they'd love to hear that."

Josh and Sean looked at each other. "Damn, she's good," Sean admitted.

"Pains me to say this, but you're right."

"*I'll* drive." She held out her hand for the keys. "But first, you guys are buying me coffee."

Chapter 23

Ten minutes later, they were working their way through a pot of coffee at the pancake house on Route 5.

"It's because of me, isn't it?" Sean couldn't get over the news about Evie resigning. "I should never have come back to Jupiter Point. I've ruined everything for Evie."

"That's not true," Suzanne said impatiently. "My cousin's a lot happier since you got here. Regular sex will do that for you."

Josh snorted coffee through his nose, then clapped a hand to his face with a moan of agony. "You should really warn a guy before tossing the word 'sex' out there."

"Sorry, big guy. I'll be more careful with your delicate sensibilities from now on," Suzanne teased.

Josh just blinked at her.

Wow—Sean couldn't remember the last time a woman had rendered Josh speechless. His estimation of Suzanne went way up. He propped his elbows on the table and rubbed his forehead. "I didn't come here to mess around with Evie's life."

"You know something, Sean Marcus? I've been wondering

just why you *did* come back."

Josh bristled at Suzanne's tart tone. "He came here to save your starry-eyed butts from wildfires."

Suzanne made a face at the tall man slouched next to her in the booth. "He can be a hero anywhere. Why did he decide to come here?"

"Why are you riding him about it? Despite the way you prance around, this town doesn't actually belong to you."

"*Prance* around? You haven't been here long enough to see me prance. *When* I prance, it will be down the aisle with my fiancé."

"And I'll be there doing the slow clap for the poor man."

"Stop it, both of you." Sean couldn't stand their bantering a second longer. "I came back because—" He broke off. Suddenly it felt strange to be saying this at two in the morning in an empty diner at a table sticky with boysenberry syrup. "I came back—"

"You don't have to explain it." Josh stepped in when he still couldn't spit it out. "Suzanne's just being a busybody. Ignore her. I have a feeling that's the best way to handle her in most circumstances."

Suzanne's nostrils flared. Sean reached for the cup of coffee in her hand before she could fling it in Josh's face. "I already told you I came back because I don't want this town thinking I'm a piece of shit."

They both turned their attention to him. Josh straightened up with an outraged expression. "*Who* here thinks you're a piece of shit? Give me names. I'll open a frickin' truckload of whoop-ass on them."

"Right, that's the solution. Go all macho." Suzanne rolled her eyes at Josh then gentled her voice. "Sean, no one thinks that about you. If anything, they feel bad for you because of the crash."

"No." He shook his head, pushing his coffee cup in circles on the laminate surface of the table. "I know how people looked at us. The fucked-up Marcus family. The hippie planning to smuggle drugs into town."

"But that was your father, not you. Sean, don't you realize half the girls in Jupiter Point had a crush on you? I…might have, too, a little bit."

Josh lifted an eyebrow at her, shaking his head. "That's Magneto for you. What is it, the dark good looks? The ripped physique? The lone-wolf act?"

Sean ignored the entire tangent. He'd just realized there was another reason he'd come back to Jupiter Point. "Here's the thing. This town was good to me. I'd lived in fifteen different states before we came to Jupiter Point. After the crash, this place took care of me. I don't mean just the McGraws. Everyone watched out for me. My teachers did, the guys on the basketball team, Hunter, the bartenders at Barstow's. I remember I got drunk one night at Stargazer Beach and a cop car came. I thought I was done for, but the officer bought me a coffee, let me cry in the backseat of the car, then took me back to the McGraws' house."

Josh and Suzanne had forgotten their quarrel and were watching him with differing degrees of sympathy and alertness.

"Leaving the way I did, skulking out of town after a night in fucking jail, I've always regretted it." He met Josh's eyes. "I thought of it during the burnover. I wanted to come back here and show everyone I wasn't a fuckup. I don't want to be the piece of shit who took everything this town gave me and threw it in their faces. I want to do something good for Jupiter Point."

The passion in his own voice shocked him. He hadn't even known he felt this way until just now. Suzanne and Josh exchanged a look.

"Holy fuck." He downed the rest of his coffee. "I must sound like an idiot."

"You don't," Josh assured him. "You're actually making sense, for a drunk guy."

Sean gave a snort. "At least I haven't married a stranger this time."

"Notice the joke." While addressing himself to Suzanne, Josh indicated Sean. "A time-tested way to avoid honest emotion."

"I'm not trying to avoid anything. If I was, I wouldn't have come near this town. I want to prove something. So far, it's going pretty frickin' well, don't you think? The police have reopened the crash investigation and I'm being accused of fucking up the Big Canyon fire. I should have stayed in Colorado."

"But then you wouldn't have seen Evie again," Suzanne pointed out. "Maybe it's destiny. Written in the stars." She made a scribbling gesture in the air over his head.

"Exactly. I wouldn't have seen Evie again. I've been nothing but trouble for her." He pulled out his wallet to pay the bill.

"I don't believe that," said Suzanne. "I know my cousin, and she's so much happier now. She's been in such a rut, I was seriously worried about her. Now she smiles and laughs and wears clothes in colors other than neutral."

"And there we have it." Josh sat back with a lazy grin. "Our work here is complete, Sean. Evie doesn't wear neutrals anymore."

Suzanne swatted him on the upper arm. "Moron. Besides, Sean Marcus, think about this. If you hadn't come back, I wouldn't have met Josh." An evil grin spread across her face. "And I so look forward to making his life hell."

Josh shot Sean a panicked look and tried to hide under the table.

Sean laughed at their clowning, but a heavy weight had settled somewhere around his heart. He tossed a twenty on the table and stood up to go. No matter what Suzanne said, if he was ruining things for Evie in any way, he should do something about it. Like leave Jupiter Point. But he couldn't leave; he'd committed to this job. He couldn't leave until the hotshot crew was up and running.

But—he could do something else. He could step away from Evie's life.

Chapter 24

Evie had a tried-and-true method for recovering from a tough day of "peopling," as she called it. Although she loved people, especially her friends and family, her naturally introverted nature required a certain amount of solitude. That was why she lived alone, and why she loved the time she spent roaming the terrain around Jupiter Point shooting photos for her mother.

In her experience, there was little that a long bubble bath, hot chocolate spiked with rum, and a pint of Ben & Jerry's couldn't improve. Add in some Netflix, and life definitely started looking up.

But she couldn't find anything she wanted to watch on Netflix, she'd poured the last of her rum into the flask she'd taken to the Point, and the jasmine scent of her bubble bath kept making her sneeze. None of it helped. She was still the woman who'd been outmaneuvered, silenced, and kicked to the curb.

Finally she gave up and tried Plan B. She called her brother. Hunter had recently gotten engaged to a famous pop star, so she never knew where he might be at any given moment. Backstage? Onstage? Tokyo? Australia?

"Hey sis," he answered. "I've been thinking about you."

"Really? Don't you have more exciting things to think about?"

"I was wondering if Sean Marcus managed to track you down."

"He did." She sealed her mouth shut so she didn't reveal any juicy details. In her fuzzy robe, curled on the couch against her newest load of clean laundry, she could feel Sean's dynamic presence in her house as if he'd never left.

"Okay then. I see we're following the McGraw family policy of don't ask, don't tell, don't say anything unless you have something nice to say, and…hmm, what am I leaving out?"

Evie reached with her big toe and hooked the laundry basket closer to the couch. Her head throbbed and she felt as if the room was closing in on her. Was she doomed to never, ever speak about anything difficult? Was that her fate in life? Was she really such a coward? "The coalition ousted me," she blurted.

"What?"

"For my own good, they said. Because I can't handle controversy." She halfheartedly folded a towel and dropped it in the laundry basket. "Is that true, Hunter? Am I controversy-challenged? Is that like some kind of disability?"

And then a flash of revelation struck her like a two-by-four to the head. "Oh my God, Hunter. I'm disabled. Not in a physical way. Psychologically. I can't deal with conflict."

"Come on, Evie—"

She picked up a blouse that had wrapped itself into a tight knot in the washing machine. "Shush. Don't try to sugarcoat it. I'm on to something here. It's not just that I'm a McGraw and our parents raised us a certain way. Look at you! You're a bodyguard. You handle conflict all the time." Giving up on the blouse, she tossed it into the basket.

"Honestly, sometimes I think I look for it. Makes me feel alive."

"I can't believe I didn't see this before. I'm Evie McGraw, and I'm disabled."

"You really think 'disabled' is the right—"

She plucked a bra off the pile and waved it in the air. "Fine. I'm Evie McGraw and I'm an addict. I'm addicted to peace and harmony. I'll do anything to avoid conflict. Even ruin *my own life*."

"Evie—"

"No, this is good, Hunter. It's really, really good. And it's not just good in an 'I feel so much better' way. It's good because I know exactly what to do now."

Tomorrow, Brad was holding a press conference.

Maybe it was time she got over her aversion to the spotlight.

Suddenly energized, she jumped to her feet and bounced up and down on the couch. Clean clothes went flying off the pile. Maybe she should feel bad because she'd just seen what a huge flaw she'd uncovered in herself. But she didn't.

She felt free and alive. Up to now, she hadn't really been living. Not fully and completely. That had to change. Immediately.

"What are you doing? I'm hearing weird sounds."

"I'm pulling a Tom Cruise. And I'm also waving a bra around. Hunter, this is amazing! You've changed everything. We should have talked like this long ago."

"You're freaking me out, sis. Do I need to call someone?"

A knock rattled her front door. "Evie," called a deep male voice.

Sean. Shivers rippled up and down her skin.

"Nope. All good. Thanks for letting me rant. I'll call you soon." She hung up, tossed the bra back on her laundry pile, and danced to the door. She flung it open. Sean stood on her front stoop. His jaw was dark with stubble, his eyes hooded and bloodshot. Despite that, he was a glorious sight. She beamed at him with pure joy.

He took a surprised step backwards—it must have been a lot of joy.

"I…uh…came to make sure you were okay. I heard about the coalition."

"Yes, they're done with me. Too bad, so sad."

She reached for his hand and dragged him inside. As soon as he was through the door, she leaped into his arms and wrapped her legs around his waist. "Let's celebrate."

He staggered backwards a half step, but managed to keep his balance. He was so strong, her Sean. Strong enough to handle fires and plane crashes and all manner of conflict.

She was pretty sure…no, almost entirely sure…that she loved him.

~ ~ ~

Clearly, Sean hadn't sobered up nearly enough. Evie's almost manic happiness made no sense to him. Shouldn't she be angry, upset, hurt, crying? Instead she was rubbing up against him like a cat, and if there was a man alive who could resist that…well, it wasn't Sean.

He walked backwards toward her couch, which looked as if a bomb had gone off in the middle of her laundry pile. Clothes everywhere. Not that he minded standing-up sex. Pinning Evie against the wall worked for him too. But he'd had just enough tequila that he didn't want to risk either or both of them hitting the floor mid-orgasm.

The back of his legs hit the couch and he fell into the cushions, his arms filled with warm, passionate woman. And a pink fleece robe with little fluffy sheep.

"I know, it's not exactly sexy," she told him, sitting back on his thighs so she could slip off the robe. "If it makes a difference, I'm naked underneath it."

His heart thudded as he let his eyes wander up and down her nudity. He touched the rosy tips of her breasts and felt her shudder. She shifted on his lap to press her sex against the hard ridge already pushing against his jeans. He groaned at the searing wave of pleasure that followed.

"Oh man. That's too good, Evie. You always feel so incredible to me." With a seductive look from under her eyelashes, she slid off his thighs and settled herself on the floor between his legs. "What are you doing?"

"Well, I only got a taste of you that night on the cliffs." She unzipped his pants and reached in to draw out his fierce erection. "It was also dark. I didn't really get the full experience. From now on,

I'm all about the *full experience*. Of anything and everything."

He held on tight to the arm of the couch. "Like what?"

"Like this." She fixed her gaze on his penis. "Your cock."

Oh God. Seeing those perfect, sensual lips say the word "cock" nearly made him come right then. But he bent his entire will on *not* coming so he could savor every bit of what she was doing to him.

She settled her mouth around the head of his cock and slid downwards, lips clasping him with wet, velvety heat. She explored his balls with light, feathery touches, then moved on up his shaft.

He flexed his hips to deepen the contact with her mouth and throat. She hummed, eyes closing halfway. The vibration traveled across the skin of his cock and directly to the pleasure center of his brain. "Holy mother of…" he breathed. It took everything in him to keep from coming. His balls tightened, energy gathered at the base of his spine. God, he wanted to come right there in her sweet, suckling mouth, explode into her throat.

But he also wanted *her*. He wanted to plunge deep into her core, to touch the part closest to her innermost being.

With shaky hands, he withdrew his cock from her mouth, trying not to look at its glistening surface because that might put him over the edge. "Stand up," he told her, voice tight and rough with lust.

She came to her feet, naked before him. He snagged a condom from his pocket, then kicked his own jeans all the way off. He drew her between his thighs. Buried his face between her legs and inhaled her heady scent. Already aroused, already wet, already trembling under his tongue. He held her tight, hands gripping her ass, while he gorged himself on her sweet juices, her swelling clit, her delicate folds, her tight channel.

He had to have her. Now. He pulled his mouth away, hearing her gasp, and stood up. Her body was so flushed and beautiful, he could look at her all night. But he had a much better idea than that. Moving behind her, he growled in her ear. "Bend over and put your hands on the back of the couch."

Eyes widening with excitement, lips parting, she did so.

"Lower down," he prompted, putting his hand to her lower back to direct her. When she'd reached the perfect angle, he widened her stance by inserting his knee between her thighs. He looked away because the sight of her in that position was almost too exciting. He might come before he even got inside her.

He slipped on the condom and positioned himself behind her. Anchoring her hips with one hand, he used the other to work his insanely hard cock inside her.

She gasped and arched her back. "So good," she whispered, looking over her shoulder at him.

A spasm lanced through him—the first warning shot of an oncoming orgasm. *Hold off, hold off.* He wanted to do this together, dammit. He reached around and found her clit. Pressed his palm against her sex, making sure the hot little kernel received plenty of friction.

He thrust into her channel, keeping his hand firmly in its position. Again. Again. Long, sleek, commanding strokes until he couldn't maintain his control any longer. He let it all loose, all the passion and lust churning inside him. He pistoned hard and fast, pinning her between his cock and his hand, working her from both sides, surrounding her, consuming her, driving both of them over the edge.

When she let out her first cry of release and her body clenched around him, he let go of the last tiny bit of his control. He exploded into an orgasm so intense, he forgot where he was. He bent over her body, held her tight and emptied himself inside her. The room spun, the world shifted. He must have made sounds, but he didn't hear.

All he knew was pleasure, release, and a deep, deep connection to the woman in his arms.

~ ~ ~

Sean slept in her bed that night, although Evie thought it might have been more a case of passing out. They entwined, naked, under her comforter. Other than the nap they'd shared the other evening, she'd never slept in the same bed with a man before.

Just one more example of how she hadn't really been *living*.

Sean conked out right way, but she had too much adrenaline cruising through her system to sleep. She wished she'd told Sean about the feelings growing inside her. The certainty that she loved him—that this was something real for her—wouldn't go away. Maybe their involvement had started as a way to reclaim her sexuality. But it wasn't that anymore. She'd fallen in love with him.

And she knew perfectly well that he wasn't interested in a relationship. For Pete's sake, he didn't even live in Jupiter Point. Their relationship was doomed. The dark fire warrior in her bed was destined to break her heart.

She could kick herself for being so reckless.

Except it was absolutely worth it. From now on, there would be no keeping silent, no holding back, no half living. She was going to live her life even when it hurt.

Chapter 25

A pounding on her front door woke Evie up bright and early the next morning. Sean sat bolt upright in bed. "My boots. Where are my boots?"

"Shhh, it's okay, Sean. It's not a fire." She slid out of bed and pulled on shorts and a Sky View Gallery t-shirt. "It's probably Brianna or Suzanne."

She hurried to her front door and peered out the peephole. Blinking, she tried to make sense of what she saw on her front stoop.

Men.

Extremely fit, very attractive men. Four of them. They didn't seem to have a spare ounce of body fat between them. She recognized Josh, but not the others.

She opened the door and gazed in amazement at the selection of male hunkiness staring back at her.

"Hi, Evie," said Josh finally. "Is Sean here?"

"Who...uh...who wants to know?" If this was some kind of firefighter gang after him, she didn't want to give away his location.

"We're friends of his." A huge, bear-like man with a beard and the kindest eyes she'd ever seen answered. "I'm Rollo. This is Hughie and Baker." He waved at the rest of the guys. "We're part of his old crew back in Colorado."

Sean stepped next to her, wearing nothing but jeans and mussed hair. He blinked at the group on the doorstep. "Rollo? Baker? What are you guys all doing here?" He whispered in Evie's ear. "I'm not still drunk, am I?"

"No, I think there really are four hotshots at my door. Do...uh...you guys want to come in? I can make some coffee."

Rollo grinned and scratched at his stocking cap. "Gorgeous and kind. You hit the jackpot, Magneto."

Sean glared at him, but Evie didn't mind. She already liked these guys. There was something unusually real and down-to-earth about them. "Remind me again what you're all doing here?"

"Word got out that someone's trying to smear the Fighting Scorpions. We couldn't let that happen."

"Not the crew, just me." Sean rubbed the back of his neck. He looked so sexy with his morning stubble that Evie wanted to kick everyone out and drag him back to bed.

"Same thing." Rollo folded his arms across his broad chest. The other guys backed him up with nods and expressions that said *don't mess with us.* "Every guy here is ready to make a statement. The others couldn't come, but I have a stack of faxes in my back pocket. We just want to know where to go and who to talk to. Then we'll let you two get back to...whatever you were doing."

Evie's eyes welled with tears. No, she didn't just like these guys. She loved them.

In a sisterly, friendly way, of course. There was only one man for her—the one standing next to her pretending he wasn't moved to the point of tears.

~ ~ ~

When he'd knocked on her door the night before, Sean had intended to slow things down with Evie. But when he caught sight of her in that fluffy robe he forgot everything except getting her naked. Now that his buddies were here, he had to put the slowing down conversation on hold again.

While the guys waited in the truck, he pulled Evie back into the bedroom. "Sorry about this. I had no idea they were going to show up. Do you want to come with us?"

She smiled and touched his shoulder. "No. You'd probably like some time to catch up with them. And I have something to do this morning."

"Your mother?"

After a micro-hesitation, she nodded.

"Okay then. I'll…see you later." He bent his head and pressed his lips to her sleep-soft cheek. "Last night…" The words to tell her about his decision refused to come out. He just couldn't say them. Especially after a night like that. "Was totally hot. I'll never forget it."

She searched his face with those wide silver-green eyes, then smiled. "Go. Your friends are waiting. And I have to get dressed. Have fun."

It was so good to be around the Scorpions again. He couldn't believe they'd flown all the way out to California just to back him up. Every time he thought about it, he had to stop talking before he lost it.

He chased Josh out of the driver's seat and steered the Ford Super Duty into town. He took them through the cute little downtown area to the Venus and Mars Cafe, which served the best coffee in town. They trouped in, talking and joking, drawing the attention of every other customer in the place. He was pretty sure the waitresses had a little tussle over who was going to serve their table. Smart move, because his hotshot crew made a point of tipping well. Good local relations were always important.

"Nice town you got here," Rollo said when they'd worked their way through a basket of homemade raisin scones.

"It's a great place," Josh told them all. "I've been scoping out the female population and I give Jupiter Point a big thumb's up."

"How's the hiring going? Are you all crewed up yet?" Baker asked.

"Just about. Still looking to fill some of the higher GS spots." He indicated Rollo with his chin. "This guy's got dibs on one of them."

"That I do." Rollo exchanged a glance with the others. "If you want some rock solid experience, you've got two more ready to transfer."

"Excuse me?"

"We want to join the Jupiter Point Hotshots." Baker spoke while Hughie, never a big talker, nodded along.

"*All* of you do?"

Baker nodded. "We're with you, Magneto. You want strong

overhead, right?" In fire-service lingo, that meant that the top positions on the crew—squad boss, captains (such as Josh)--had plenty of experience.

"Of course."

"You won't get better than us. You're looking at over twenty years of experience right here."

Sean scanned the array of faces, more familiar than his own. Bearded Rollo, with his stocking cap and favorite lucky sweater, hand-knitted by his sister. Baker's mahogany face, always filled with laugh lines. Hughie had a new ring on his finger—he must have proposed to Cindy after all. They'd all cut line together, worked their asses off, then survived a face-off with hell. He knew them, he trusted them.

Then he remembered the one who hadn't trusted him. The one who'd run into the ravine rather than stick with the crew. "Did Finn send one of those faxes?" He asked Rollo.

"He did."

Again, that inconvenient surge of emotion kept him from answering. The brotherhood of hotshots hadn't let him down. He hadn't spoken to Finn since he'd told him to take his movie and shove it. But even Finn had come through for him in a crisis.

"I'll run it by Vargas, the operations supervisor," he finally said when he could squeeze out a word. "Jupiter Point, watch out."

~ ~ ~

After a breakfast of catching up and a lot of joking around, the group of hotshots emerged into the sunshine of mid-morning. Rollo wanted to go straight to the police department to deliver their statements, but Sean nixed that. The burnover had nothing to do with the crash investigation.

As they walked down Constellation Way, past the pretty awnings and storefronts, Josh said, "Isn't that Merry, Evie's friend? The reporter?" He snapped his fingers. "A reporter! That's exactly who we need right now. We can show her all the faxes of support. It's a great news story."

But Merry turned out to be in a huge hurry. Her brown eyes sparked with energy as she explained that she was on her way to cover a press conference. "I absolutely want to interview all of you, but we'll have to do it later. Brad White is making a big announcement. Everyone's saying he finally got the endorsement he wanted."

Sean's happy mood evaporated. So the dickface had won after all. Brad had gotten Evie ousted from the coalition and secured the group's support. He'd done it in the most underhanded, backstabbing way possible. Sean couldn't help but think that Jupiter Point deserved better.

Suddenly he remembered Evie's hesitation this morning when he asked her what she was doing. He'd asked if it was about her mother, and she hadn't answered right away. Was it possible it had something to do with Brad's announcement?

"Wait." Sean snagged her arm before Merry could disappear. "Where is the press conference?"

"Outside his campaign headquarters. Not far, just a few blocks away."

"I'm coming too."

"Suit yourself. The whole town's invited." Merry glanced at the guys still trooping behind them. "Them too, I suppose. Hotshot's gotta have a posse."

"You guys want a crash course on local politics?" Sean asked the group.

Rollo have him a thumb's up. "We're with you, Magneto."

They all trooped down the street after Merry. At the foot of Constellation, they turned the corner and hurried past the 7-Eleven. Up ahead, a small crowd was already gathering.

"Damn, I hope I haven't missed anything." Merry sped up until she was practically running, her kitten heels slapping against the pavement, her messenger bag bouncing against her ribs.

"Here, let me." Rollo shoved past Sean and scooped Merry into his arms.

"What the heck—" she yelped. "What are you doing? Who *are* you?"

"Champion running back in college. Third runner-up for the Heisman." And Rollo was off, sprinting down the sidewalk with Merry still squawking in his arms.

The rest of the group convulsed with laughter as they followed the odd spectacle. Only Rollo could get away with something like that.

"I bow down to the master," Josh said. "I'd be tripping over my shoelaces if I tried something like that."

They jogged after Rollo and Merry until they reached Brad's campaign office. A lectern had been set up on the sidewalk outside. A huge royal-blue banner with white lettering proclaimed that "Brad

White will Fight for You!"

Yeah, right. Sean had a better slogan for Brad. "Brad White's a Dickface Who Will Fight Only for Himself." He squeezed through the crowd of reporters and curious town residents. Near the lectern, he spotted Brad, in a light gray suit with a bright blue tie to match his banner. He was chatting with the fire chief, Doug Littleton, which gave Sean an uneasy feeling. Littleton had kept his distance since the mud-slinging had started. He hadn't taken a side one way or the other. Was Brad pouring more of his poison into his ears?

Even though Brad had gotten what he wanted, Sean was still a potential threat to him. And proud of it. Just to make sure Brad saw him, he maneuvered so the candidate couldn't avoid him. He folded his arms across his chest and nailed him with a scornful stare.

He was happy to see Brad's plastic smile slip, just for a moment.

Campaign volunteers wove through the crowd passing out flyers and buttons. Sean passed on the button, but took a brochure from a pretty young redhead. Something about her rang a bell, but he couldn't place her. And then someone tapped on the microphone at the lectern and the press conference began.

Chapter 26

Before heading downtown, Evie drove to her parents' house. She had to prepare them for what was to come. She found them in the living room. Her mother lay back in her recliner, an afghan draped over her legs. The Dean sat on a footstool while he trimmed her toenails. Light classical music played in the background and she sniffed the perpetual scent of chamomile tea.

The tenderness of the moment hit Evie like a crossbow to the heart. She was about to shatter their peace of mind into a million pieces. Was there any way she could avoid telling them? Allow them to stay in their protected bubble?

No. This was Jupiter Point. No one kept a secret for long. In fact, she probably held the local record for secret-keeping. Thirteen years of never saying a word—that was plenty long enough.

The Dean gave her a vague smile over his half-moon glasses as she knelt on the carpet next the recliner. She picked up her mother's hand and held it to her cheek. Molly turned her head in Evie's direction and her lips curved up at the corners. Molly's smiles had changed as the Parkinson's advanced—more deliberate, less spontaneous, as if they required thought—but they still warmed Evie's heart like nothing else in the world.

She couldn't bear to cause her mother pain. She couldn't do this.

Closing her eyes, she rubbed her cheek against Molly McGraw's fine-boned hand. To her surprise, those thin fingers uncurled so her mother cupped her chin. She felt her face being tilted upwards and when she opened her eyes, she was looking directly into her mother's. They were alive with mischief.

"Never thought I'd see that," she whispered in the raspy voice the Parkinson's had left her with. "The Dean...pedicure!"

Evie chuckled. The Dean raised an eyebrow and graced them with an indulgent smile. They all shared a glorious moment of appreciation of the absurdity. And all of a sudden it hit Evie—her parents were pretty remarkable. They were dealing with *Parkinson's*. Life challenges didn't come much tougher than that. Maybe she was underestimating her family.

"I need to tell you both about when Sean left," she began.

~ ~ ~

The press conference had already started when Evie found a parking spot on Constellation Way. She sprinted down the sidewalk, which was nearly empty because so many people were clustered around Brad's campaign office. Someone was already speaking. The feedback from the microphone echoed off the buildings. She didn't recognize the voice, but it sounded like it might be Jack Drummond.

As she approached the crowd, she spotted Merry near the lectern, holding up a small recorder. If only she'd had time to talk this over with Merry first. Maybe Merry would have had a better idea about the best way to drop this bombshell.

Not a bombshell, she reminded herself. Her parents hadn't shattered under the impact, so why should anyone else? The Dean had been outraged, yes, but not with her. Molly hadn't quite followed her story, and maybe that was for the best.

"You do what you need to do, Evangaline," the Dean had told her. "I have only one request."

"What's that? Keep it quiet? Don't go public? Keep the McGraw name out of it?"

"None of that, my dear. My request is that you not worry about us."

On the far side of the press conference, closest to the building, Evie spotted Sean and his entourage of hotshots. They were hard to miss, with their easy confidence and rugged masculine magnetism. She wasn't sure why they were there, but she was glad for it.

"I'm sure many of you have been wondering when the Jupiter Point Business Coalition would get around to issuing its endorsement," Jack was saying in that easy, authoritative way of his.

Brad, standing just behind him, gave a comic "what, me worry?" gesture with his hands. Laughter rippled through the group.

Evie swallowed hard, anxiety washing away the confidence she'd gained from that moment with her parents. The spotlight was definitely not her comfort zone, but to Brad it was like a second home. Maybe a first home. He loved the spotlight, reveled in the attention. Was that why he wanted to run for office? Was it for the power? The status?

It definitely wasn't to help anyone except himself.

That thought gave her strength. She put her hand to her cheek, where her mother's fingers had ghosted across her skin. Her mother might be mostly silent these days, but her spirit was as strong and beautiful as ever. Just because someone was quiet didn't mean they ought to be trampled over. Sure, Evie was an introvert who shunned the spotlight. But her experience still mattered.

She'd make it matter.

Jack was gearing up for the climactic moment of his speech. "If something's worth doing, it's worth doing right, you know? So we hope you'll forgive our slow pace, Brad. All it means is that you and the California voters can be assured that the process was thorough. Doing things right is important to us."

Evie took a deep breath. She couldn't imagine a better moment than this. She raised her voice and called over the heads of the crowd. "I couldn't agree more, Jack."

Heads swung her direction. The attention felt like a flock of bats flapping around her head. She fixed her gaze on Jack's surprised face. If she allowed her attention to wander, she might lose her nerve and flee.

"As the person responsible for the delay in endorsing Brad White, I'd like to explain myself. I know you've all been curious about it."

Brad was whispering frantically in Jack's ear. Jack bent to the microphone. "I'm not sure this is the right time, Evie."

"I know it isn't, Jack." She walked toward the lectern. Curious bystanders stepped aside to clear a path for her. "The right time was thirteen years ago."

A *fizz* passed through the crowd. The flapping bats had apparently transformed into buzzing bees. *Keep going*, she told herself. *One step after the other.* She reached Merry's side. Her friend reached out and touched her elbow, but kept her recorder going. Questions filled her big brown eyes. Evie gave her a thumb's up and a slight smile. She wanted Merry there with her recorder.

Brad spoke into the mic. "You had your chance to influence the coalition's decision. You chose to resign. I'm sorry, Evie, but you have no say in it anymore."

She reached the edge of the lectern and turned to face the crowd. Wide eyes, rampant curiosity, whispers, iPhones. She spoke to them, not to Brad or Joe. "I'm speaking as a private citizen of Jupiter Point. Everyone is welcome to dismiss what I'm about to say, or not. The coalition can still award its endorsement if it wishes to. I'm speaking up for *myself*, and what I went through with Brad White when I was fourteen. Brad thinks I'm afraid to speak out. And I was. I still am."

She gave a nervous laugh. Brad grabbed the opportunity to drown her out with the microphone. "You're interrupting a press conference, Evie. Security, can you take care of this situation?"

"Let her speak," Sean called as he wound through the crowd. "What are you afraid of, Brad? I want to hear what she has to say, don't you?" He addressed the second question to the crowd, which clapped and whistled.

Evie looked back at Sean and felt a current of strength flow from him to her. A security guard stepped forward, but didn't get far.

The group of hotshots blocked his path. Every time he took a step, a barrier of big strong firemen managed to be right in the way.

She probably didn't have much time, she realized. *Do it. Now. Speak.*

"When I was fourteen and Brad was seventeen, he pretended to take me for ice cream and instead he assaulted me."

The crowd went dead silent.

Behind her, she could feel waves of fury radiating from Brad.

"If he hadn't been interrupted by Sean Marcus, I have no doubt he would have raped me. Afterward, he threatened, intimidated and manipulated me so I wouldn't tell anyone. Not my parents, not my friends, no one. In many ways, that was even harder, because I couldn't put it behind me."

She couldn't look at the faces arrayed before her. Instead she fixed her gaze over their heads, on the traffic light at the intersection of Constellation Way and Pine. Its steady pattern of flashing red, green and yellow grounded her.

"When Brad asked the coalition for its formal endorsement, I assumed that we'd grant it. Of course, why wouldn't we? He's a local boy, he's one of us. He's going places. But I couldn't do it, because I know a different Brad White. I know the boy who didn't care that I was terrified. The boy who wouldn't stop until he got what he wanted—or until someone punched him."

Her eyes flicked down to meet Merry's. Her friend's brown eyes shone with tears, but her recorder hadn't budged. She was a reporter; she knew the best thing she could do for Evie was bear witness.

"If Brad had apologized to me, if he'd found some way to demonstrate that he knew what he did was wrong, I might be saying something different right now. But he didn't do that. Instead, once again, he threatened me. He said nasty things in the newspaper. He tried to smear Sean Marcus, the only other witness to his actions. He's still the *same Brad White*. He'll still do anything to get what he wants. But this time…"

She took a quick glance in Sean's direction. He was watching her steadily, sending silent support.

"I'm the one delivering the punch. You all know me. I'm a McGraw. Do you think I'd be standing up here unless I absolutely had to? I dragged my feet as long as I could. I rationalized. I delayed. I lost my position as president of the business coalition. All because I *didn't* want to speak up."

A murmur passed through the crowd. Her points were hitting home, she could feel it. She could also feel Brad about to explode behind her. The mic crackled as he snatched it up.

"That's a very interesting story, but it's *just* a story— completely unsubstantiated, slanderous and unsupported by facts."

"I support it," came Sean's deep voice. "One hundred percent."

Brad ignored him, maybe hoping no one heard. "It's funny how a spurned lover will do anything to get revenge, isn't it?" He tried a laugh, but Evie thought it fell flat. "If there was anything to these ridiculous accusations, why didn't she file a report? Why come out with it now? My lawyer is going to laugh when he hears about this."

Evie gripped her hands tightly together but held her head high. A *lawyer*. She hadn't thought about that. Could Brad sue her for this? She didn't have any physical proof. It was so long ago.

No matter--whatever the consequences were, she'd deal with them.

A pair of black boots stepped into her field of vision. The security guard had finally escaped the blockade of hotshots. He took her by the arm and guided her away from the lectern. She didn't resist; she'd said her piece. She'd accomplished what she came to do. If she made trouble for the security guard, she might end up in jail. *That* might be a little much for the McGraws.

Brad talked into the mic as the guard led her away. "It's a sad day when someone can sling mud like this. You know me. I grew up here. I went to Jupiter Point High. Won some football games. My family owns the bank. Does anything she said sound like something I'd do?"

"It does to me, you sleazy slimeball!" A young female voice rang out from the direction of the campaign office. Evie caught a glimpse of red hair and a furious face. Craning her neck, Evie recognized the intern who'd shown her to Brad's office. Then the guard was hustling her away from the scene and she couldn't see past the crowd. But the girl kept yelling while Brad's microphone-amplified voice tried to drown her out.

"Oh my God," she said out loud, realization striking hard. "I'm not the only one. Of course I'm not the only one. Oh no, that poor girl." She started shaking from the adrenaline coursing through her body. It was a good thing the security guard had a firm grip on her arm, or she might be a puddle on the pavement by now. To ground herself, she kept on talking. "That's the problem with not speaking out. You think you're all alone. But you might not be. How will you know unless you speak up?"

"You're not talking to me, are you?" the security guard asked. She recognized him as a retired member of the Jupiter Point PD. "I'm just doing my job here."

"I know, I know." She sucked in a deep breath, trying to stop her teeth from chattering from the aftershock. "I completely understand."

They reached her parking spot on Constellation. A parking ticket stuck under the windshield wiper flapped in the breeze. Perfect. Ejected from a press conference and awarded a parking ticket in the space of an hour. What other damage had she unleashed on her life? She turned to the guard, who still held her by the elbow.

"This is my car. I'm not going to cause any more trouble, sir, and I'd be surprised if I actually broke any laws back there. It's a public sidewalk, and I don't think interrupting Brad White is against city ordinances. Not yet, anyway."

The security guard snorted, but he released her arm. He watched as she unlocked her car and got into the driver's seat. His expression was completely unreadable. Had he heard what she'd said at the press conference? Did he believe her? Did he care? Did any of it matter? If this one man represented all of Jupiter Point, how was her hometown reacting to what she'd said?

Based on the guard's impassive face, she had absolutely no idea.

Chapter 27

Brad called a quick end to the press conference, since it had turned into a referendum on his sex life. The teenage redhead collapsed into heartbroken tears. Sean whispered to Josh that her mother was one of the nurses they'd partied with. "Go take care of her and make her call her mother. I'm sure she'll come get her."

As Josh whisked the girl away, Merry darted through the crowd toward Sean.

She aimed her recorder at him. "Sean Marcus, would you like to respond on the record to what Evie McGraw just said up there?"

He grinned at her. This woman sure knew her job. "Yes. I'd like to say that I confirm Evie's account of what happened thirteen years ago."

"Can you explain what you saw, in our own words?"

"I saw Brad White pinning Evie McGraw to the backseat of his car and exposing himself to her. I opened the car door and punched him in the face. The rest is pretty much on file at the police department."

Merry's eyebrows soared. "Do you intend to make a statement

to police?"

"I'll make any statement anyone wants from me. The only reason I didn't back then was because Evie didn't want me to. She didn't want to upset her family." He wanted to make sure she got that point into her article. "You know Evie."

"I do," said Merry softly. "I guess not as well as I thought I did." She clicked off the recorder. "Listen, I need to get this story written up, but do you still want me to do a piece on you and your crew? I think it's even more relevant now."

Rollo stepped close to them. "We're here to back up Sean, so just name the time and place. We're ready to go."

"You know, I wonder..." Merry's eyes sparkled as she got an eager newshound look on her face. "I wonder if we could make a little ol' deal here. I do a big puff piece on the new hotshot crew. I'll include your stories about the burnover. I'll make sure Jupiter Point gets your side of the story. I can't control what anyone else says, obviously. But I'll get you your ink."

Sean narrowed his eyes at her. "And in exchange?"

"I want to be embedded with you guys."

Rollo reared his head back, narrowly escaping the corner of a campaign sign someone was carrying past them. "What did you say?"

"Embedded," she repeated impatiently. "I want to go with you to a wildfire and write a story about it."

Rollo flexed his shoulders, cracking his neck a little in the process. "Oh, that's just a genius idea. What do you think we do out there, roast marshmallows? You have to be in peak physical shape.

It's dangerous, especially for someone your size. I carried you down the street like a football."

When Merry's glare threatened to incinerate him on the spot, he turned to Sean. "Magneto, talk some sense into her."

Sean lifted an eyebrow at him. It wasn't a *crazy* idea. Other reporters had spent time with wildfire crews. Maybe they weren't as petite as Merry, but she looked plenty tough to him. "I'll do my best, but I can't guarantee anything," he told Merry. "It may not be my decision. But I can advocate for you."

"Fair enough." Ignoring Rollo, she smiled sweetly at Sean. "Okay, then, how about we meet in two hours out at the base? You can show me everything you've been doing to get the crew ready."

"Sounds good."

She turned to go but he snagged her arm before she disappeared. "Any sense of how the town is reacting to Evie's statement?"

She glanced around at the quickly dispersing group. "I think we'll have to see. Brad is pretty respected around here. But so is Evie. And Tara O'Neill, that intern, she's a wild card."

He nodded, trying to keep a lid on his anxiety. What if Evie had spilled her guts for nothing? Would she be okay?

"I'll tell you this much," Merry continued. "I sure am glad you were there for her back then. And I'm glad you're here for her now."

Sean let her go and she tore off in the direction of the *Mercury News-Gazette* offices.

Sean's phone buzzed and he answered right away, thinking it might be Evie. Instead it was his immediate supervisor from the

Forest Service. *Hell.* Matt Vargas had been trying to reach him since yesterday. Between the tequila, Evie, and the arrival of his old crew, he hadn't had a chance to call him back.

More accurately, he hadn't *wanted* to call him back. But now he was stuck.

"Marcus," he answered.

"What the fuck is going on there?" Vargas thundered. "Neither you nor Marshall is answering the phone. I'm getting weird-ass calls from people I never heard of. Asking me questions about the Big Canyon burnover. Is there something I'm missing here? Your local connection was supposed to be an asset, Marcus."

Vargas was talking so loudly that even Rollo could hear. People in the next street over could probably hear. Sean ducked around the corner, Rollo close at his heels. "I'm on it, Vargas. I have a media outreach plan already in place."

Rollo gave him a thumb's up, and Sean made a face at him. As of one minute ago he had a media outreach plan, thanks to Merry.

"There's some political stuff going on here that I can't control. I'm doing what I can."

"Not good enough. One more flare-up and I'll have to put someone else in charge. I have actual fires to worry about, and so do you. I need you to focus, Marcus. This is a big job and thirty-one is damn young for a superintendent. Don't make me look like an ass for putting you in that position."

"No, sir. I'm one hundred percent focused, sir."

He hung up and stuffed his phone back in his pocket. Rollo was still keeping pace at his side. "Good talk?"

"One for the memory banks."

His phone buzzed again. He considered stomping on the damn thing until it could never bother him again. Instead, he pulled it out and glanced at the new text. He didn't recognize the number, but he had no doubt who had sent it.

You and me, Marcus. Airstrip, two hours.

~ ~ ~

In his time with the fire service, Sean had noticed something about the typical firefighter personality. In order to get along in such tough working circumstances, firemen developed a certain sensitivity to each other's moods. When a guy needed some space to work through his shit, he got it. When he was ready to talk—or maybe just drink—he could do that too.

The guys seemed to pick up on his need for a break because no one talked about Evie or the press conference as they drove out to the base.

When Merry arrived, Sean beckoned Josh to join them. "Show her around the base, would you, Marsh?"

"Sure thing." Josh grinned at her and offered his arm. "It's a thing of beauty, this place. You're probably going to want to move in."

Sean forced a smile. "Merry, I think you should interview the rest of the crew first. They'll speak more freely if I'm gone."

"Where the hell are you going?" Josh asked.

"Got something to take of."

Josh raised an eyebrow, but Sean ignored him. Of course his friend assumed he was going to see Evie, to offer support after that incredible soul-baring moment at the press conference. He'd been so proud of her. He'd watched with his heart in his mouth the entire time. Right now, he'd love to get her alone in a room and wrap his arms around her.

But if Brad was going to the airstrip, he was going too. He didn't trust that guy for a second.

The waving grasses and wildflowers welcomed him back as if no time had passed. He drove by the spot where Evie had taken photos for her mother and parked just outside the barrier.

Sean ducked under the barrier and walked down the runway. He noticed a ragged windsock still hanging from a pole, a green distance marker now lying on its side. At the end of the runway, he stepped onto grass.

This was the spot. Thirteen years ago, after checking the direction of the wind with that same windsock, he'd flung his father's ashes into the air. His mother's had gone to her family in Florida. But no one had asked for Jesse Marcus's.

A black BMW coupe zoomed into view and jerked to a stop outside the barrier. The door opened and Brad White got out. A quick scan told Sean that Brad was alone, and that he didn't seem to be armed and dangerous. Brad shaded his eyes and scanned the property, not spotting Sean until he raised his hand and started forward.

They converged in the center of the runway, keeping a careful distance between them. Sean waited for Brad to speak first. The candidate wore the same business suit as earlier, but the tie was unknotted and sweat stains darkened the armpits.

"You think you've won, don't you, asshole?"

Sean snorted. "I'm not running for anything. That's your gig."

"Sure you are. You're running for respect. You want this town to like you. You want everyone to forget your father was a fucking hippie-ass criminal."

Sean clenched his jaw to keep from responding. It was one thing for *him* to badmouth his father. Listening to Brad do it was a different story. "If you think I care what you say about my father, forget about it. I heard enough crap back in high school."

"Yeah you did. And it was all true. Want to know why your father crashed that plane?"

Sean's stomach did a sick, slow roll. He didn't answer. Brad was going to say whatever he wanted. And he'd hear it, because that was why he'd come.

Brad reached into the back pocket of his trousers and pulled out a sheaf of papers. "It's all here. Drug money. It came through our bank. My dad had just figured it out and was about to bring in the police. He knew. Your father knew. He was going to jail, and your mother too because he put her name all over everything. Nice, huh? He would have brought your whole family down. If you weren't a minor, you would have gone to jail too."

Sean stared at the printouts, which were covered with numbers. A booming sound rang in his ears. The blood pounding? His world shifting?

Brad snickered. "Wait, you *did* go to jail. I forgot. It's where you Marcuses belong. So what do you think? Did your dear old loving dad crash that plane on purpose because he just couldn't handle the heat? Sounds about right, don't you think? I looked into his life history from what's on file at the bank. Seems like he crossed state lines every time things got a little hot for him."

Sean couldn't drag his gaze from those papers. "What…" He cleared his throat. "What are you going to do with that?"

"I don't know. What should I do? I don't want to go public with this shit. It is *our* bank, after all. Makes us look bad that we ever had anything to do with your slimy family."

Sean clenched his fists so hard his knuckles cracked.

Brad's face relaxed into his trademark charming smile—the one Sean particularly hated. "Tell you what? Let's make a deal. I'll keep this information to myself. And you," he paused for the drama of it, "you sell me this piece of property."

Sean's jaw dropped. He hadn't seen that coming at all. "Why?"

"You need to ask? This is prime real estate here. Ocean view, lots of space. I'm seeing vacation condos or a fucking golf course. Does it matter? I want it. Call it a backup plan in case people take Evie seriously." There was a dangerous, reckless gleam in his pale gray eyes. "You don't need it. What would you do with an old airstrip? It's practically a fire hazard."

Sean narrowed his eyes at him. Was that a threat? What exactly was Brad up to here? It was hard to believe this was just about a real estate deal. "What about Evie?"

"Evie? What about her? You can have her. There, I just sweetened the deal. Are we good?"

Sean itched to wipe the nasty smirk off his face. "I'll need to think about it." He held out his hands for the sheaf of papers.

After a slight hesitation, Brad handed them over. "These are just printouts, so don't bother to get your matches out."

Still holding the papers, Sean folded his arms across his chest. "Anything else before I kick you off my property?"

Brad took an involuntary step back. "Going caveman again?"

He took a step forward, then another. "Why not? It felt damn good the last time."

With one last sneer, Brad turned away and headed for his BMW. Just before he reached it, he called out one more thing. "This town is never going to accept you, Marcus. You should sell and get out. Move to a place where no one knows the whole Marcus family circus. If you keep hanging around Evie, I feel for the McGraws. They're a good family, and they sure have been through a lot."

Mentioning the McGraws was the last straw. Sean started after him, energy surging through his body and into his fists. Brad ran the last couple of steps to his car and slid inside. Before Sean could reach him, he drove off, sticking his left arm out the window, middle finger raised.

Sean let out a howl of pure fury. His whole body vibrated with it. It rang through his voice, his throat, his lungs. Fucking little twit.

But after the first red flash of rage, he knew the truth. His anger wasn't really about Brad. It was about his own flesh and blood.

"Jesse, what the fuck did you do?" He kicked at the pavement of the runway. "You selfish, foolish idiot. What did you do?"

Chapter 28

The next day, Evie's first two hours at the gallery seemed to last about a week. No one came through her door. The tourists and honeymooners were probably sleeping late. But the Jupiter Pointers…where were they? What were they thinking? Was Brad busy trashing her in every way he could?

By the time the door jingled open, her heart just about jumped out of her chest. Chief Becker walked in with his long, loping stride.

"Chief," she said faintly, the blood pounding in her ears. "It's nice to see you."

"It's nice to finally get the real story of what went down that night." With his height and imposing stature, he made the gallery look like a dollhouse. "I wondered if I'd ever know."

Her heart jumped again, this time with hope. He'd said "the real story." That must mean he believed her.

"I'm sorry—"

He held up a hand to stop her. "No need. It's not really unusual for victims to be afraid to speak out. I came by to ask if you want to pursue any charges at this point in time."

"No," she said quickly. "Absolutely not."

"It's the only way to make him pay for his actions."

"Oh, he's already paying!" At the sound of Mrs. Murphy's cheerful voice, both Evie and Chief Becker swung toward the door. The bookstore owner practically skipped across the polished floor toward the espresso bar.

"There's been a run on White Savings and Loan!" she declared, triumph shining from her eyes. "Everyone's closing their accounts!"

"Everyone?"

"A lot of people. *I* certainly did. Everyone's saying his campaign is dead as a doorknob. Jim is trying to get him into some treatment center just to get him out of town."

Evie drew in a long, unsteady breath. "Treatment for what?"

"I'm sure I don't know. They say treatment, that's all."

"I don't think there's a treatment for what ails him," Chief Becker muttered, turning to go. "Have a good day, ladies. Keep me in the loop. Seems I'm the last to know these days."

As soon as the chief was gone, Mrs. Murphy got down to business. "Evie, you've really stirred things up. Tara O'Neill has an interview in the paper today, and they say more girls are coming forward. And it's all because of you. People will be talking about this for years!" Delighted at that pleasant picture of the future, she hitched one hip onto the stool.

"Wait." Evie rushed around the counter. "I got this for you." She snapped open a camp chair she'd ordered online. "It has cup holders and everything."

"For me?"

"For you." She smiled affectionately at the older woman. Mrs. Murphy might be a gossip, but she had a kind heart, and right now Evie was all about kindness. Was there anything more important, when you came right down to it?

"Evangaline McGraw, you are an angel sent from heaven. Now." She settled her wide rear into the canvas seat and sighed happily. "I'll take a cappuccino for this darling little cup holder. Oh, and did you hear about the coalition? We're having another meeting tonight…"

After Mrs. Murphy's visit, a steady flow of Jupiter Point residents came through the gallery. Even if they didn't reference the press conference directly, they said things like, "We're behind you, Evie," and "You need anything, let us know."

Feeling that degree of support from her hometown was nearly overwhelming.

But one person didn't show up that day…or the next. Or the next. Evie didn't hear anything from Sean over the next few days. He'd texted her a sweet message of support after the press conference, but nothing since then.

~ ~ ~

Three days after the fateful press conference, Brad officially ended his campaign and checked into a sex addiction treatment center. According to Merry, insiders were saying that he could survive this scandal, in time. His plan, according to people in the know, was to lay low for a while, then come back and try to rebuild his reputation and the family finances. Apparently he already had a few projects in mind.

But Evie no longer cared. She'd done her part, and the sense of power and freedom was sweet indeed.

After four days of no communication with Sean, she gave in and drove to the hotshot base. On her way into the front lot, she spotted a group of men running with heavy-looking packs strapped to their backs. They were running hard, sweat dripping down their faces, feet pounding the trail that ran through the woods near the lot. At the head of the pack, staring at a stop watch, was Sean. Shirtless, sweaty, magnificent Sean.

With her heart in her mouth, she parked and leaned against her Jetta as they burst into the parking lot, one by one. Sean called out their times as they collapsed onto the grass.

"Hey, Evie," Josh called from his prone position on the ground.

Sean whipped around.

"Hi, hotshots." She waved and gave Sean a tentative smile. He wrapped things up with the guys—it sounded like a pep talk, but she couldn't make out all the words—then jogged over to her.

"Hi, Evie. I'd…uh…come closer but I'm a little grimy right now."

She nodded, throat tightening. Grimy or not, she would love to be pressed against him right now. The sight of his spectacularly muscled chest, still heaving from the exertion of the run, made her light-headed.

But obviously something wasn't right between them. His smoky eyes held a remoteness she hadn't seen before—or at least not since he'd come back to Jupiter Point.

"It looks like you're pretty busy," she said, proud of how calm she sounded.

"Yeah, it's been nuts. All the forecasts say the wildfire season's going to kick in any day now. We want to be ready. We *will* be ready."

"That's great. Jupiter Point is grateful. Merry showed me her article. It makes you guys look pretty good. Like saviors."

He laughed, the white of his grin flashing against the newly tanned skin of his face. All those outdoor runs, she imagined. Of course they had to make him even sexier. "She's angling for a special assignment. She wants to be embedded with the crew on one of our trips."

"Wow, that's brave."

"Yup. Well…" He glanced back at the other hotshots, who were now downing bottles of water and performing cool-down stretches. "I don't know how much time I'm going to have. We have a lot of training exercises coming up, and as soon as the fire season gets underway, I'll be gone a lot. But we should get together—"

"I love you, Sean."

He went a little white under his tan.

She snapped her mouth shut, stunned that those words had come out of her mouth. She hadn't come here to say them. If she'd known they were going to burst out like that, she would have driven off Jupiter Point instead of coming here. But now, there they were, hanging between them like a fireball about to slam into their faces.

"I…" He started to speak, but couldn't get any words out.

"That's okay. Don't worry. It's okay. You don't have to say anything." She fumbled behind her for the door handle of her car. Where was the damn thing? Had it decided to play hide-and-seek just to torture her? "I hope everything goes well with the rest of the…you know…fires…and…"

Finally her fingers encountered smooth chrome. Light-headed with relief—or maybe from the stricken look on Sean's face—she tugged the door open and slipped inside her car.

She turned the key in the ignition. The engine sounded very far away. Everything felt strange and warped. She pushed the button to raise the window, putting a desperately needed barrier between her and Sean.

Unable to fully meet his eyes, she cast him a lopsided smile. Waved her fingers in a cheery goodbye gesture she'd never used before in her life. And drove blindly from the parking lot.

Chapter 29

Merry's article came out near the end of the week and it made the hotshots look like heroes. Normally Sean would have celebrated with the rest of the crew. But he just couldn't get excited about it. The only thing on his mind was Evie, the McGraw family, Brad's offer, and the mess Jesse had left behind.

When he walked into the reception area and found the headline, "Jupiter Point: New Home for Heroic Fire Suppression Crew" plastered on every available wall, he just gritted his teeth and ignored it.

"It's a damn good photo, don't you think?" Josh stood admiring a blowup of the front page on the bathroom door. It included a shot of the old Colorado crew, as well as a close-up of Sean with the caption "Hometown Hero Returns to Lead Crew."

"It's fine." Sean shrugged. "Do you mind? I have to take a leak."

"Hometown heroes have to pee too, I guess."

Sean flashed his middle finger, then shoved past him.

"Hometown heroes have a temper." Josh grinned. "Hometown

heroes need to get laid."

Sean slammed the door in his face. Josh had it all wrong. It wasn't about the sudden evaporation of his sex life. Not even close. It was about the soft, sure look in Evie's eyes when she'd said, "I love you."

And the terror that had gripped him right afterward.

She had no idea what a mistake she'd made. Sean was not "love" material. He'd *told* her that. Just look at his parents. Jesse had dragged his family around like tin cans tied to a dog's tail. As a hotshot, Sean needed to be free to jet off at a moment's notice— without making someone else suffer for that.

Just like Brad had said, he couldn't drag the McGraws into the Marcus family mess. Those bank statements sat under his cot in the dorms like a neutron bomb about to go off. No way would he let anyone else get hurt by the fallout. Especially not someone as amazing and perfect as Evie.

When he was finished in the bathroom, he pushed open the door to find Josh just outside. He loped alongside Sean and read from the newspaper article as they headed for the next training session.

"Hotshot firefighters are often referred to as 'elite.' While they are highly trained, what really sets these backcountry firefighters apart is their toughness. The physical demands are intense, but the true test of a hotshot is his or her inner strength. To work at such a grueling pace for sixteen plus hours a day, then do it again the next day, and the next, and the next, until the work is done, requires a special kind of mental toughness. That strength was put to

the ultimate test on July 24 of last year, when the Big Canyon wildfire defied all predictions and the twenty crew members of the Colorado Fighting Scorpions were trapped between a wall of flames and a wall of stone."

Josh whistled. "Wow, she really has a way with words. I'm starting to think I'm pretty hot shit, reading this." He scanned the rest of the article. "LCES, blah blah blah… Escape routes…pre-determined safety zone such as an already-cleared or burned area."

"Has she gotten to the part where I apparently made the terrible decision to deploy where we were, rather than try to make it to the black?" Sean asked as they strode through the base toward the area they'd designated for training drills.

"Yup. But that's not how she put it. *Crew boss Sean Marcus was faced with a terrible choice. Keep running the quarter mile to the safety zone or deploy the fire shelters. He'd lost contact with the lookout, who could have told him how fast the flames were traveling. And the helicopters had been called back to base. The decision rested on his shoulders. As Marcus put it, "I had to go with what I was seeing, and I saw and heard a forest fire that was moving faster than anticipated. We had predicted that it would take an hour to go from the first trigger point to the second. It took fifteen minutes."*

Sean shuddered as the visceral memory of that moment came flooding back. He hadn't felt this way when he'd recounted the story for Merry. But now, hearing his own words read out loud, he could practically smell the smoke and burning brush.

"She goes into an explanation of trigger points here…blah blah," continued Josh. "Okay, here it is. *Not far away, another crew boss made the opposite choice. As we all know, three firefighters couldn't outrun the fire.* Then she has a quote from the National Fire Safety Board that says you made the right call under the circumstances, but they're investigating the supervisor of the Arizona crew."

"I hate all the second-guessing," Sean muttered angrily. "You do the best you can. If a single one of us had panicked and ditched his shelter, I'd be the one taking all the blame. If Finn had died, I'd take the blame."

"Mental toughness," said Josh wisely, tapping his skull. "Speaking of Finn, she talks about him, too."

"Oh yeah? Conference call from Hollywood?"

"Guess so. See here? His quote is, *'Sean did a good job and saved some lives.'* When asked why he chose to try to outrace the fire instead, deploying his shelter in a gravel stream bed, he refused to comment. Full disclosure: a production company owned by Finn Abrams's father is fast-tracking a movie about the events of the Big Canyon burnover. Its tentative release date is in the summer of next year."

Josh crumpled up the paper and tossed it in a burn barrel as they jogged toward the hotshots doing pushups on the grass. "How the fuck did Finn manage to get a plug for his movie into this article?"

"Are you surprised?" Sean made a mental note to be nowhere near a movie theater next summer. He had no interest in watching Finn's father's version of events. Finn would probably end up looking like the lone wolf hero instead of the guy who panicked and got lucky. Whatever. It didn't matter what Finn said or did.

He wasn't even sure if it mattered anymore what Jupiter Point thought of him. *Hometown hero.* Wasn't he the hometown fuckup just last week?

Merry's article was just the icing on the cake, he knew. The one person who had really restored his reputation was Evie McGraw.

He hadn't paid for a single cup of coffee or a single beer since she'd made her dramatic appearance at Brad's press conference. Everyone in Jupiter Point loved Evie, and now they were embracing Sean.

While he felt like a piece of dog crap on the bottom of someone's shoe. That look on her face...

He shook it off. *Focus, asshole.*

If Jupiter Point knew about the bank statements and Brad's suspicions about Jesse and the crash, he'd be back on the "bad boy" list again.

"Okay, kids. Time for some fun," he called to the crew. The Jupiter Point Hotshots were now fully staffed. Nineteen men and one woman, ranging in ages from twenty-two to thirty-six, a mix of fire veterans, military veterans, and six local hires. One superintendent, two captains, two crew bosses, three sawyers. As required for a Type 1 crew, a full eighty percent of them had at least one fire season under their belts, which made training a lot easier.

"Packs on," he directed them.

The firefighters shouldered their fully loaded packs, which weighed forty-five pounds.

Sean pointed toward the trail that led up Heart Attack Hill, as they'd nicknamed it. The wind was a steady fifteen knots, perfect for a deployment drill. "As some of us can verify, you need to be able to deploy your shelter in winds that feel like a hurricane. I want you to run three and a half miles up that trail. When you reach the lookout, you set up your shelter. The wind should be pretty fierce up there. Wait sixty seconds, then pack up your tent and run back down the hill. This is a timed exercise. It should take you no more than ten seconds to deploy under any conditions. We'll be practicing this over and over. But first, you two."

He pointed to the two rookies on the squad, who were both locals.

"What's the proper method to deploy a shelter in fifty-mile-per-hour winds?"

Tim Peavy raised his eyes to the sky as if looking for the answer. "Um…you lie down first?"

"Correct. If you're standing up, it'll turn into a kite. Okay, everyone ready? And…go!"

The group took off toward Heart Attack Hill. Sean ran ahead at full speed. Without a pack, he could move faster than the rest, and he needed to reach the top before they did so he could time their deployments. Besides, he needed the burn. He needed to feel his muscles pumping and oxygen pounding through his bloodstream.

He needed to obliterate the image of Evie's crooked smile behind the window of her car.

Why couldn't he forget about it? He'd done nothing wrong. He'd tried to help Evie in any way he could. Because he cared about her.

Then why hadn't he told her that?

Yes, that's how the conversation should have gone.

I love you, Sean.

And I really care about you, Evie.

Yeah, no. That definitely wasn't any better.

I love you, Sean.

I wish I could say the same, but I'm not really sure what it means and the word terrifies the living crap out of me.

Nope, even worse, if more accurate. One more time.

I love you, Sean.

If I could love anyone, it would be you. I feel things for you I can't put into words or explain and I can't stop thinking about you, but can you hold that "I love you" thought until I can work it out my Neanderthal brain?

Oh, for fuck's sake. He slammed up the trail, branches whipping against his face. This was why he didn't bother with relationships. This was why his only attempt at marriage had been an unmitigated, embarrassing disaster.

He should leave Evie the hell alone. Nothing he said would make things better at this point. He'd stood there like an ice statue while she'd opened her heart to him. And even if he did get a do-over, would it really be any different?

If only he could get rid of this longing to see her again. Touching would be even better. But he'd lost the right to touch her when she'd rolled up her car window. Just to see her face, bask in her smile one more time. Even from across a room or a street. He needed some other image of her to replace the one playing on a torturous loop in his head.

Yeah. That was all he needed. Then he could go on with his life.

Chapter 30

The Sky View Gallery had never done this kind of business before. For the next week, Evie was slammed from the moment she walked in the door to the moment she flipped her sign. Her town wanted to show its support in the most material way it could. She appreciated the dollar vote, of course, but mostly she was grateful to be busy. The more she worked, the less she thought about Sean.

Theoretically, anyway.

Jack Drummond and Belladonna came by the gallery with an official apology from the business coalition.

"We want you back, sweet-pea." Belladonna leaned both elbows on the counter and fixed her purple-ringed, pleading gaze on Evie. "Your resignation is like an open wound in our hearts. We miss you, our dear fearless leader."

Evie snorted. "Now that's a description I definitely don't deserve."

"She's right, Evie." Jack lowered his voice so none of the lingering honeymooners could hear. "We need you back. Since you left, we've had more squabbles over pettier things than you can imagine. No one can agree on the new posters. Some people want the town motto, others don't. We need your calming presence and sense of perspective."

Evie kept her focus on the lemon she was peeling for twists to add to espressos. "Of course you need the motto. We've always used the motto."

"But it might be changed at the next meeting."

"It will never be changed. It's a great motto. 'Remember to Look Up at the Stars.' That's Jupiter Point in a nutshell. Every time someone tries to change it, there's a full-scale revolt. Keep the motto. Trust me."

"See, this is why we need you." Belladonna batted her eyelashes. "We're lost without you."

"You're just embarrassed because Brad had to withdraw."

"I'm embarrassed because we should have trusted you," said Jack softly. "We should have known you weren't just playing games. I take full responsibility for my role in this debacle."

Evie scooped her pile of lemon twists into a ceramic container. "It really wasn't your fault. I shouldn't have been so…reserved. I'm trying to change that part of myself."

"Well, don't go changing too much. We love our Evie." Belladonna reached over and pinched her cheek. "Think about it, sweet-pea. It would mean a lot to us, and I think you can really make a difference for Jupiter Point. Your fellow business owners need you. We want you. We love you."

Well, it was nice to hear words of love from someone, although she would prefer them to come from a strong and sinfully handsome firefighter.

"I'll think about it," she promised. "And believe me, I do appreciate the gesture."

"It's not a gesture." Jack shook his head gloomily. "If you don't come back, you're going to doom me to an early grave. The poster alone will be the death of me."

Evie laughed. "You have no conscience, do you?"

He grinned at her. "Is it working?"

"When's the next meeting?"

Belladonna let out a whoop of glee and the two of them danced a little polka across the gallery floor, nearly mowing over Brianna as she burst through the door. She made a wide, wary circle around them.

"I'm not even going to ask," she told Evie.

"I think I just agreed to be president again."

"Well, good, I hope you made them beg."

"Not really." She spoke over her shoulder as she steamed a hot chocolate for Brianna. "I want to be president."

"Get it, girl. Go for what you want."

She passed the mug to Brianna, then went to ring up a sale for one of the honeymooning couples. "I love this one," she told them, admiring their choice, a close-up shot of the dense atmosphere surrounding the planet Venus. "It's so mysterious, you know?"

"We're going to hang it in our bedroom," the bride confided. "It's supposed to remind us that love is an enigma."

"So very true. Also, its atmosphere contains toxic gases," Evie pointed out. At the espresso bar, Brianna snorted into her hot chocolate.

The groom laughed. "Luckily, we've known each other since high school. We know all about each other's toxic gases."

"Shht." The bride swatted his arm and he pulled an "I'm in trouble now" face.

After they'd left, Evie returned to Brianna. "Newlyweds are so *adorable*," Brianna deadpanned. "Seriously, I thank the Goddess every day that I work with plants and not people."

"Hey, I'm the reserved introvert around here. And I think they're sweet."

"That's because you're a *sweet* reserved introvert. Which is why I forgive you. Not that there was ever any doubt about that." Brianna's freckled face twisted ruefully. "It might be harder to forgive myself."

"Brianna, stop that." They'd been moving in and out of this conversation over the past few days. "You aren't a mind reader. How would you have any idea unless I told you?"

"I just think I should have known. Granted, flowers are a lot more predictable, and I understand them much better than human beings. But you're my *best friend*, Evie. And I let you down."

Brianna's woebegone expression, so different from her usual sunshiny mood, ripped at Evie's heart. Why couldn't Brianna understand that Evie was the one who'd made the mistakes?

"You didn't let me down. I promise. You're the best friend I could ever wish for. Ever. And now I need you to help me with something."

"Really?" Brianna perked up. "What can I do? Name it."

"I need to figure out a casual way to run into Sean Marcus. I hate the way I left things with him. I don't want him to think I can't handle being around him, you know what I mean? I want us to be friends."

Surprisingly, she actually sounded as if she meant it. And she did, in a way. She'd rather be friends with Sean than feel this horrible awkward tension every time she thought about seeing him.

Brianna nodded, a frown of concentration creasing her forehead. "So you haven't seen Sean since you broke up?"

"It wasn't exactly a breakup, but…" She shook her head, unwilling to explain all the ins and outs. "No, I haven't."

"And you want to. I just want to make sure I have this straight. Because my track record lately is a little shaky."

"Yes. I want to see him. I need to get that first random encounter out of the way. Except I don't want it to be random. I want to be prepared. But I can't think of a way to accomplish it. Any ideas?"

"Well, as a matter of fact…" Brianna glanced over her shoulder toward the door. "Can you be ready in about five minutes?"

"What?" Evie knocked a pile of napkins off the counter. They went fluttering to the floor in a shower of "Sky View" light blue.

"I ran into Sean on the street. He said he'd see me in here."

"You're just telling me this *now*?"

"I'm sorry! I didn't know you were worried about seeing him!" Brianna dropped her head onto her folded arms. "I'm the worst friend ever," she wailed.

"You're not, you're not. Just stay here for a minute while I make sure I look okay."

"You look ridiculously beautiful, as always," Brianna called as Evie ran toward her back office. She threw herself in front of the old gilt-framed mirror she'd stumbled across at a thrift store. Usually, she appreciated its cracked and slightly warped reflection. Now, she desperately wished for a normal mirror. She met her own panicked eyes. She looked like a Picasso painting, with one half of her face an oddly shaped cube.

"What are you doing?" she whispered to herself. "Is falling in love something to be embarrassed about?"

No. It wasn't. People fell in love all the time. Every day. She saw them trooping into her gallery, nuzzling and holding hands and whispering to each other. It was normal. *She* was normal.

For the first time since she was fourteen, she'd opened her heart and made herself vulnerable. She should be proud of that!

With her head held high, she glided back toward the gallery. She might have stumbled a bit when she saw Sean's tall figure next to Brianna, head bent down to listen to her friend. Brianna, cheeks turning pink, was chattering a mile a minute. She did that when she got nervous; she and Evie had that in common.

Sean looked up when she came toward him, his green eyes flying to scan her face. She kept her determined smile fixed firmly in place even though her heart performed several consecutive jumping jacks.

"Hi, Sean."

"Hi. I was, uh, just walking around town and I thought I'd stop in and say…well, hi."

Brianna piped up. "I'm going to take off, you guys. I have some mulch to deliver. Too much information, probably. I mean, who wants to hear about mulch? Even the word is unappealing, isn't it? 'Mulch.' It's like a combination of 'mold' and 'gulch.' Neither of them are attractive words and when you put them together—"

"Brianna," Evie interrupted, for all their sakes. "Sean and I could really use a minute to catch up."

"Right." Bright as a firefly, Brianna whisked herself out of the gallery. Miraculously, the place was momentarily empty.

"How've you been?" Evie tried to sound normal and ignore the deep longing that gripped her soul. Sean didn't feel the same as she did; that was crystal clear.

"Bad," he said bluntly. God, she'd forgotten how he always got straight to the point. "I felt bad about how we left things."

"Don't." Unable to hold his gaze, she decided this would be the perfect time to replace the photo of Venus that the honeymooners had purchased. Crossing to a stockpile of framed photos from the Observatory, she flipped through them blindly. "There's no need."

"So we're cool?"

"Of course we're cool." So cool. Just look at her—cool and calm and collected. "Perfect Evie," as Brianna would say.

"Yeah. Listen, Evie, I owe you for what you did."

"Excuse me?"

She gave him a sidelong glance. He stood a few steps away from her as she extracted a framed print of the Horsehead Nebula. He was dressed more formally than usual, in light wool trousers and a creamy sweater. Did he really have to look this good? Was he trying to kill her?

"I know that you wanted to stop Brad's bullshit before it snowballed on me. That's one of the reasons you decided to crash his press conference. I haven't really thanked you. So, thank you."

"Maybe I should thank *you*. It was the best thing I ever did."

Maybe the simulation of a supernova imploding would be better. She pulled that one out too, then stared at it for a long moment. The intense colors, the vivid flares of pure light and energy…

A thought flashed through her head. She and Sean were together in the same room. When would that happen again?

This is your life, Evie. Live it.

She abandoned the photos and closed the gap between her and Sean. Startled, he stepped back, but she grabbed him by the shoulders and stood on tiptoe. She pressed her lips against the firm, curved contours of his.

Fire streaked between them, hot and real and all-consuming. He let out a groan and devoured her mouth as if it was the only thing standing between him and starvation. He put one big hand on the small of her back and tugged her close.

This was where she wanted to be, the *only* place she wanted to be. This was where she belonged, and every rapid beat of his heart told her "*yes, yes, yes.*"

Relief and joy sent her head spinning. She'd wondered, late at night, sleepless in bed, if she would ever kiss Sean again. Now she was kissing him *and* he was kissing her back. He *did* feel the same as her. He felt the same passion, the same longing, the same love.

It was all there in his kiss.

Until he stepped away.

He dropped his hands from her body, his face going blank as the empty space on her gallery wall. "Sorry, Evie. I'm sorry."

Her jaw fell open. Her stomach gave a sickening plunge. Part of her wanted to run away and hide under the desk in her office. But the other part, the more important part, refused.

"You coward," she told him in a low voice. "You feel the same things I do. But you're afraid to face them."

He watched her silently, not agreeing, not disagreeing. She wanted to pick him up and shake him. Or maybe toss him to the ground and pummel him. Her frustration felt almost violent.

"And the only reason I can say that is that I used to be afraid too. I know how it feels. And I know it when I see it."

With a tormented look, he scrubbed a hand through his hair. "I didn't mean...I came here to..."

"Don't bother with trying to concoct some kind of line. That's not you. That's why you can't spit it out."

"Look, Evie, it's not..." He trailed off, which proved her right. Whatever he'd come here to say, he couldn't do it.

"I know you, Sean. You don't tell lies. So look me in the face and tell me you don't feel something for me."

He said nothing. His gaze dropped to the floor, to the wall, to anywhere but her.

"Goodbye, Sean."

She spun on her heel and snatched up the first photograph her hand landed on. Turning her back on him, she carried it to the fastener protruding from the wall. It fit perfectly in the space.

His footfalls echoed through the gallery on his way out the door. She kept her gaze fixed on the photo, even though she couldn't see anything through her tear-blurred eyes. Her entire being was focused on Sean disappearing from her life.

When the door jingled closed, she finally allowed herself to blink. Slowly the photograph came into focus.

Jupiter filled the frame, big and bold, with the distinctive eye-shaped giant storm dead center. That storm had been raging for hundreds of years. It was bigger than the entire planet Earth.

And yet it was nothing compared to what was going on inside her heart right now.

Chapter 31

Every kiss from Evie seemed to change Sean's life.

This one was no different. He left the Sky View Gallery and drove right to the station house. He had no trouble finding Chief Becker's office—the station practically felt like a second home. The chief was on the phone, but Sean didn't need to actually talk to him.

He pulled out the papers that had been burning a hole in his pocket since Brad dumped them on him a week ago. If the choice was sell the airstrip to Brad or he'd leak the bank statements—well, he'd save Brad the trouble.

He planted the sheaf of papers on Becker's desk. Right away he felt a huge burden roll off his shoulders. He snagged a notepad and scrawled a message for Becker. "More material for your Marcus investigation."

He watched as Becker scanned the note, registered the meaning of the bank statements. When the police chief, who still had his phone to his ear, finally met his eyes, he gave the man a little salute, and a thumb's up.

Whatever happened next was up to the Jupiter Point Police

Department, and Sean was more than okay with that. Whether it looked bad for him, or Brad, or Jesse, or all of the above, it didn't matter.

Unless he was cleansed of the past, he'd never be worthy of Evie McGraw and her kisses.

Over the next few weeks, Sean threw himself into work. The weather forecasts were alarming; the entire fire community was on watch. Even though it was only mid- April, this part of California was like a tinderbox, and a wildfire could spark at any moment. As he'd promised Vargas, from now until the fire season began, he intended to be one hundred percent focused on getting the Jupiter Point Hotshots ready.

Working nonstop, he completed all the paperwork required for a Type 1 Interagency Hotshot Crew. He and his two captains—Josh and Baker—began planning an initiation ceremony that would mark their crew's official entrance into the firefighting world.

In the meantime, they trained, and trained, and in their spare time, trained.

Chief Littleton had finally stopped keeping his distance and invited Sean to meet with him about coordination between the hotshots and the JP fire department.

"Gotta tell you, I'm glad you guys are here," the chief said as he showed him around Station Eleven. "These dry conditions are making me antsy."

"You and me both." Sean nodded to one of the firefighters, who he recognized from that drunken night at Barstow's Brews. "Hey, Rabbit, how's it going?"

"Not bad, man." They exchanged fist bumps. "Good to see you slumming it here with the locals."

Littleton excused himself to take a phone call. "Rabbit, do you mind showing Marcus here the rest of the rigs? He needs to know what resources we can offer up if need be."

"Sure thing, Boss."

Rabbit, a good-looking, lanky guy with a cocky grin, led the way into the apparatus bay. It was empty and its back door wide open. In the sunny open lot behind the station house, several firefighters were busy polishing a ladder truck and an engine until they shone.

"Guess you missed your chance with Suzanne, huh?" Rabbit said as they walked through the apparatus bay. "I'm thinking that night at Barstow's was one of her last nights of freedom."

"Sorry?"

"Suzanne Finnegan. The blond you left with that night. I heard she's engaged to some lawyer from the Bay Area."

"No kidding." He'd probably know this news already if he was still spending time with Evie. "She's a good kid, I hope she's happy."

"So…uh…I heard you were seeing her cousin. Evie McGraw."

Sean's entire body tensed at the sound of Evie's name. "Yeah, I guess you could call it that."

Rabbit was watching him curiously. "Not anymore?"

"No, I haven't seen her recently."

The other firefighter blew out a breath and beamed at him. "So I'm clear to step in, right? I'm just checking as a courtesy, one firefighter to another. Which is more than some of the others are doing."

Sean froze, nearly stumbling over a crack in the apparatus bay floor. "What are you talking about?"

"Asking Evie out. Following protocol, dude. You were seeing her, so—I want to make sure that's all in the past before I make my move." He kept moving toward the lot, not waiting for Sean.

Sean shook himself out of his paralysis and hurried to catch up. "I wouldn't waste your time. Evie isn't interested in dating. She despises dating."

"You're behind the times, bro." Rabbit laughed as they stepped out of the apparatus bay into the sunshine. "Evie has entered the singles scene. She's put out her single shingle. And you know what that shingle says? 'Open for business, but you better take a number.' I heard she's been seeing a cop. That ain't right. She deserves better." He winked and put out his fist for another bump, but Sean ignored it this time. "Anyways, we're cool, right?"

"Yeah, yeah, we're cool." Sean made himself speak those words because what else could he do? He didn't have any say in what Evie did or who she dated. But he walked through the rest of the firehouse tour like a zombie.

Evie was *dating*? Why hadn't she told him?

Of course she hadn't told him. He'd walked away from her and lost all right to know about her life. When a girl told you she loved you, and your only response was, "I'm sorry," you pretty much lost all say in her love life.

Love life.

He hated the sound of those words. How far was Evie planning to take this? Who was she going out with—the police officer who had written a poem about her pearly teeth? It could be anyone—half of Jupiter Point probably wanted to date her.

She'd put up all those emotional walls and he'd helped tear them down. And now she was dating.

Of course she would want to find someone else. She was a warm-hearted, caring, passionate, kind, sensitive woman who deserved to find true love. Her physical attractiveness was just icing on the cake. Her true beauty lay within. But would the "pearly teeth" guy even recognize that? Would all these dudes asking her out see her as the miraculous woman she was—or as some kind of trophy? Would any of them feel a fraction of what *he* felt for her?

~ ~ ~

Without bothering to say goodbye to Littleton, Sean left the firehouse and drove straight to the police department. As he walked through the bullpen area, he looked daggers at each police officer he passed. Which one was Evie going out with? The one who looked like a *GQ* model in blue? The good-looking Latino guy speaking rapid-fire Spanish into his phone? The one who looked like he could lift a Harley with each beefy arm?

When he reached Chief Becker's corner office, the man unfurled himself to his full six-foot-seven height and reached over the desk to shake his hand. "Good to see you, Marcus. You look like you've seen a ghost."

Sean raked a hand through his hair. "In a way."

"Sit down." Becker gestured him to a chair, but Sean couldn't bear to sit yet. The need to be doing something had transported him here. He didn't know exactly *what* to do, but here he was.

He paced back and forth in front of Becker's desk. "I don't want to take up your time. I just…I've been hearing some rumors about your guys."

"My guys?" Becker raised his eyebrows up to his grizzled hairline. "Someone doing something they shouldn't?"

"Yes. No. I mean, I'm sure they're doing their jobs just fine. Serve and protect. Solve crimes, keep Jupiter Point safe. All that."

"Uh-huh." Becker got that look Sean had seen on many a police officer's face, that wary, 'ready for whatever the crazy person might do' look. "I hope so. That's what we're paying them for."

"Yeah, but are you paying them to pester your female citizens?"

Becker walked to his office door and closed it. "What's on your mind, Marcus?"

"Word has it your officers are lining up to go out with Evie McGraw. I have to question their motives. As their superior, you should keep them under control. Tell them to back off. Evie's a sensitive person and she doesn't need a bunch of Neanderthals beating down her door. No offense."

"Oh really? What about *your* guys?" Becker folded his arms across his chest. "Are you going to tell them to back off?"

Sean came to an abrupt stop at the random spot he'd reached, halfway across the office. "*My* guys? What are you talking about?"

"I'm pretty sure that was your boy Josh Marshall I saw with Evie at the Orbit the other night, when I took my wife out for her birthday."

Josh and Evie…*dating*? "He wouldn't do that. He fucking wouldn't."

"That's between you and him. I'm just the police chief. And I'm pretty sure, no, almost a hundred percent sure," Becker scratched his head as if trying to remember some obscure police regulation, "that I have no say in who my subordinates go out to dinner with, or who they fall in love with, or who they marry."

"*Marry?*" Horror flashed through Sean with the force of a lightning bolt hitting an oak tree. "Who said anything about marrying?"

"That's generally what people do when they love each other. Unless they have problems with the institution or deep-seated issues they haven't worked through."

Sean stared at the older man, who seemed to be struggling to hold back a laugh. "You're saying I have issues?"

"You saying you don't?"

"You don't even know me."

"Boy, you put your fist in my face. I arrested you." He jabbed a finger in the air toward him. "I interrogated you. I listened to you rage in a jail cell all night. I investigated your parents' death. That means I investigated them and I investigated you. I *know* you."

Sean swallowed convulsively. That night in jail, he'd released years' worth of anger within those four walls. Becker had let him vent. Brought him a glass of water. Told him he'd get through it. Even though his jaw was swollen from Sean's punch, he'd treated him fairly.

He could trust this man.

"Fine," he said in a hoarse voice. "What issues do I have?"

Becker squinted at him. "Do I look like a therapist?"

"Is that some sort of game? You want me to say what my issues are? Well, fine, I don't think I have any. I'm my own person, and I'm nothing like my father. Duty, integrity, respect." He emphasized the words by pounding one fist into the opposite palm. "That's the hotshot motto, *that's* what I live by. It's the opposite of how Jesse lived. He lived for himself, and he wanted his family to be his fan club. Follow him everywhere. Laugh at his jokes. Like the things *he* liked. He didn't love us. He didn't love me. He just wanted a slave."

He stopped, breathing hard. He slid a glance at Becker, but like that night Sean had spent in jail, the man was just letting him vent.

"Jesse never listened to me. I told him he wasn't cut out to be a pilot. He barely had enough flight hours to get his license, let alone fly other people around. If he'd listened to me, just once, just one fucking time in his whole life, maybe he wouldn't have crashed. Unless he crashed on purpose, because he didn't want to go to j—"

The chief watched closely as Sean fought to get a grip on his emotions. When Sean said nothing more, Becker walked to his desk and picked up a fat olive-drab file folder.

"I took a look at the bank statements you gave me. Interesting stuff. I've had a detective digging around and our guess is there's money hidden somewhere. Not in here, though."

Sean frowned, not understanding.

"There's nothing in these accounts that would have sent Jesse Marcus to jail. And the crash wasn't his fault."

"*What?* Of course it was." Sean had never once questioned that. A momentary lapse in attention, a detail left unattended to, a desire to show off for his wife on their anniversary. He couldn't say exactly how it had happened, but he knew it had to be Jessie's doing.

"I gotta admit, I assumed it was, too, knowing Jesse Marcus. But after Brad White got the investigation reopened, I assigned one of my best detectives to it. He found a report from the NTSB that never got made public. Several fishermen reported unpredictable winds that day. They said it kept changing direction. The conditions weren't bad enough to ground a plane. But there's a good chance that wind shear brought it down. Investigators were leaning toward that conclusion, but didn't have enough evidence to make the call. So they left the final cause undetermined."

"They think it was wind shear?" Sean had been inside the school gym playing basketball when the crash happened, not monitoring the weather. He didn't remember anything about the wind conditions.

"Yeah, it's a sudden change in the direction of the wind—"

"I know. I know what it is."

"From what I've heard, it can happen to anyone," Becker added. "Not much he could have done."

Sean nodded slowly. Hotshots dealt with gusty, unpredictable winds all the time. They were a fact of life. If you got caught on the wrong side of a sudden change, you could pay with your life. None of this was news to him.

The possibility that a force of nature had taken his parents' lives and not some bad decision on Jesse's part?

Yeah, that actually was news.

"It's like anything," Becker was saying. "You do what you love and you take your chances."

"Uh-huh." Sean cleared his throat. He needed to think this through. For thirteen years he'd pinned the blame on his father. And no matter what had caused the crash, it didn't change anything. Jesse was still a selfish, controlling husband and father.

But maybe it *did* change things. Maybe Jesse wasn't as reckless as he'd thought. And maybe he could move forward now that he knew the truth.

"And listen, Sean. It says a lot that you brought this evidence in even though you didn't know how it would turn out. I respect that, son. You earned a lot of goodwill around here, for that and for everything else."

Respect. The word entered his bloodstream like a shot of B-12. Respect. That was all he'd ever wanted.

"So…anything else you wanted to discuss? You can take this file if you want. I told you the highlights but you might find it interesting. Seems the plane was perfectly maintained and mechanically sound. I was going to pass this on to the newspaper to see if they wanted to do one more write-up on the crash. Put all the rumors to rest. But if you want to look through it first, have at it."

Sean automatically took the folder. He imagined wading through all those reports in there, all those interviews and photographs and transcripts.

No. He had work to do, a crew to run—a future to claim.

He handed it back. "Think I'll pass. I appreciate it though. Thanks for filling me in."

"You got it. So what are you going to do with that piece of property? The old airstrip?"

"Brad White wants to buy it."

Becker nodded. "My gut tells me there's a reason for that. I wouldn't let him near it, if I were you."

Sean shoved his hands in his pockets. The same thought had occurred to him. Why had Brad wanted to blackmail him into selling it? There had be something going on under the surface. "Yeah, I think I'll hang on to it a while longer."

"Good. So, Marcus—I don't want to rush you, but if you want to catch Evie before Officer Blaine picks her up for dinner at the Seaview, you'd better run." Becker gave him a ghost of a wink.

"Officer Blaine, huh?" Sean's eyes narrowed. "What's his story?"

"Ninety percent clearance rate. Never married. Keeps a picture of his nephews on his desk. Even-tempered, methodical. That's about all I can tell you."

For no real reason, Sean already hated the guy. He didn't have an embarrassing divorce in his background, he was into kids. Even-tempered…Evie could also be described as even-tempered. She and Officer Blaine were probably a perfect match.

He reached the truck and realized he didn't even remember saying goodbye to Becker.

In the sky above, long streaks of blood orange and apricot lit up the underside of the clouds. A beautiful Jupiter Point sunset. The terrace at the Seaview Inn was probably jam-packed with honeymooners sipping cocktails and holding hands.

Maybe Evie was already there with Officer Blaine. He pictured her sitting at one of the Inn's white-linen-covered tables, the candlelight turning her eyes silver. She'd be listening to Blaine's police work stories with her full attention, in that way of hers. Blaine was probably telling her—methodically—how beautiful she was and how much he loved children.

Evie.

He wanted her. More than he'd ever wanted anything or anyone in his life. And he was a stubborn jackass for not admitting it until now.

Chapter 32

Sean drove back to the base in a fog. The first person he laid eyes on was Josh, who was busy setting up the new gas grill they'd just acquired.

"Magneto, where the hell have you been? We're thinking cookout to kick off the season."

Sean suddenly remembered that he hated Josh. He strode up to him, chest to chest. "Why'd you take Evie out, you asshole?"

Josh held up a spatula in self-defense. "I didn't. She took *me* out."

"What is that supposed to mean? Why would she take you out?"

Josh stepped behind the grill, so it separated them. "You seem upset, Sean." His teasing tone made Sean want to inflict actual damage on him. "The last I heard, you and Evie were through. What's it to you who she goes out with?"

The look on Sean's face, which must have been terrifying, made him raise the spatula again, this time in surrender.

"I helped Evie out with some stuff for her mother. She needed a new ramp for the back porch but none of them are all that handy with power tools. When we were done, we went for a bite to eat. There was something I wanted to talk to her about."

"What?" The pit in Sean's stomach made no sense. Why would it matter to him what Josh and Evie talked about? As long as it didn't involve kissing…or touching…or… "What did you talk about?"

"It's personal." The unusually serious look on his friend's face made Sean even more worried.

"We're like brothers, man. What can you talk about with Evie that you can't tell me?"

"Look, asshole." Josh stopped hiding behind the grill and came around to face Sean. "I'm only going to tell you this because you clearly have it bad for Evie and don't know what the hell to do about it. But you can't say anything. Not one word, not to anyone. I was talking to Evie about her cousin. That's it. That's all I'm saying."

"Her cousin?" Feeling slow-witted, Sean searched his mind for the other time Suzanne's name had come up that day. "The one who just got engaged?"

With a scathing look, Josh turned back to the grill and pressed the primer button.

Oh. *Ohhh.* Josh had a thing for Suzanne? Sheer relief made Sean let out a laugh. He was an idiot. Of course his brother in arms wouldn't stab him in the back and go after Evie. That wasn't Josh's style. He was getting paranoid. He really needed to get a grip on himself. He couldn't keep acting crazy like this.

Josh released the button and a flame ignited in the depths of the grill. "Sean, did it ever occur to you that if you want Evie, you actually need to go get her? And if you don't, someone else probably will?"

"You can go back to worrying about your own love life," Sean grumbled. "I'm good now."

"Yeah, but is *she*? She told me that her whole attitude is different now. Now that she's broken away from the whole Brad situation, she's ready and eager to see what's out there."

"I'll tell her exactly what's out there—" He glanced up at the hills where the Seaview was located. A halo of reddish light glowed above the darkening slopes. He squinted, trying to bring it into focus.

Josh followed his glance. "Sunset glow?"

"It's about the same color. Maybe it's reflecting off the clouds."

"Yeah." Both of them fell silent, watching the light. If it was a refraction of the fading rays of the sun, it would die out very soon. It was nearly night already. If it was more than that...

"Maybe I should call Littleton," Sean said uneasily. "At least check with dispatch. Keep an eye on it, would you?"

Josh nodded as Sean jogged toward fire dispatch, which was staffed twenty-four hours a day. If it was an early brushfire, the Jupiter Point FD would check it out first, then call it in if they needed more resources.

Just in case, he put a call in to Chief Littleton to let him know the hotshots stood ready.

~ ~ ~

Evie dragged a steamed mussel through the pool of white wine and butter sauce on her plate. She was determined to wring every ounce of enjoyment out of this dinner. If it had to come from the deliciousness of the food rather than the man across the table, so be it. She'd take what she could get.

"So this guy, after I collared him, he started yelling, 'I want my nanny.' I thought he meant Mommy, but that wasn't it. He wanted his damn nanny."

Evie frowned at Danny Blaine, who was so clean-cut he could have been chiseled from a bar of soap. "I don't understand. Was he still a kid? Why did he have a nanny?"

"Got me."

"You never asked what he meant?"

"Nope. It sounded like a 'don't ask, don't tell' kind of situation, if you know what I mean."

Evie nodded wisely, even though she really didn't see the point of the story. Where was the payoff? Whatever. It didn't matter. She was *dating.* She was *getting out there.* This was what Brianna, Suzanne and Merry had meant when they'd all met at the Venus and Mars Cafe the other day.

"It doesn't matter if it's fun," Brianna had insisted. "Think of it as shaking the rust off."

"Kind of like WD-40," Suzanne agreed. "Like we used to use on our bicycle chains."

"I refuse to think of a man as a can of WD-40." Evie had to draw the line somewhere.

Brianna snickered. "I'm trying so hard not to say the word 'lubricate' right now."

Everyone groaned and Suzanne pretended to throttle her. "That's a terrible comparison anyway," said Merry. "I like to treat dates like research. It's all about observation. You seek out all the little details that tell you who a person really is."

"No, no, no. Your approach is all wrong, Merry, which is probably why you're still single." Suzanne shifted her right hand so her engagement ring caught the light. She'd been doing that nonstop since she and Logan had announced their engagement. "Evie's not writing an article, she's trying to find her soul mate."

"I thought you didn't believe in soul mates," said Evie. "That's why you got engaged to Logan."

"Ohh, burn." Brianna, wide-eyed, sucked down half her iced latte.

"No no, she's right. I don't believe in soul mates—for me. I'm more practical. I'm marrying Logan because he's exactly what I've always wanted in a husband." Suzanne turned to Evie. "But you're a different kind of person. Really, you're a romantic at heart, Evie."

Everyone had agreed with that, no matter how much Evie protested. Since when was she a romantic? She'd just spent the past thirteen years avoiding close relationships. She was the opposite of romantic.

Now, gazing across the table at Danny Blaine's warm brown eyes, she tried to think like Merry. Details. Research. She made mental notes on what she'd noticed about him so far. He was very organized. He'd given the waiter a rough schedule of when the main course should arrive and how long they should wait before dessert.

Well organized. That was good. She appreciated a well-organized person. Although insisting on finishing every bite of steak before moving on to the potatoes seemed a little rigid.

"Can I ask you something, Evie?" Danny asked.

"Of course."

"Why did you finally say yes to me? I kept a running tally of how many times I asked you out. I was up to eight. I was honestly pretty shocked when you called me back."

That was definitely true, based on the lengthy silence that had greeted her call. "Well, I guess I was focusing on other areas of my life."

"And that's one of the qualities I find appealing about you. You're a successful businesswoman. That takes discipline and perseverance. You're living your dream because of all your hard work. Hard work is the key to success."

Hard-working.

"Mm, hmmm." She popped another mussel in her mouth and savored the flavor. "Actually, owning the gallery was never my dream. I had a different dream. I wanted to travel the world and take photographs everywhere I went."

"Is that right?" He made a little face that showed he didn't think much of that idea. "I think you made the right choice. The only reason to travel is that it makes you appreciate how good we have it here."

Unimaginative. She imagined writing that down in a little notebook like one of Merry's. "Well, I guess I wouldn't know. I haven't been anywhere besides Jupiter Point."

"And that's another thing I like about you. You stayed close to home, close to your roots. That's how it should be. Family first, don't you agree?"

"To be honest, I think it depends. Everyone's different. My brother would have gone crazy if he'd stayed here." Not to mention Sean Marcus. If he'd stayed…

Stop thinking about Sean.

Evie pushed her mussel shells to the side of her plate. Everything she hated about dating came rushing back to her. The tedium of stilted conversation. Biding her time until she could gracefully leave. Fear of hurting someone's feelings by revealing her lack of interest.

"Some people are more different than others." Danny smoothed his neatly trimmed moustache. "Me, I like to stick with what I know. Jupiter Point, born and bred, no plans to go anywhere else. Although if you pushed me, I might make an exception for a cruise."

She smiled sweetly at him. "You mean those cruises where you eat all your meals onboard and only get off to pick up some souvenirs?"

"Yes, that sounds about right. Now that, to me, is a nice honeymoon. Relaxing, stress-free, clean. Everyone speaks English. I heard you can get anything you want on those cruise ships. All the food you can eat, games, shows…" As he rattled on about the glorious features of cruises, Evie cast a desperate glance around the restaurant.

Wasn't there anyone here who could rescue her? She hadn't set up an escape call this time, because her friends had accused her of not giving her dates a chance. Well, she was giving Danny a chance and he was droning on about Princess versus Norwegian Cruise Lines, and how a Caribbean cruise was on his bucket list.

You know what was on her bucket list? Getting out of here with her sanity intact! Maybe she could make a call. Or pretend to get a call. Or throw herself through the plate-glass picture window that looked out on the terrace. If only something would save her, anything...

The terrace...something was going on out there. She squinted past the reflections moving across the glass. Everyone was crowded to one side of the terrace and pointing toward the hills. She craned her neck to see what they were looking at, but couldn't get a good angle on it.

Danny's phone beeped. "This only rings for emergencies," he told her as he pulled out his cell phone. A frown gathered on his square forehead. "Yeah, I'm here at the Seaview. What's going on?" He listened, nodding, to the rapid-fire voice on the other end.

When he hung up, he was all business. "We have to evacuate the Seaview. There's a brushfire one hill over."

"Oh my gosh." Suddenly, her desire to end the date suddenly seemed trivial compared to an emergency. "How can I help?"

"The best thing you can do is follow my orders."

Evie tried not to feel put in her place. Danny beckoned to the manager, who hurried over to their table. As Danny filled him in, Evie's own phone buzzed.

It was her father on the line. "I don't like interrupting your date, Evangaline, but your mother's getting agitated. We've heard some sirens and people shouting outside and she's becoming quite distressed."

"I'll be there as soon as possible," she promised. "Make her some chamomile tea and tell her I'm on my way."

It was only after she'd hung up that she realized she didn't have her own car, since Danny had picked her up. Her stomach tightened as she pictured her mother getting more and more upset and stressed. She tapped Danny's shoulder, but he was already gearing up to address the diners.

"Attention, Seaview guests. I'm Officer Blaine from the Jupiter Point PD. It looks like dinner is going to have to end early. There's a small brushfire within about two miles of here. The fire department has requested that we evacuate this restaurant as a precaution. There's no need for concern. The most important thing is to stay calm and execute an orderly exit from the premises. I need everyone here to do exactly what I say."

Even though his tone was calm, it inspired a cacophony of worried questions and chairs scraping across the floor.

"I said orderly!" Danny yelled. "That means please follow my orders!"

"Danny." Evie tugged on his arm again. "Can I help?" The sooner they got the place evacuated, the sooner she could get to her mother.

"Yes, you can talk some sense into these people." He dug into his pocket. "Actually, there is something you can do. Set an example and head in an orderly manner to the parking lot. Take my car." He pulled out his keys and handed them to Evie. "Take my Tacoma and lead the way down the hill."

She stared at the keys—her ticket back to her mother's side. "But how will you get back?"

"There are emergency vehicles on the way. Don't worry about me, this is my job. Just go."

Evie had to admit that Danny Blaine was a lot more appealing when he was taking charge. She leaned up and kissed him on the cheek.

"Thank you. You're a good man. Stay safe."

His face twisted. "That doesn't feel like the kiss of attraction."

She bit her lip, because of course he was right. There was only one man she wanted to kiss on the lips. But he wanted nothing to do with her.

"I'm sorry." Which was exactly what Sean had said to her after that passionate kiss at the gallery.

When would Sean Marcus get out of her mind once and for all?

She palmed Danny's keys and walked as calmly as she could manage toward the exit. Outside, she smelled a warning in the night air. Warm, slightly smoky, animated by a rising wind. She picked up her pace, careful to maintain an "orderly" appearance for the steady stream of exiting diners. Everyone was pointing to the red haze lighting up the clouds over the next hill.

She found Danny's Toyota Tacoma, and hopped inside. She rolled down the window as she drove through the lot toward the exit road. "Don't forget—keep it orderly!"

A man in the red car next to her rolled down his window. "We don't have a choice. The road's jammed up. No one's going anywhere. This is a fricking mess!"

Crap! Evie craned her neck to see up ahead. The man was right. A sea of red brake lights and bumpers clogged the exit. It looked like the kind of traffic jam you might see in a city.

Her phone beeped again. Her father had texted, *She threw off her blankets and I can't keep her in bed. She keeps asking for you.*

Evie stared at the mess up ahead. Surely other police officers would arrive to help direct traffic. The line of cars would start making their way down the hill, one by one. But how long would that take? In the meantime, her mother needed her. She couldn't just sit here and wait. Danny had told her to be orderly and set an example.

Well, screw that.

Decision made, she tapped the accelerator and turned the Tacoma toward the back road, the one she'd used to deliver mulch for Brianna. The turnoff was tucked behind a tall grove of cypresses at the back of the terrace. With a quick glance, she saw that diners were still crowding the terrace—Danny's orderly evacuation didn't seem to be going as planned.

She nosed the Tacoma down the road and the terrace, restaurant and gardens quickly disappeared from sight. The road curved around the steep hillside. To the left was a dark scrubby slope, to the right a sweeping view of the shoreline and the low-lumen lights of Jupiter Point. She ignored both, keeping her eyes on the gravel road illuminated by the Tacoma's headlights.

The road was much bumpier than she remembered. When was

the last time it was graded? She hadn't been down this road in four years. Wasn't it maintained anymore? She hit a pothole that jarred the entire vehicle, and cursed under her breath.

Maybe she should go back and join the traffic jam instead. But the road was too narrow to turn around easily. With a shudder, she imagined accidentally backing the Tacoma off the edge onto the steep downward slope.

Nope. It was much better to just keep going. Get off this hill and to her mother, as soon as could be.

Thinking of her mother, she unconsciously picked up speed. The road seemed to improve, and she relaxed, rolling her neck to release the tension.

And then came a sharp left-hand curve. She almost missed it, then yanked the steering wheel just in time. The Tacoma skidded on the gravel, the tires spinning as they lost purchase.

Fighting to keep control, she fishtailed across the road. One side, then the other, and then—*slam.*

The back of the truck went *crunch*—into a pothole?— and the engine stalled out.

She jerked backward, her head slamming against the head rest.

For a moment she stayed right where she was. Adrenaline pounded through her. That pothole must be huge. It had practically swallowed up the vehicle, like a sinkhole. Should she get out of the car and check it out? Try to restart the engine? She whooshed out several deep breaths and picked up her cell phone. She should call Danny…but no, he was in the middle of evacuating a restaurant.

Carefully she got out of the Tacoma and surveyed the

situation. The rear left tire was so deep in a cavernous pothole that the bumper was twisted up like a snarling mouth. No way was it going to be able to drive anywhere.

She pulled out her phone to let Danny know what had happened. It seemed very wrong to bother him when he had a whole inn full of people to juggle. But it was his truck and he might be interested to know it was stuck on the back road. As she started to dial, one side of the pothole collapsed and the truck settled even deeper into the road.

Oh great.

She sniffed the air. Gas.

She took a step back, then another, and then—she was flying backwards on a blast of light and sound.

Chapter 33

The road to the Seaview was a mess. Sean had to drive half on the shoulder, half on the upslope to make it past the bottleneck of vehicles. As soon as dispatch told him the JPFD was checking out the fire, he'd called Chief Littleton and offered their help.

"It's small, Type Four, nothing we can't handle. Looks bigger than it is because of the overcast."

"Come on, Chief. You expect us to sit on our hands out here watching you guys do all the work? Give us something."

"Fine. Get on out to the Seaview and help the PD evacuate the place. It's just a precaution but he could use a couple extra hands out there. Traffic's clogged up."

"Sure thing. Who's in charge up there?"

"Officer Blaine. He happened to be there on a date, go figure."

Evie.

Maybe it was petty of him, but he was almost relieved that her big date was being interrupted by an evacuation. As Sean worked the Super Duty through the mess of cars, he kept a careful eye out for Evie. As soon as he saw her, he'd tell her...

Forget telling. He'd just haul her up against him and kiss her. Kisses said more than words ever could.

The scene in the parking lot was even more chaotic, with so many vehicles trying to leave at once. A bottleneck had developed at the entrance of the lot. An older man in a Camry was yelling at a car full of teenagers. A young mother was trying to soothe her sobbing baby. No one seemed to be in charge, so Sean told Josh to go play traffic cop at the main parking lot exit.

"Shouldn't we check in with Blaine first?"

"I'll do that. We don't want things getting out of hand out here."

With a nod, Josh did as Sean directed. With Rollo following behind, he ran into the inn to look for Officer Blaine.

Inside, more chaos reigned. Confused guests argued with an overwhelmed-looking manager at the reception desk. Sean caught raised voices, an edge of panic, a buzz of confusion.

Finally he found Blaine outside on the terrace, trying to herd the guests inside. Most of them seemed more interested in taking photos of the glow on the hillside. It was definitely something to see. Wisps of smoke drifted across the valley between the Seaview's hill and the next rise. The low overcast flickered with a deep crimson light.

"Chief Littleton sent us," Sean told the police officer. He tried to block out the fact that this young, good-looking guy had dared to take his Evie out to dinner. "How can we help? I got one of my guys directing cars out in the lot."

"Good, that works." Blaine glanced at the hillside. "Do you

think it's going to make it this far?"

Sean checked the direction of the wind, sniffed the light scent of burning pines. "Hard to say. The wind is dying down, so that's good. I checked a map and there are several roads between here and there. With luck, it won't jump any of them."

"Amen to that. Okay, since you guys are the firefighters, how about you two check the premises for any potential gas leaks or other hazards while I handle crowd control?"

"Roger that." Sean gave a little salute and he and Rollo headed back toward the interior of the inn. "Kitchen first, I think—"

Boom!

The sound of an explosion ripped his thought in half. "What the hell—"

"That sounded like a gas explosion." Rollo ran back to the terrace and leaned over the balustrade to search for signs of fire. "I don't think it was here, though."

"Parking lot?" Sean clicked his comm to call Josh. "Everything okay out there?"

"Yup. No exploding vehicles. Sounds like it came from down the backside of the hill."

Officer Blaine got off his phone and raised his voice to penetrate through the din of alarmed chatter. "Please remain calm, everyone. The Seaview has not sustained any damage. The evacuation is still underway. Please follow directions and do exactly as you are told."

He gestured to Sean and Rollo. "That includes you two. I want this place checked in the next ten minutes so we can shut it down."

Sean nodded. He wanted desperately to ask where Evie was, but managed to refrain. She was probably somewhere in that traffic bottleneck. Although he hadn't seen her, and he'd been looking…

Followed by Rollo, he ran into the kitchen, where an alert waiter was already shutting down the gas line.

"Good man," Sean told him. "You're a step ahead of us."

"Did you hear that explosion?" The young waiter's hands were shaking. "I was afraid the kitchen would be next."

"Do you know where it happened?"

The waiter pointed toward a door at the far end of the kitchen. "Sounded like it came from that direction. There's a road back there."

"The back road? The one that curves past all those overlooks?"

"Yeah. Hardly anyone uses it anymore."

Sean glanced at Rollo, knowing they were thinking the same thing. If someone had driven down that way, they were probably on their own. The emergency workers had their hands full here.

"You should go join that mob trying to get down the hill," Sean told the waiter. "We can take it from here."

The waiter nodded with relief and headed for the door.

"Wait," Sean called after him. "Was Evie McGraw here tonight?"

"Yeah, she had dinner with that cop. But I think she already left. He told her to take off when he first got the call. She would have gone down the main road, that's where the officer was sending people."

An uneasy feeling settled into Sean's gut. He'd scanned every car they'd passed on the way to the Seaview and he hadn't seen her. He'd looked for her in the parking lot and inside the restaurant. No sign of her anywhere.

He pulled out his phone and dialed her number. No answer.

Uneasiness gave way to dread. Had Evie taken the back road, despite Blaine's instructions?

He knew his Evie. She wasn't always the rule-follower everyone thought.

He bolted for the back door. "I gotta go."

Rollo grabbed his arm, jerking him to a stop. "What about Blaine? The PD's in charge and they told us to do a safety check."

"Tell him I went down the back road to check out the explosion."

"Isn't Vargas still all over your ass? Better do what the locals say."

Sean forced words out of his suddenly tight throat. "Evie knows that back road."

Finally Rollo understood and let him go. "I'll handle things here. Go." He pushed him out the door.

Sean ran across the back lawn. Blaine was the least of his worries. Vargas was maybe the second to least. They could demote him, fire him—hell, kick him out of the fire service. The whole town could say it was one more Marcus fuckup. And he wouldn't care. The only thing that mattered right now was Evie.

Outside, he ran for the trail he'd taken the last time he was here, when he'd been following Evie after she fled her disastrous dinner with Brad. He pounded downhill until he saw the back road.

He leaped over a rosebush and scrambled through some hedge whose fragrance reminded him of that night with Evie. Stumbling as he landed, he barely kept himself from doing a header onto the gravel. *Run, run.*

He launched himself down the road. When he rounded the next curve, he spotted a small column of smoke rising into the air. From the smell of it, it wasn't a brushfire. He'd sniffed a thousand brushfires in his lifetime and knew the aroma well. He could identify the makeup of the forest—birch, pine, juniper—from the odor of its smoke. This smoke didn't come from wood. It came from man-made materials—steel and plastic and fabric. It came from a car.

Faster, faster. Like some kind of hurdling champion, he leaped past potholes and patches of gravel as he careened down the road. Smoke stung his eyes and seared his lungs.

Finally, he spotted the wreck. The burning frame of an SUV filled the center of the road, a flaming skeleton pouring smoke and licks of flame into the night air. It looked almost demonic, a metallic skeleton.

Evie didn't drive an SUV. This wasn't her cute little white Jetta. For a moment, relief flooded him. Someone had wrecked their car, but it wasn't her. He ran closer, covering his mouth with his elbow to protect his lungs from the hot, smoky air. He scanned the terrain—scrub-covered hillside to the east, a downslope to the west, vegetation interspersed with bare rock.

A dark figure lay sprawled along the side of the road. He jogged toward it, blinking away smoke fumes. As he got closer, he switched on his head lamp and played the beam across the victim.

A woman, tall, dark-haired…*oh my God.*

His heart beating like a snare drum, he turned the victim's head to feel her pulse, and saw her face. *Evie.*

Shoving down his sheer automatic terror, he checked her pulse. Strong. She was alive. Unconscious, but alive. He ran his hands over her, checking for other injuries. Nothing obvious jumped out, but she could have internal injuries, wounds he couldn't see, a concussion. He grabbed his comm. "Josh, I have Evie down here on the back road. She's unconscious and possibly injured. I have to get her medevacked out."

"On it."

Sean hunched over Evie, shielding her from the heat pulsing from the smoldering vehicle. He should get her farther away. What if there was more fuel waiting to ignite? Moving her was a risk, but so was leaving her. *Shit.* He smoothed the hair away from her face. God, what he wouldn't give to see her smile right now.

"I'm sorry," he whispered. "I'm sorry I ever let you go, even for a second."

Lovely and still, her face displayed no response.

"Please, Evie." He cupped her cheek, willing her to wake up. "It's Sean. The idiot who's completely in love with you but didn't know how to say it. Please, wake up."

A blast of hot air grabbed his attention. He looked up and saw that a patch of scrub grass had caught a spark from the SUV fire and was now burning merrily away.

"Evie, I have to leave you for a second. I'll be right back." He set her back down and ran to the patch of grass. Stomping it with his boots, he chased down every smoldering blade until nothing was left burning. He turned back to Evie.

Shit. Another fire had sprung up, even closer to her. And a third, just past her. The breeze must be carrying sparks from the vehicle to the grassy margin. He quickly called Josh again as he dashed back to her, leapfrogging over the flames between them. Crouching down, he gathered her into his arms.

He rose to his feet, grunting under the dead weight of an unconscious woman. Now what? Fires crackled on both sides, consuming fuel like young demons released from hell. He could try to run through the flames and down the road. He was wearing his Nomex pants and a padded jacket, but Evie had nothing like that. The wind was picking up, but its direction was variable. Now it seemed to be heading straight down the road, but in the next instant it was pushing flames down the hillside.

He had to make a decision. *Now.*

He tightened his grip on her limp body and hunched around her so that his fireproof jacket protected them both as much as possible. Then he plunged between the smoldering vehicle and the fire crackling through the grass. Sparks landed in Evie's hair but he batted them away. *Go, go, go.* Past the flames, down the road.

Carrying Evie in his arms, he jogged around a curve in the rutted road. He couldn't go far while holding her like this. It was probably ten miles to the end of the road. His thigh muscles burned, his lungs heaved. Evie's weight seemed to get heavier and more awkward. He needed to find some kind of shelter in case the flames did the unpredictable.

A roar from behind him grabbed his attention. He looked back. *Holy shit*. The fire was really going now, eating through the dry brush along the side of the road. It would probably spread to the downslope next. The entire hillside would catch fire. And maybe the other side of the road would be next. There was no way he could outrun it.

He flashed on Finn, who had taken shelter in a gravel stream bed. This back road, even badly maintained, was pretty similar to a stream bed. Gravel and dirt, clear of all vegetation. It was their best chance right now.

If only he had his fire shelter with him.

But he had his fireproof jacket, and maybe that would be enough. As the flames leaped and danced only a few feet away, he lowered Evie to the ground. He took off his jacket and nudged her into a fetal position, then covered her with his own body. He curled tight around her, like a football he'd just intercepted. He made his own body as small as possible and pulled his jacket over both of them. He tried to pin it to the ground the way he would with his aluminum shelter, but it wasn't quite big enough.

He took shallow breaths of the heated air. If they were in the heart of a wildfire with nothing but a jacket for protection, they'd be doomed. But this fire was just getting started, and they were smack in the middle of the road. There was limited fuel out there. Once the flames passed, they'd be okay…

Please, Lord, let Evie be okay.

The crunch and crackle of the flames just outside made the hair on the back of his neck rise. The smell of burning sagebrush mingled with the scent of Evie's hair under his nose.

Once again, there he was in the middle of a burnover. This time, Evie's life was in his hands. He'd die before he let that fire get her. He squeezed his eyes shut and huddled in a tight ball over her unconscious body.

During the Big Canyon burnover, all kinds of crazy thoughts had gone through his brain. His family, his past, his need to set things right, all of it coalescing into one conviction: he had to go back to Jupiter Point.

Now, only one thought pounded through his brain. *Save Evie. Love Evie. Evie, Evie, Evie…*

As if the power of his plea reached from his cranium to hers, she stirred underneath him and moaned.

"Evie, sweetheart, it's Sean," he whispered, trying to keep his voice as calm and even as possibly. "I'm here. I'm right on top of you."

"What…?" All her muscles tensed as she regained consciousness. She tried to lift her head, but he used gentle pressure to hold it close to the ground.

"Listen to me and *don't move*. Do you trust me?" He felt her nod. "You were knocked unconscious. Your gas tank must have gotten damaged when you hit the sinkhole."

"D…Danny's car." She still sounded confused.

"Right. Danny's car. Thank God you weren't still inside it. I found you about ten yards away from it. The explosion triggered a brushfire. You can smell it and hear it, right?"

"Oh my…God." She struggled against him again. "My

mom…"

"You have to trust me," he said firmly. "We're in the safest possible place for now. We're in the middle of the road and we're covered by my jacket. It's fire resistant. You need to keep your face close to the ground because that's where the cleanest air will be. You have to stay still because if you stick an arm out or a leg, you might catch a spark. Think of us as a turtle hiding in its shell. You're the turtle, I'm the shell."

After a long moment, she gave a breathless little laugh. His spirits lifted at the sound. If she could laugh, maybe they had a chance—as long as the fire didn't get them.

"Tell me if I'm squashing you too much. I can give you a little more space, but you have to promise not to panic or make any moves at all."

Her breath came in quick little pants, but she did as he said. With her face to the ground, slowly she relaxed and lay quietly under him.

"Good girl," he murmured. "I'm seriously impressed. Not many people would wake up in the middle of a brushfire and keep their cool."

"How…long…will it take?"

"Most likely just a few minutes. This isn't yet a fully engaged brushfire, luckily. I've notified Josh and they should be sending some backup down here."

"There was a fire in the hills…"

"Yup, they're on it. Apparently someone's campfire got out of control."

She fell quiet, and for a moment, the only sound came from outside their little shelter. The hisses and crackles sounded almost conspiratorial, as if the flames were plotting with each other.

"Why are you even here?" she asked finally.

"I just had a feeling you might have come this way. I'm supposed to be back at the Seaview assisting with the evacuation. But once we heard the explosion and I realized you might have driven down this road, I had to come after you."

He felt her warm breath drift against his hand. "You saved my life."

"Just one more impossible situation." He murmured the wry words into her hair. The soft strands brushed against his lips. "I have a way with those."

"You came after me. You're my turtle shell. You're risking yourself for my sake." She trembled underneath him. Her warm body, sheltered in the nest of his arms and torso, felt like...like everything. Like life itself. Like everything he ever needed or wanted, curled up in a ball under his protective crouch.

Just a few feet away, the fire was building momentum, cackling like a mad alchemist, turning live plants into smoke and debris. If he didn't tell Evie how he felt now, he might never have another chance.

"I could say it's my job. But that's not the whole truth," he whispered to her. "The truth is, you are my life."

She tried to turn her head again, but he stopped her.

"Let me finish. Keep breathing that nice air so you can hear this. I love you. You're the only one for me. You're the one who sets me on fire. Who lights my way. You're the one who makes life mean something. I want to be with you, only you."

"But you said…'I'm sorry.'" She gave a little hiccup of a sob. "I thought we were through."

"I know what I said, and I was an idiot. I couldn't admit how hard I'd fallen for you. I've had all this shit hanging over me from the past, and I didn't want to mess up your life with it. And you were right. I was afraid. I haven't had feelings like this for anyone before."

"And now?"

"I'm not afraid. And I'm not going anywhere. Not without you."

Her body trembled again and he tightened his hold on her. "I can't leave Jupiter Point."

"Sweetheart, right now, you can't leave this road. Neither of us can."

They both laughed. Crazy to be having this conversation while a fire raged around them. He lifted his head, listening to the flames. The crackling sound had lost its energy. He no longer felt such intense heat on the part of his butt that wasn't covered by his jacket. "I think the fire might by dying out. Stay right where you are."

Cautiously, he lifted one edge of his jacket and peeked out. The moon lit up an eerie landscape of gray smoke and charred hillside.

"It moved past us," he whispered.

"So we can go?"

"I think so, but let me make sure it's safe first."

As he made a move to get up, she gripped his arm. "Do we have to go anywhere? I kind of like it here with you."

He laughed, releasing all the fear and tension of the last hour. They were okay. And they were together. "It's definitely the best burnover I've ever experienced." He lowered his head to rain kisses onto her cheek. "I still have to make sure you weren't injured in the explosion, so please don't move."

"I won't move. I trust you, Sean."

I trust you. That was a start, but he wanted much more from Evie. First, though, he had to get them to safety.

He pushed back the jacket and raised his head. Smoke blew right in his eyes; the wind had shifted again so it was blowing toward them. That was actually a good thing; the fire had already burned through the fuel behind them.

He uncoiled himself from his hunched position and sat back. All his muscles burned and complained, but his heart sang with relief.

He helped Evie sit up. "Does anything hurt?"

She brushed gravel from her cheek. "Probably just about everything, but right now, absolutely nothing." A smile brighter than the moon spread across her face. "We made it. Thanks to you."

"We made it," he agreed, savoring every detail of her tousled, gritty appearance. He fingered a lock of her hair, noticing the burnt end where a spark had landed. "Can I just ask you one question?"

"Of course."

"Do I still have a chance with you? Or did I ruin everything by being such an ass?"

She cocked her head, looking dreamily into the distance, as if weighing the options. "Well, on the one hand, you broke my heart and forced me to start dating, which you know I detest. So that's definitely a big black mark against you. On the other hand, you saved my life. There's also the little fact that I'm—" She broke off and tugged her lower lip between her teeth, tears filling her eyes. "The fact that I'm completely and utterly in love with you. So I guess, all things considered, you didn't ruin anything."

On his knees, he took her face between his hands—it felt like the most precious thing in the world. Their lips joined in a kiss so soft and tender, every barrier between them vanished like a wisp of smoke.

"Thank you," he whispered. "I love you, and I won't be so stupid again."

She smiled against his lips. "That's quite a promise."

"I won't be so stupid about *you*. You think you hated dating? Imagine how it was for me *hearing* about you dating."

"Aw, poor baby." Laughing, she nipped at his lower lip. "At least I had steamed mussels and tiramisu to make up for it."

He jumped to his feet and put out his hand to help her up. "Dammit, as soon as we get back to a scanner, I'm putting the word out. You're with me. The rest of Jupiter Point can just get used to it."

As she gained her feet, she wavered, holding tight to his forearm. "Is everything spinning or is it just me?"

"You might have a concussion. Hang on." He checked her pupils. Same size, not dilated. "You're probably still in shock. Give yourself a moment to adjust."

"Yes, I'm definitely in shock. Sean Marcus telling me he loves me? That's a bigger shock than an exploding car." The mischievous gleam in her glorious silver eyes made him grin.

"If you can make fun of me, I think you'll be okay. Try taking a step forward."

She carefully put one foot in front of the other, then looked at him in triumph. "I'm totally fine. Nothing really hurts! Either I'm so happy I'm feeling no pain, or I got really lucky. Or both."

He wrapped one arm around her for added support, thinking that "lucky" didn't even begin to describe it. They'd both gotten incredibly lucky. He made a vow to never forget how close he'd come to losing Evie. To losing the love of his life.

"Up or down?" He glanced both directions. The roadside fire had lost most of its energy and now existed only as sparks and flickers in the grass. The Tacoma still smoldered, a column of black rising into the sky. They could hike back up the road to the Seaview; it wasn't far, but it was all uphill. Or they could make their way down the road.

Evie tugged at his arm and gestured toward the sky. The smoke had cleared enough to unveil the points of light scattered across the velvet darkness.

"Any minute now, someone will come," she said softly. "Let's just take a breath for a moment. You know what we say here in Jupiter Point. Remember to look up at the stars."

He did the Jupiter Point thing and glanced up at the sky. But its stunning beauty didn't hold him for long. He turned his gaze to her instead. To the woman he wanted beside him for the rest of eternity. "That's nice, but I have something even better to look at, babe."

She smiled and rested her head against his chest. "Do burnovers always make you so romantic?"

"I'm a rough-and-tough firefighter. Only one thing can make me romantic. You."

He wrapped his arms around her and breathed in the smoky, citrus scent of her hair. He caught the sound of an engine approaching. Help was on the way. His hotshots, or other Jupiter Point first responders, or maybe a volunteer. And that's when it struck him.

This was his place. He belonged here, in this town, with this woman.

So he did look up at the stars. And he promised to remember.

Chapter 34

"I present to you…the Jupiter Point Hotshots. Our mission is to provide a professional, mobile, highly skilled crew for all phases of fire management, here and elsewhere. In other words, to keep as many people as possible safe from wildfires. Our motto is Duty, Integrity, and Respect." Sean stepped back and joined hands with the other crew members.

"And fun," added Josh, with a wink.

Evie watched in delight as the crew members lifted their arms in the air and whooped. The lineup of rugged, ripped, attractive men—and one woman—was downright dazzling. Like a smorgasbord of fitness and insane physiques.

None of them could compare to Sean, of course.

If anyone in town had harbored doubts about Sean Marcus, those doubts vanished after he saved her from the fire behind the Seaview. His hotshots were also feeling the love after they helped beat back the brushfire started by the campfire. In the season's first scare, no lives had been lost, no property damaged.

Well, except for Danny's car.

At first Officer Blaine had made noises about how Sean had disobeyed his orders and ought to be reported to his superiors. But Chief Becker must have put a stop to that pretty quick. Sean was pretty much a local hero these days.

Everywhere he went in Jupiter Point, someone wanted to shake his hand. It didn't seem to bother him to be in the spotlight. Evie thought he was adapting well to his new status. Or maybe he was just adapting well to his new life in general. He was with her now, heart, soul and body. He'd sold his house in Colorado and planned to move in with her when the fire season ended.

She'd promised to tidy up before then.

Evie had never imagined so much happiness would come her way. Life with Sean promised to be one long adventure. After the fire season, she intended to close the gallery for a month so they could travel together. Hunter would be back by then and could provide backup care for their mother. She and Sean planned to start in the Himalayas and go from there.

The crowd applauded as Sean broke a ceremonial champagne bottle over a chainsaw.

"We've got the grill going, we have hot dogs and soda, enough potato salad to feed the entire state, and you're all welcome to help yourselves." Sean put a hand over his heart as he addressed the guests. "Thank you for coming out today. Let's have a safe fire season, everyone!"

The ceremony broke up, and the guests meandered in the direction of the food. As Chief Littleton approached him, Sean caught Evie's eye and gestured that he'd join her in a few minutes.

Evie sighed happily. Whenever she looked into those smoky green eyes, everything was right with her world.

Suzanne appeared at Evie's elbow. "So…double wedding…what do you say?"

"Would you stop with that? We're not even officially engaged yet."

Suzanne snorted. "Whatever, cuz. That man can barely keep his hands off you. You'll get married, it's just a matter of when. So why not make it at the same time as us?"

"Why does it matter so much to you?"

Her tall, blond cousin shrugged. "I just think it would be fun," she muttered. Not for the first time, Evie wondered if all was right with her cousin's engagement. Something seemed a little off. But every time she asked, Suzanne insisted she was on cloud nine.

"Come on, let's get a hot dog. Josh claims he makes the best dogs in the world."

Suzanne rolled her eyes. "Typical macho Josh boasting. A hot dog is a hot dog. How can one person make them any better than another person?"

"Since it's Josh, I wouldn't be surprised. He does a lot of things really well."

Suzanne's gaze strayed to the grill, where Josh wielded the spatula. With a bandanna holding back his sun-streaked hair and a big apron wrapped around his lean body, he laughed and flirted with a constant stream of girls.

"Pass," Suzanne muttered. "Anyway, I should call Logan."

Evie was about to ask her if everything was okay when a

strong arm came around her. All thoughts of anything other than the man at her side vanished. "Hey, hotshot."

"Hey, love of my life."

They smiled at each other. Evie felt as if visible beams of happiness must be shining from her. It was almost embarrassing to be this happy. After so much time hiding behind her well-behaved, cool facade, being so open made her giddy. "How long do you have to stay and socialize?"

"Well, I still have to butter up the president of the Jupiter Point Business Coalition."

"I do hope you mean that literally."

His eyes darkened with desire and he pulled her tighter against him. "As you wish, milady."

She felt suddenly breathless. Sean actually took her breath away. "Hey, someone once offered to show me the cots around here."

"Hotshot on a cot. Coming right up, sweetheart."

Shivers of excitement rippled through her. She was joking about the cot, but it didn't really matter where they ended up that night. Her bed, a picnic blanket, an overlook, or in the middle of the road next to the burning wreckage of an SUV…with Sean, it was all good.

So she waited patiently as more Jupiter Pointers stopped them to congratulate Sean. She laughed when the other hotshots gathered around to throw out the latest ridiculous ideas for a mascot.

A Roman god in a toga? No.

A space probe? No.

She smiled and held Sean's hand and reveled in the town's support. She could be patient, because the wait would be worth it. When darkness fell, she and Sean would be alone together, somewhere, somehow, and between the two of them, they'd set the night on fire.

About the Author

Jennifer Bernard is a USA Today bestselling author of contemporary romance. Her books have been called "an irresistible reading experience" full of "quick wit and sizzling love scenes." A graduate of Harvard and former news promo producer, she left big city life in Los Angeles for true love in Alaska, where she now lives with her husband and stepdaughters. She still hasn't adjusted to the cold, so most often she can be found cuddling with her laptop and a cup of tea. No stranger to book success, she also writes erotic novellas under a naughty secret name that she's happy to share with the curious. You can learn more about Jennifer and her books at JenniferBernard.net.

Also by Jennifer Bernard

Jupiter Point

> Seeing Stars
>
> *(Prequel and Hope Falls Kindle World Novella)*

The Bachelor Firemen of San Gabriel

> The Fireman Who Loved Me
>
> Hot for Fireman
>
> Sex and the Single Fireman
>
> How to Tame a Wild Fireman
>
> Four Weddings and a Fireman
>
> The Night Belongs to Fireman

> *Novellas*

> One Fine Fireman
>
> Desperately Seeking Fireman
>
> It's a Wonderful Fireman

Love Between the Bases

Made in the USA
San Bernardino, CA
31 January 2017